Praise for Deb Caletti's

wild roses

★ "With its profound observations and vivid . . . language, this multifaceted and emotionally devastating novel will stick with readers."
—*School Library Journal*, starred review

★ "Cassie's first-person narrative will sweep up readers, and her exploration of the fine line between madness and genius alternates between humor and painful truth."
—*Publishers Weekly*, starred review

"Caletti's perceptions on divorce are crystalline, [and] the story is populated with delightfully oddball yet solidly real characters and shot full of genuine wit."
—*Kirkus Reviews*

"Readers struggling with their own turmoil will find Cassie a kindred spirit."
—*Bulletin of the Center for Children's Books*

"Caletti hits the 'wow' factor. . . . She writes . . . without pretension."
—*Romantic Times*, A Top Pick

A New York Public Library Book for the Teen Age
A Bank Street Best Book of the Year
A PSLA Top Ten Young Adult Book

ALSO BY DEB CALETTI

wild roses

by DEB CALETTI

Simon Pulse

New York London Toronto Sydney

This book is a work of fiction. Any references to historical events, real people, or real locales are used fictitiously. Other names, characters, places, and incidents are the product of the author's imagination, and any resemblance to actual events or locales or persons, living or dead, is entirely coincidental.

SIMON PULSE
An imprint of Simon & Schuster Children's Publishing Division
1230 Avenue of the Americas, New York, NY 10020
This Simon Pulse paperback edition March 2010
Copyright © 2005 by Deb Caletti
SIMON PULSE and colophon are registered trademarks of Simon & Schuster, Inc.
Also available in a Simon & Schuster Books for Young Readers hardcover edition.
For information about special discounts for bulk purchases, please contact
Simon & Schuster Special Sales at 1-866-506-1949 or business@simonandschuster.com.
The Simon & Schuster Speakers Bureau can bring authors to your live event.
For more information or to book an event contact the Simon & Schuster Speakers
Bureau at 1-866-248-3049 or visit our website at www.simonspeakers.com.
Designed by Yaffa Jaskoll
The text of this book was set in Berkeley Book.
Manufactured in the United States of America
10 9 8 7 6
The Library of Congress has cataloged the hardcover edition as follows:
Caletti, Deb.
Wild roses / Deb Caletti.
p. cm.
Summary: In Washington State, seventeen-year-old Cassie learns about the
good and bad sides of both love and genius while leaving with her mother and
brilliant, yet disturbed, violinist stepfather and falling in love with a gifted musician.
ISBN 978-0-689-86766-8 (hc)
[1. Mental illness—Fiction. 2. Love—Fiction. 3. Stepfathers—Fiction.
4. Remarriage—Fiction. 5. Violinists—Fiction. 6. Musicians—Fiction.
7. Washington (State)—Fiction.] I. Title.
PZ7.C127437Wi 2005
[Fic]—dc22
2004023230
ISBN 978-1-4169-5782-9 (pbk)

ACKNOWLEDGMENTS

Thank you to my dear friends and partners—Ben Camardi and Jen Klonsky. It's a privilege to be part of your intelligence, humor, and insight. Thanks as well, to Jenn Zatorski, Leah Hays, Sam Schutz, and all the fine folks at Simon & Schuster—you guys are the best. Gratitude also to Kirsty Skidmore and Amanda Punter and U.K. Scholastic.

Doug Longman, music teacher extraordinaire—thanks for essential information, and for your dedication to teaching. And to all those organizations that assist writers and, more importantly, get the word out about books, my appreciation and admiration. Thank you Artist Trust; National Book Foundation; PNBA, with special thanks to Rene Kirkpatrick; California Young Reader Medal Program; PSLA; International Reading Association; YALSA, and to libraries everywhere, particularly King County Library System. Librarians are awesome, and KCLS is home to my favorites.

Anne Greenberg; the beautiful and singular Muriel Diamond; "Magic" friends; Rick Young; and the Flo Villa houseboat gang—life is happier with you in it. Love and endless thanks to my clan in Virginia, California, Chicago. And to my new family in Denver, Seattle, Phoenix, L.A., and Mineral Point—oh, lucky girl am I.

Finally, deep and forever love and gratitude to Evie Caletti, Paul and Jan Caletti, Sue Rath and family. And to my Sam and Nick, who make every day a present.

CHAPTER ONE

To say my life changed when my mother married Dino Cavalli (yes, *the* Dino Cavalli) would be like saying that the tornado changed things for Dorothy. There was only one other thing that would impact my life so much, and that was when Ian Waters drove up our road on his bicycle, his violin case sticking out from a compartment on the side, and his long black coat flying out behind him.

My stepfather was both crazy and a genius, and I guess that's where I should start. If you've read about him recently, you already know this. He was a human meteor. Supposedly there's an actual, researched link between extreme creativity and mental illness, and I believe it because I've seen it with my own eyes. Sure, you have the artists and writers and musicians like my mom, say, who are talented and calm and get things done without much fuss. The closest she gets to madness is when she gets flustered and calls me William, which is our dog's name. But then there are the van Goghs and Hemingways and Mozarts, those who feel a hunger so deep, so far down, that greatness lies there too, nestled somewhere within it. Those who get their inner voice and direction from the cool, mysterious insides of the moon, and not from the earth like the rest of us. In other words, brilliant nuts.

I guess we should also begin with an understanding, and that is, if you are one of those easily offended people who insist that every human breath be politically correct, it's probably best we just part company now. I'll loan you my copy of *Little House in the Big Woods* (I actually loved it when I was eight) and you can disappear into prairie perfection, because I will not dance around this topic claiming that Dino Cavalli was joy-impaired (hugely depressed), excessively imaginative (delusional), abundantly security conscious (paranoid as hell) or emotionally challenged (wacko). I'm not talking about your mentally ill favorite granny or sick best uncle—I'm not judging anyone else who's ill. This is my singular experience. I've lived it; I've earned the right to describe how it felt from inside my own skin. So if your life truths have to be protected the same way some people keep their couches in plastic, then ciao. Have a nice life. If we bump into each other at Target, I'm the one buying the sour gummy worms, and that's all you need to know about me.

Anyway, madness and genius. They're the disturbed pals of the human condition. The Bonnie and Clyde, the

2

Thelma and Louise, the baking soda and vinegar. Insanity just walks alongside the brilliant like some creepy, insistent shadow. Edgar Allan Poe, Virginia Woolf, Charles Dickens. William Faulkner, Dostoevsky, Cézanne, Gauguin. Tolstoy, Sylvia Plath, Keats, and Shelley. Walt Whitman and F. Scott Fitzgerald and Michelangelo. All wacko. And we can't forget the musicians, because this story is about them, especially. Schumann and Beethoven, Chopin and Handel and Rachmaninov and Liszt. Tchaikovsky and Wagner.

And, of course, Dino Cavalli.

In that group you've got every variety of creation: the ceiling of the Sistine Chapel and *Farewell to Arms* and the epic poem, "Ode on a Grecian Urn," which, if you ask me, finds its true greatness as a cure for insomnia. You've also got every variety of crazy act. You've got the gross—van Gogh slicing off his earlobe and giving it to a woman (you can just hear her—*Damn, I was hoping for chocolates*), and the unimaginable—Virginia Woolf filling her pockets with stones to hold her down in the river so that she could do an effective job of drowning. And even the funny—the reason our dog is named William, for example, is because Dino Cavalli bought him during a particularly bad bout of paranoia and named him for his enemy and former manager and agent, William Tiero. He liked the idea of this poor, ugly dog named William that would eat used Kleenex if he had the chance. He liked yelling at William for getting too personal with guests. I can hear his voice even now, in his Italian accent. *Get your nose out of Mrs.*

3

Kadinsky's crotch, William, he'd say with mock seriousness, and everyone would picture William Tiero with his bald head and beetle eyes, and they would laugh. Man, oh, man. You didn't want to get on Dino Cavalli's bad side.

Some people think the brilliant have been touched by God, and if this is true then Dino Cavalli got God on the day he was wearing black leather and listening to his metal CDs, feeling a bit twisted and in the kind of mood where you laugh at people when they fall down. God wearing a studded collar. Because, sure, Dino Cavalli was a world-renowned composer and violinist, a combination of talent virtually unheard of, but there were days he didn't get out of bed, even to shower. And, sure, he wrote and performed *Amore Innamorato,* said to, "have moments of such brutal tenderness and soulful passion that it will live forever in both the hearts of audience members and the annals of modern composing,"[1] as well as the unforgettable *Artemisia* ("breathtaking and heart-stopping work with the brilliance of the seventeenth-century masters."[2]), but he also had the ability to make you feel small to the point of disappearance. His perfectionism could shatter your joy like a bullet through a stained glass window.

What I'm saying is, he possessed magnificent and destructive layers. Either that or he was just plain possessed. I mean, it all got toned down in the papers, but we all know what could have happened to William Tiero that day. We all now know what happens when you self-

---

[1] Dawson Cook, "Cavalli Strikes a Perfect Note" *Strad Magazine* (April 1996): 12–15.
[2] Alice Lambert, "The Season's Best" *Strad Magazine* (May 1989): 20–22.

destruct. Yet I've got to say, listening to his music can make you cry. Goose bumps actually rise up along your arms.

Everyone wants to get close to genius and fame, claim pieces of it, mostly because it's the closest they'll ever get to fame themselves. You learn this when you live with someone renowned. Those who know that Dino Cavalli was my stepfather think I'm near enough to fame to call it good. Fame, the nearness of it, the possibility of it rubbing off, seems to turn people into obsessed Tolkien characters, hypnotized not by a ring but by the thought of getting on TV. Luckily at my school, most of the kids who hear the name Dino Cavalli will think it's some brand of designer shoes. To the majority I am just Cassie Morgan, regular seventeen-year-old trying to figure out what to do with my life and hoping my jeans are clean and swearing at myself for cutting my own bangs again. Few know my stepfather was once on the cover of *Time* magazine, or was also well known for the journals in which he wrote of his sexual adventures as a young composer in Paris. Everyone is too involved in the school game of How Orange Is Tiffany Morris's Makeup Today to care, even if they did. But the teachers and orchestra students, they know who I am, and I see what it means to them. Once during a school concert this kid was staring so hard at me that he accidentally stepped into an open viola case and wore it like an overgrown shoe for a few seconds on the gym floor.

And then there's Siang Chibo, who used to follow me home every day. She would walk far behind me and duck

5

behind trees when I turned around, like some cartoon spy. She once tripped over a tree root in the process and spewed the contents of her backpack all over the place. You couldn't find a more incompetent stalker. I went over to her after she fell, and her palms even had those little pockmarks on them from landing on gravel. Now we have a Scrooge-Tiny Tim partnership of reluctant giving and nauseating gratitude. To Siang, I'm second in line in the worship chain of command, right after Dino. If people look at the famous as if they've been touched by God, then they look at those close to the famous as the ones who have seen Jesus' face in the eggplant.

You would have never recognized the Dino I lived with in the books that had been written about him before the "incident." No one had a clue. No one seemed to see what was coming. His demons were the real truth, but those who clutched at his fame made him into someone else. Just listen to Irma Lattori, a villager from Sabbotino Grappa, interviewed in Edward Reynolds's *Dino Cavalli—The Early Years: An Oral History,* the much-quoted source of Dino's childhood. It's his only authorized biography, in which the people who knew him then tell the events of his life.

Everyone in Sabbotino Grappa knew Dino Cavalli had that special light, Irma says in the book. *From the time he was an infant. I would see his mother, Maria, walk him around in his carriage. She was a beautiful woman with round, warm eyes. She always dressed elegantly, oh, so rich. She had tucked a peacock feather in the back of his carriage. It rose up, like a grand flag. You want to know where he got* Un Cielo Delle

6

Piume Del Peacock? *That was his inspiration. Maria always appreciated the unusual. She wore hats, even when no one wore hats. Stunning. No wonder he became a ladies' man. He was born, you see, taking in the world and using it in his work. Born to beauty and greatness. He couldn't have been more than six months old, this time I am remembering. He reached his hands up to me when I bent to look at him. He wanted me to hold him. He wouldn't let my sister Camille go near him.*[3]

And Frank Mancini, gardener, another one of the villagers from tiny Sabbotino Grappa: *A beautiful garden, beautiful. Four hundred years old. Magnolias in the spring. Plumbagos, hibiscus in the summer. Lemon trees and figs. An olive garden. I worked my fingers to the bone. Now I cannot tie my own shoe, my fingers are so crippled. But it was a beautiful garden, and you could hear the child playing the violin through the open window. Small boy, not more than four years old, and he played the violin! A divine gift. His mother played the piano. Music was in his veins. And the smell of lemon trees. I didn't mind that the father was cheap and barely paid me enough to buy food.*[4]

All in all, as gagging as a dental X ray.

"No one ever mentions that he is a wife-stealing psycho," my father said once after Dino was featured in the entertainment section of the newspaper—FAMED MUSICIAN SEEKS LOCAL INSPIRATION. He tossed the paper down on his kitchen table. "With bad breath."

[3] Dino Cavalli—*The Early Years: An Oral History.* From Edward Reynolds, New York, N.Y. Aldine Press, 1999.
[4] *Dino Cavalli—The Early Years: An Oral History.* From Edward Reynolds, New York, N.Y. Aldine Press, 1999.

7

"You haven't even been close enough to him to smell his breath," I said.

"Who says you have to be close," my father said. Let's just say my father didn't read the divorce books that say you are not supposed to talk badly about the other parent and the other parent's partner. Actually, I think he probably did read them, but has somehow convinced himself that only my mother is required to follow these rules. He ignores the other Divorced Parenting Don'ts too, the ones where you aren't supposed to grill your kid about what happens in the other home. Sometimes he tries to be casual about his fishing around, and other times it's like I'm in one of those movies where the criminal sits under the bare light-bulb in a room and after twelve hours confesses to a crime he didn't commit.

My parents were divorced three years ago, and my mother married Dino five days after the divorce was final. Do the math and figure out what happened. If you've been through this, you know the vocabulary. Parenting plan, custody evaluation, visitation, court orders, mediation, transfer time. And can anyone say *restraining order*? I can talk with my friend Zebe about these things. Ever since I met her in Beginning Spanish we've spoken the same language, in more ways than one. Her new stepfather may not be famous, but we understand the most important things about each other. She knows that you really don't give a crap about who gets you on Labor Day, that *no-fault divorce* are the three stupidest words ever spoken, and that you are not split as easily as your parents' old

Commodores albums, and there was even a war over those.

"Barry Manilow, in my house. Not Commodores," Zebe told me once. "Which they both hated, by the way. For a week they were flying e-mails at each other over the goddamn F-ing *Copacabana* LP. They each accused the other of taking it. 'Did your mother find my "missing" album yet?' 'Next time you go to your father's, look for my stolen record.' God."

"Was anyone hurt?" I asked.

"Aside from the e-mail bloodbath, the only thing that was hurt was both of their egos when one of them finally remembered that they brought the album to some party back in the seventies and left it there on purpose."

"You wonder why they ever got married."

"*Mi mono toca la guitarra,*" she said. *My monkey plays the guitar.* It's what she wrote on every Spanish test question she didn't know the answer to. I cracked up. Zebe's the greatest.

If my father treated my time at my mother's house as if he were the gold miner panning for The Dirt of Wrongdoing, my mother, on the other hand, would listen to any news of my father the same way someone who had plans to stay inside listens to a weather forecast. Hearing just enough to make sure there was no tornado coming. This is one difference between the leaver and the left, the dumper and the dumpee. The dumpee has the moral righteousness, and the desire to hear every dirty fact that will prove that *You get what you deserve in the end.* The

9

dumper has the guilt, and wants to know as little about the other party as possible, in case they hear something that will make them feel even more guilty.

"Dad's got a new client. Some big Microsoft person," I told Mom once. It was after she and Dino had first gotten married, and I was starting to get a real clear picture of what she'd gotten us into. I guess I was hoping she was seeing, too, and that a little nudge in Dad's direction might help along the underdog. I hadn't learned yet that in terms of divorce, your only real hope is not to play team sports.

"Oh, really. Good for him," she said. She was braiding her long hair. She had a rubber band in her teeth. *Oh, weewy. Ood for him.* She finished the braid, put her arms down. "I need to find my overalls. I'm planting tulip bulbs today. Planting just calls for overalls." She went to her closet, flung open the doors.

"It'll bring him a lot of money," I said. My father was an accountant. He was a white undershirt in a world of silk ties and berets and pashmina. He was a potato amongst pad Thai and curry and veal scallopini. He was still madly in love with my mother. He didn't have a chance.

"Great," she said. "My God, look at this mess. The man is incapable of hanging anything up." She said this with a great deal of affection, poked a toe at a pile of Dino's shirts. "Overalls, overalls. Bingo." She held them up.

"You're not even listening."

"I'm listening, I'm listening. You're just making me feel like I'm in some *Parent Trap* movie. You're not going to put frogs in Dino's shoes or something, are you?"

Mom's unwillingness to get involved may have also had to do with her own experience of her parent's divorce. Thirty-two years after the end of their marriage, she still can't tell one of her parents that she's visiting the other, or she'll be punished with coldness, hurt, and upset. Thirty-two years later, and her mother still refers to her father's wife as That Tramp.

"I thought you'd like to know. Jesus, Mom."

"Good. Thanks for telling me. You're not the *Parent Trap* type anyway. What was the name of that actress? Started with an H. Heather. Hayley! Mills. God, how'd I remember that? You, girl, are not Hayley Mills. I'd like to see them put you in a remake. Disney'd ditch the hemp bracelet. Don't you think? Too edgy."

"I hope squirrels dig up your tulip bulbs," I said.

She socked my arm. "You know how much I respect you. I *like* your hemp bracelet."

Respect—that was what was lacking in the other member of our household. Dino didn't respect me, or my mother, either, for that matter. Or anyone who wasn't his own perfect self. See, Dino hadn't always acted crazy. For a while, he was just plain arrogant. Dino was fluent in criticism, as generous in spirit as those people who keep their porch lights off all Halloween. If my mom was dressed up to go out and looking beautiful, he'd point out her pimple. If you opened the wrong end of the milk carton, he'd make you feel you were incapable to the point of needing to be institutionalized. After I'd bought this jacket with fur around the collar and cuffs at Old Stuff, Dino had pointedly told me that people who tried to make some statement of individuality were still only conventional among those of their group.

"I'm not trying to make a statement," I said. I was trying to keep the sharpness out of my voice, but it was like trying to hold water in your hands—my tone was seeping through every crack and opening possible.

"I didn't say you were. Did I say you were? It was a commentary on dress and group behavior," he said in his Italian accent. He chewed a bite of chicken. He was a loud, messy eater. You could hear the chicken in there smacking around against his tongue. His words were offhand, casually bragging that they meant more to me than they did to him. "By avoiding conventions, one falls into other conventions." He plucked a bit of his shirt to indicate someone's clothing choice. I felt the ugly curl of anger starting in my stomach.

"I'm sorry, I just don't want to be one of those See My Thong girls who bat their eyelashes at boys, rah rah rah, wearing a demoralizing short skirt and bending over so a crowd sees their butt," I said. "That's convention." Anger made my face get hot.

"Be who you like. I was simply making an observation. You don't need to bite me with your feminist teeth."

Honestly, I don't know how my mother didn't poison his coffee. Certainly I wondered what the hell she was thinking by loving him. If this is what could happen to a supposedly charming, romantic guy, then no, thank you. And this was before everything happened, even. Before

Dino's craziness became like a roller coaster car, rising to unbelievable heights, careening down with frightening speed; before he started teaching Ian Waters; before he began composing again and preparing for his comeback after a three-year dry spell. But in spite of what must have been perfect attendance in asshole classes, Dino was one of those people who got under your skin because you cared what they thought when you wished you didn't. So after that conversation I did the only thing I could. I wore the coat the next day, too. The truth was, I wasn't sure I liked it either. It was vaguely Wilma Flintstone and Saber Tooth Tiger. Little hairs fell into my Lucky Charms.

Because I wanted his approval and hated that fact, I did what I could to make sure I didn't get it at all. One of those things you should be in therapy for. Before I met Ian Waters, for example, I had no interest in music, which was an act of will living in a house where my mother was a cellist and my stepfather a prominent violinist and composer. But Ian Waters changed that about me, and everything else, too. Before I met Ian the music I liked best was something that sounded, if Dino was right, *like your mother hunting for the meat thermometer in the drawer of kitchen utensils*. My interest was in astronomy—science, something that was mine and that was definite and exact. I felt that the science of astronomy existed within certain boundaries that were firm and logical. If you think about how vast the universe is, this gives you some idea of how huge and wild I thought the arts were.

After three years of living with Dino Cavalli, I had had enough of people of passion. Passion seemed dangerous.

I'd seen the tapes of his performances, the way he had his chin to his violin as if he were about to consume it, the way his black hair would fly out as he played, reaching crescendo, eyes closed. It made you feel like you needed to hold on to something. I'd never felt that kind of letting go before. It all seemed one step away from some ancient tribal possession. And that crescent scar on his neck. That brown gash that had burned into him from hours and hours and hours of the violin held against his skin. He had played until the instrument had made a permanent mark, had become part of his own body. If Chuck and Bunny are right, and everyone should *hunger for life and its banquet,* I would rather have the appetite of my neighbor Courtney and her two brothers, over Dino's. All Courtney and her brothers hungered for in life was a box of Junior Mints and MTV, fed straight through the veins. Dino, he could inhale an emotional supermarket and still be ravenous.

Right then, the only thing I was hungry for was to have Dino Cavalli, this flaming, dying star, out of my universe. It was the only thing I would dare be passionate about. That is, until Ian Waters veered into our driveway on his bike, his tires scrunching in the gravel, scaring Otis, the neighbors' cat, who ran across the grass like his tail was on fire. Otis was running for his life. In a way, that was when I began finally running to mine.

CHAPTER TWO

Edgar Allan Poe watched his mother bleed from the mouth as she died from consumption, as he and his two siblings lay in bed beside her. Hemingway committed suicide with the same gun his father had used to kill himself. Lord Byron's father had an incestuous relationship with his own sister, and his mother's relatives were a toxic mix of the depressed and suicidal. When you look at the families of crazy geniuses, you start to understand where their pain comes from. You start to get their need to paint it away, write it away, compose it away.

But Dino Cavalli's childhood in Sabbotino Grappa (population 53) sounded like one of those lush movies filmed in hazy golden-yellows with a sappy soundtrack that makes you cry even though you know it's just music manipulation. It sounded close to perfect. Reading *The*

Early Years snapped me right up from Seabeck, the island where we live, just a ferryboat ride from Seattle. It lifted me from the salty, wet air and the evergreens and the cold waters of the Puget Sound, and landed me in the warm orange tones of a Tuscan hill town. *I would open the shutters in the morning,* said Antonia Gillette, wife of town baker Peter Gillette. *And I would see little Dino walking to school in his white shirt, holding his mother's hand. I remember the smell of the lemon trees, and the smell of the baking just done, coming up warm through the floorboards. Peter would hurry out to give a frittelle to Dino, and one to his mother, no charge. Always no charge. He should have charged the mother, but she was too pretty. And the father—ah. Handsome, like from a magazine. And a beautiful voice. Dino, we all knew he was special. His hair shined; his fingers were magic on his little violin. We knew he would bring us fame. I heard him from the open window, Grazie, Zio. That's what he called Peter. Uncle.*[5]

"It's too good to be true," my father said once. "You mark my words. If it sounds like a duck and looks like a duck and smells like a duck, it *is* a duck."

"Quack," I said.

The stories of Dino's childhood glowed like firelight or radiation, one or the other. You could see those townspeople sitting at their kitchen tables, remembering a time past, smelling of wine and salami, a thick, wrinkled hand grabbing the air to emphasize a point. You grew to love those old Italians, and that ragged town with its winding

[5] Dino Cavalli—*The Early Years: An Oral History.* From Edward Reynolds, New York, N.Y. Aldine Press, 1999.

streets and good intentions, more than you liked Dino himself. I did anyway. The only real nasty thing that was said came from Karl Lager, Sabbotino Grappa grocer. *The child was a monster. Spoiled and sneaky. He stole candy from me. Later, cigarettes. Slipped them up the sleeve of his jacket as he looked at me and smiled. I tried to grab him, took off that jacket, but nothing was there. Born of the devil, and any idiot could see it.*

Karl Lager is a drunk and a bastard, Antonia Gillete said. *He'd accuse the pope of stealing.*

Karl Lager had no business in Sabbotino Grappa, Peter Gillette agreed. *He is a German, after all.*[6]

You imagined a childhood like that creating a genius. You did not imagine those two beautiful and perfect parents and the adoration of a village creating a Prozac-ed pit bull.

"Is Mr. Cavalli home?" Siang Chibo said the day that I first saw Ian Waters. She was whispering, following me around the house as I dropped my backpack on a kitchen chair and looked around in the fridge for something that might change my life. If you want a good picture of Siang Chibo, imagine that little boy in *Indiana Jones and the Temple of Doom*, that kid that rides around with him in the runaway mine car. She's not much taller, and has that same squeaky voice—*"Indy, Indy!"* But Siang's surprised me a few times. For example, she and her father love to watch monster trucks on the weekends. For another

---

[6] Dino Cavalli—*The Early Years: An Oral History*. From Edward Reynolds, New York, N.Y. Aldine Press, 1999.

example, she's a fierce flag football player. I once saw her nearly knock out Zane Thompson's perfect teeth as she reached up to catch a pass in tenth-grade PE. Zane had to rush to a mirror to see if he was still beautiful. Go Siang.

"Dino's at the symphony offices," I said. I didn't want to let Siang down, but the truth was, I had no idea where Dino could be. He might have been at Safeway, for all I knew. Being a violinist was not a regular nine-to-five job, I guess—in fact, lately he didn't seem to have any job at all except for being famous and giving interviews about his past glory days. He gave one concert that I knew of, traveled to Chicago for it with Mom. I stayed with Dad a few extra days, days that were mostly spent trying to talk him out of searching the Web for every nasty comment or review about the event. He even printed out one *Chicago Tribune* article and posted it to the fridge with this glittery macaroni magnet I made in preschool. RERUN PERFORMANCE BY MASTER DISAPPOINTS.

What Dino spent most of his time doing was hiring and firing new managers. Since he ditched William Tiero three-plus years ago, he just went through these poor guys like you go through a bag of M&M's when you've got your period. Consume, and on to the next. One of the first exposures I had to Dino's temper was when we had all just moved in together and this manager got booted. I heard only a part of the enraged conversation before I left and walked down toward the water, went far enough so that the cries of the seagulls and gentle voices on the beach—*Olivia! Roll up your pants so they don't get wet—*

18

replaced Dino's shouts. The few pathetic imaginings I was trying to hold onto about a stepfather—new beginnings, new adventures, new life—were instantly shot to shit and replaced with a deep distrust of the word *new*. It is bad enough to be suddenly (even if it is not so sudden, it feels sudden) living with a male stranger who sleeps in bed with your mother and eats off of your forks and who farts with an unearned degree of familiarity. But when the male stranger *yells* loud enough to shake your baby pictures in their frames, too, then, God, where have all the boarding schools gone?

Anyway, almost six months before Ian Waters first came, Dino got this new manager, Andrew Wilkowski, this skinny guy with music notes on his tie. It was practically a long-term relationship. Andrew Wilkowski flattered Dino's ego, talked to him about writing again. I heard them when Andrew came over for dinner. They could take it slowly, he told Dino. But the world was ready. Dino was ready. I'm sure Andrew Wilkowski only had staying power because his ass-kissing skills were so perfected, his lips were chapped.

If I had to create a job description based on Dino's behavior before he really went nuts, I'd say being a violinist and a composer meant spending some days in bed, some holed up in your office, occasionally playing music and stopping over and over again, and storming around the house as your wife walked on eggshells. Oh, and seeing your psychiatrist. Mom said this was necessary for Dino to deal with the stresses of his work, but to keep that information private for the sake of Dino's reputation. It was okay to look like a tyrant, I guess, but not to talk with Freud about what your id did. Basically, a genius composer/violinist meant being a tantrum-throwing toddler with an expensive musical instrument. My mother should have given him the spaghetti pot to pound on with a wooden spoon instead.

I wouldn't tell Siang any of those things, though. I could have destroyed him in an instant for her, but it seemed too cruel. To her, not to him. "Apple?" I offered. Mom was on a diet kick. I hated when the adults in my life went on a diet kick. There was never anything good to eat in the house. I hoped Dino *was* at Safeway.

"Okay," Siang said. She took the apple, but didn't eat it. She put it in her sweatshirt pocket. I imagined a Cavalli Collection—empty TP rolls from our bathroom, pebbles from the insides of Dino's shoes left by the front door, William's squeaky rubber hamburger dog toy that had vanished without a trace. "Can we go in his office?"

"I worry about you, Siang, I really do."

I took the key to Dino's office out of the sugar canister that was empty of sugar. Mom put it there because she was sure that Dino, in a distracted state, was going to one day lock himself out. That there was a key at all should tell you that Dino would have gotten furious had he known we were in his study, but I couldn't let Siang down. I had a little problem saying no to people with eyes as pleading as in those ads Feed a Starving Child for as Little as One Dollar a Day. She practically left offerings on his desk blotter.

20

The room always felt cool when you first opened the door, cool and musty. There was a fireplace in that room, though it was never lit except when guests came over. The fire showed off the room for what it was—one of the best in the house, with big windows that had a peek of the waters of the sound, if you stood on your toes and looked high over the neighbor's hydrangea bush. His desk was dark walnut, and a mess—papers and books, mail and clippings, piles of sheet music. There were three clocks on it, only one which you could hear ticking, sounding like a metronome, and an old coffee mug with a ring of dried brown on the bottom. Assorted objects lay among the clutter—a robin's egg, a golf tee (Dino was not a sportsman), a cigar box (Dino did not smoke cigars). There was a paperweight with a white dandelion puff saved perfectly in glass, and a spare pair of Dino's glasses worn sometime in the seventies, if you judged by their size and thick black frames. Above the desk was a painting of white flowers against a dreary green background, and in the corner of the room sat a globe that always settled toward the side revealing the African continent. An antique music stand, ornate silver, delicately curved, stood in another corner, and there was a bookcase, too, filled with Cavalli biographies, volumes of music theory, history, and art, and one of those enormous dictionaries.

Siang strolled by the desk, her fingertips lightly touching the edge. She looked up at the painting, tilted her head to the side and examined it for a moment. Her eyes moved away to a frame facedown on the desk. She took hold of the velvety frame leg, rubbed her thumb along it. "What's this?"

"How am I supposed to know?"

Siang raised the picture carefully, the way you lift a rock when you're not sure what's underneath. It was an old black-and-white photo of a young man. He was standing in front of a building, a theater, maybe, as you could see a portion of a poster in glass behind him. He was beaming, hands in his pockets.

"That's William Tiero," I said. "At least I think it is." I squinched my eyes, looked closer. "Same beaky nose. A much younger William Tiero. He still had hair. I never knew the guy ever had hair." I chuckled.

"William Tiero became Dino Cavalli's agent shortly after Cavalli won the Tchaikovsky competition in Russia when he was nineteen," Siang said.

"Jesus, you give me the creeps sometimes," I said. "Put that back down."

"They say it was a partnership made in heaven." Siang set the photo on the desk the way it was.

According to Mom, William Tiero had been dismissed no fewer than five times before the final break a little more than three years ago. I could only imagine what that firing must have been like. Before Andrew W. came on the scene, the last poor manager that was booted got a wineglass thrown in the direction of his head. I saw the delicate pieces of it, sitting on top of the garbage can, and felt the silence that lay heavy as a warning in the house. I remember the drops of red wine on the wall, looking as if a crime had been committed there. If being fired five times by Dino was a partnership made in heaven, I wondered what a bumpy working relationship would look like.

"Siang, really. You need a hobby or something. Crochet a beer-can hat. Learn fly-fishing. Whatever."

"The pursuit of understanding genius is always a worthwhile endeavor," Siang squeaked in her *Temple of Doom* voice.

"Did some famous person say that?"

"No. I just did."

"Shit, deprogramming necessary. We are going to walk down to 7-Eleven. We are going to have a Slurpee. Corn Nuts. Or one of those scary revolving hot dogs. We are going to take an *Auto Trader* magazine, just because they're free."

"I hear the door," Siang said.

I froze. Listened. "You're right. Damn it, get out of here."

We hurried out. My heart was pounding like crazy, and my hand was shaky on the key as I locked the door again.

"Cassie!"

"It's just Mom," I said.

My chest actually hurt from the relief. We walked casually into the kitchen. At least I did. God knows what Siang was doing behind me—probably putting her hands up in the air like a captured criminal in a cop show. Mom was filling a glass of water. Wisps of her hair were coming loose from her braid. "What are you doing here?" I asked. Mom

23

was in a rehearsal period with the theater company of her current job. By the time she took the ferry home from Seattle afterward, she didn't usually arrive until dinnertime.

"Hello, my wonderful mother. How was your day?" she said.

"That too," I said.

"I got off early," she said. It seemed like a lie, but I let it pass. "What are you two up to?"

"I was just heading home," Siang said. "Chemistry test to study for."

Mom shuddered. "God, I'm glad I'm done with school."

"Then she's starting a new hobby," I said.

"Crafts," Siang said. I smiled. It was pretty close to a joke.

"Puff paint. Shrinky Dinks," I said.

"Cool," Mom said. She took a long drink of water. You could usually count on her to make her best effort to one-up your jokes. Obviously she was distracted.

Siang left, and I went up to my room, turned on a few of my lamps. My head was achy and tired—I'd slept like shit for the past few nights. Dino kept turning down the heat below zero to save money, and in a few days my nose and toes were going to turn black and fall off from frost-bite. Far as I knew, Dino had a lot of money, but he was really attached to it. Any time he had to spend any, he acted like he was parting with his cardiovascular system.

I looked at my homework and it looked back at me, flat and uninspiring, growing to impossible proportions right in front of my eyes. Sometimes a little math and science is as easy as tying your shoes, and other times, it feels like an Everest expedition, requiring hired Sherpas and ropes, oxygen bottles, and crampons, which always seemed like an especially unfortunately named word—a mix between cramps and tampons. I picked up a book of poetry beside my bed instead, thumbed through e.e. cummings, my favorite poet for probably the same reason he was other people's favorite poet—he chucked grammar and got away with it. It was like thumbing your nose at every one of those tests where you had to underline once the main clause, and underline twice the prepositional phrase. I stank at those. Grammar words were so unlikable—*conjunctive,* some eye disease you need goopy medicine for; *gerund,* an uptight British guy. *Gerund would like his tea now!*

I amused myself with these inane thoughts until I heard Dino's car pull up. He had a Renault, and it made a particular *clacka-clacka-clacka* sound so that you always knew it was him (okay, *he,* for the above-mentioned grammar neurotics, although no one really talks like that). The engine was still on when he came through the front door. Then he went back out again and shut it off. It was entirely possible that he forgot that he'd left the engine running, as this was pure Dino, distracted to the point of barely functioning in the real world. Mom sent him to the store once for dinner rolls for a small party they were giving, and he came back two hours later with a glazed expression and a pack of hot dog buns. Another time, he tried to catch a bus from one part of Seattle to another, and ended up across the lake, calling my mother for rescue from a phone booth. He can play the first page of any major concerto off the top of his head, but doesn't understand that it's time to cross the street when you see the sign change to the little walking guy.

I heard my mother and Dino talking downstairs, which for some reason actually spurred my sudden desire to do my homework after all. We were maybe a month into the school year, and every teacher was beginning to pile homework on as if they had sole responsibility for keeping you busy after school and therefore out of jail and drug-free. My head was really hurting now. I worked for a while, then I heard the crunch of bike wheels down our road. This was not an uncommon sound, as Dino also often rode his bike; we Americans drove our cars too much, he said. Growing up in Italy, it was the only way people got around, he said. It was no wonder Americans had such fat asses, he said. You could often see him pedaling to town and back with a few grocery items in his basket. Yes, he had a basket on his bike. It wasn't a tacky one with plastic flowers or anything (thank God), but a real metal basket. The whole bike itself, old and quaint and squeaky, looked snitched from some clichéd French postcard, or stolen from some History of Bikes museum.

The sound of bike wheels on gravel might not have been out of the ordinary, but Dog William (versus Human William) barking crazily at the sound *was* unusual. I pulled up my blinds and here is what I saw: the curve of our gravel road, and the line of maple trees on each side framing the figure in the center. I saw a boy about my age, in a long black coat, the tails flapping out behind him, with a violin in a black case in a side compartment. I saw a yellow dog running alongside him grinning, his tongue hanging out in a display of dog joy.

I cannot tell you what that moment did to me. That boy's face—it just looked so *open*. It was as if I recognized it, that sense he had—expectation and vulnerability. He looked so hopeful, so full of all of the possibilities of a perfect day where a yellow dog runs beside you. The boy's black hair was shining in the sun and his hands gripped the handlebars against the unsteadiness of the bike on the dirt road. Are there ever adequate words for this experience? When you are suddenly overwhelmed by a wave of feeling, a knowing, when you are drawn to someone in this way? With the strength of the unavoidable? I don't know what it was about him and not someone else. I really don't know, because I'm sure a thousand people could have ridden up that road and I would not be abruptly consumed with a longing that felt less like seeing someone for the first time than it did meeting once more after a long time apart.

I watched him as he veered into our driveway, causing a snoozing Otis to bolt awake and flee maniacally across the lawn. What was he doing here? He was about my age, but I'd never seen him before. Was this a Dino pilgrimage? A fan wanting his violin signed? He parked his bike, set it on its side on the ground. He said something to his dog, who looked up at him as if they'd just agreed about something.

The boy lifted his violin case. He ran his fingertips along it, as if making sure it was okay—a gentle touch, a caring that made me rattle the blind back down and sit on the floor suddenly like the wind had been knocked out of me.

Here is something you need to know about me. I am not a Hallmark card, ooh-ah romance, Valentine-y love kind of person. My parents' divorce and my one other experience of love (Adam Peterson, who I really cared about. Okay, I told him I loved him. We hugged, held hands. He told me I was beautiful. He told half the school we had sex.) has knocked the white-lace-veil vision right out of me. Love seems to be something to approach with caution, as if you'd come across a wrapped box in the middle of the street and have no idea what it contains. A bomb, maybe. Or a million dollars. I wasn't even sure what the meaning of the word was. Love? I loved my telescope. I loved looking out at the depth of the universe and contemplating its whys. But love with some-one else, an actual *person,* was another matter. People got hurt doing that. People cried and wrapped their arms around themselves and rocked with loss. Loving words got turned to fierce, sharp, whip-cracks of anger that left per-manent marks. At the least, it disappointed you. At most, it damaged you. No, thank you.

So I sat down on that floor and grabbed my snow globe, the one that had a bear inside. I have no idea where I got it; it's just something I've always liked and have had forever. Just a single bear in the snow. He used to be anchored to the bottom, but now he just floated aimlessly around, and maybe that's why I liked him so much. I related. I turned it upside down, let him float and drift as the snow came down, down. *Oh shit*, I thought. *Holy shit*. My heart was actually thumping around in some kind of heaving-bosom movie-version of love. I could actually hear it. God, I never even came close to experiencing anything like this for Adam Peterson, and look where that got me. I breathed deeply, but it was like a magnet had been instantly surgically implanted in my body, drawing everything inside of me toward that person out there.

My headache had hit the road, replaced with some super energy surge. I told myself I was insane and an idiot and a complete embarrassment to my own self. The snow settled down around the bottom of the globe as the poor bear just floated, his head hitting the top of the glass as if in heartfelt but hopeless desire to rise above his limited world. I got back up and peeked out the blinds. The yellow dog sat on the sidewalk with the most patient expression I'd ever seen on animal or human—just peace and acceptance with his waiting, appreciating the chance to enjoy what might pass his way. The boy had come inside, I guess. And then it finally occurred to me—he'd come inside. True enough, there were voices downstairs. I opened my door a crack, heard Dog William being forcibly removed from the house, his toenails sliding against the wood floor.

"We'll work in my study." Dino.

"Can I get you or your dog something to drink?" Mom asked.

"That'd be great—my dog would love some water," the boy said.

29

"What's his name?" Mom again.

"He's a she. Rocket."

"Shall we not waste valuable time?" Dino said. You should have heard his tone of voice. That's what could really piss you off. I sent a silent curse his way, that his tongue would turn black and fall out. I heard my mother fish around in the cupboard, probably for a bowl for the water. My heart was doing a happy leap, prancing around in a meadow of flowers, tra la la, without my permission. His dog's name was Rocket. I liked astronomy. It was that thing you do when you first fall in love. Where you think you must be soul mates because you each get hungry at lunch time and both blink when a large object is thrown your way.

I started to put the pieces together. Boy with violin, Dino and his study. Maybe Dino was giving him some kind of lesson. But Dino wasn't a teacher. First, the best music teachers weren't necessarily virtuoso players. I knew that. Teachers are usually teachers and players are players. As far as I knew, Dino had never taken a student before. But more importantly, Dino didn't have the patience instructing would require. He would get irritated when he couldn't figure out how to turn on the television, for God's sake. You'd think he of all people could locate a power button.

I got a little worried for that boy now, alone with Dino in his office. I went downstairs, caught Mom coming back inside from giving Rocket her water. She had little gold dog hairs on her black skirt.

"What's going on?"

"Dino's taking a student," she said to me.

A student. He was going to be Dino's student. I thought about what this would mean. He'd be coming back. And back again. I swallowed. Wished my jeans were a size smaller. Wished my hair was something other than brown, that I had a better haircut. Shorter, longer. Anything other than medium length. I forced the casual back into my voice. "Why's he taking a student? He's not a teacher."

"Well, one, because the opportunity came up, and two, the boy needed someone."

"Dino's not exactly patient," I said.

"He's a master. The boy's lucky to have him. And Dino's not charging a cent. A friend of Dr. Milton's set him up." Dr. Milton was Dino's psychiatrist. "God, I'm starving. It's a good thing I'm not home during the day. I'd weigh three hundred pounds." Mom rooted around in the cupboards.

Dino teaching for free surprised me. I knew how he glared when I threw away a bread crust. "That's generous of Dino," I said.

"Well, they both get something out of it. Andrew Wilkowski's got this deal in the works with Dino's old record company and the Seattle Symphony. He's got to have three pieces ready to perform for a taped concert to be held in March. He's got two that he started a long while back, but they need more work. I guess the composing has been torture in the past and he's only got six months."

"So, what, the student helps him?"

"Aha!" she said, and held up the last Pop-Tart she

found. She removed it from the foil, threw away the empty box, and took a bite without bothering to warm it up. "No, the student doesn't help *literally*. The lessons just provide a structured environment—another focus, a place he's got to be. They're trying to avoid all of this open time spent obsessing about creating and not creating."

"Maybe he should pay the student, then."

Mom devoured the Pop-Tart like Dog William devours a . . . well, anything. "Ian needs Dino. That's his name. Ian Waters. He's preparing for an audition that's coming a couple of weeks before Dino's concert. Sometime in March, too, I think. You know who he really should have? Someone like Ginny Briggs. He's that good, from what I hear. But you've got to mortgage your house to get her."

"What's he auditioning for? The youth symphony?" I asked. It was a hopeful question. If he was that good the answer could be Julliard, which meant he was heading to New York.

"No. Curtis."

"Wow," I said. My heart sank. It more than sank; it seemed to clutch up and evaporate. The Curtis Institute of Music. Only the best of the best went there. Better than Julliard, lots of people thought. Every student was on full scholarship. He was heading to Philadelphia.

"Yeah. Ian was asked to perform at the Spoleto Festival in Italy last year. He was only sixteen. You know who else performed there at that age."

"Clifford, the Big Red Dog?" I guessed. "No, wait. Donny Osmond."

"Very funny," Mom said.

"Is it George Jetson?" I'm sorry, but it just always bugged me how everyone was supposed to know Dino's entire history. Dino composed his first piece of music at twelve. Dino made his first armpit fart on June 12, 1958.

"Okay. Never mind," Mom said. "You asked."

"No, I'm sorry. Okay? I'm sorry."

"Anyway," Mom said. She paused for a moment, deciding whether to forgive my brattiness. "That's why he's taking Ian on. He and his mother moved here when she lost her job. From California. You know that little house by the ferry terminal? Shingles? The one that used to put the sleigh in the yard at Christmas?"

"And keep it there until spring? Yeah."

"They moved in there. Whitney Bell taught him in California. For little or nothing."

"He'll be going to my school."

"Kids like that don't go to school. They have tutors. They learn at home. He's probably working on his GED now. They get into college early. More time for the music. I think the plan is, he applies in March and if all goes well, he moves to Philadelphia in June."

"Lucky," I said. Nine months. That's as long as he was going to be here.

"I don't know. This prodigy business . . . look at Dino. The ultimate love-hate relationship with that violin. I hope this teaching really does help. He'll have to start writing, and he hasn't picked up his instrument in weeks."

"Or his socks," I said. Lately, whenever Dino arrived in

33

the front door, his shoes and socks would come off immediately. They lay in the entryway like they'd just had a
thoroughly exhausting experience.

"He always went barefoot growing up. It's hot in Italy."
Italy, Italy. That was another thing you got sick of
hearing about in our house. How much better it was than
evil and endlessly annoying America. How Italy had per
capita more beautiful and intelligent people than here,
how they invented the human brain, how they could take
over the world using fettuccine noodles as weapons if they
wanted to.

"Well, I hope Dino's nice to him," I said.

"I know."

"So *that's* why you're home early."

"Just keeping an eye on things."

It was my personal opinion that my mother didn't
have a relationship as much as she had a babysitting job.

Mom went upstairs, probably reading my mind and
trying to prove me wrong. From the kitchen I couldn't
hear anything coming from Dino's office. I lingered outside the door for a while, listening to the rumbles of conversation without the definition of actual words, and then
I heard the tuning of a violin. I did something I shouldn't
have. I sat down right there with my back against the door
so that I could hear better. They discussed music, what
piece the boy should begin with, and then he began to
play.

I can tell you that I have heard Dino play many times,
and have heard the best of his performances on his

recordings. As I've said, they send chills down your spine, even for someone like me who still chuckles when some musician mentions the G string or the A hole. Dino's playing was a storm thrashing waves against rocks; all of the earth's emotion jammed into a cloth bag, then suddenly released.

But Ian Waters's playing was different. It was tender as that hand brushing the violin case, as open as his face as he rode down that road with the maple trees on either side. There was a clarity, a newness. A hopefulness that made your throat get tight with what could be tears.

From what I have learned from my mother all of these years, no one pretends to understand musicality, that certain something that a human being brings to the playing of his instrument. A machine can play an instrument, but it is that something of yourself that you bring to it that makes a player really good. That piece of your soul that you reveal as the music comes through you. I know nothing of this personally—I played the tissue paper comb in the kindergarten band—but you can hear it. You may not have words for it, but you can hear it. Maybe *feel* it is more accurate. There is a communication going on at some ancient and primitive level when music is played from somewhere else other than simply the fingers. This playing—it was his energy and heart rising from the notes. His dreams lifted from the instrument and carried out to where I heard them.

I don't even know what he was playing, and that's not even the important thing to this story anyway. I shut my eyes; it was as if he was painting with sound. I saw tender, vulnerable pictures. I was a child in a village, a child who'd just plucked a tangerine from a tree. Around me were the sounds of a town, Sabbotino Grappa maybe, voices speaking in Italian. I watched other children playing under a fig tree, and because it was so orange and shiny, put my teeth into the tangerine peel before remembering that this is not a good thing to do; it tasted terrible.

"Stop, stop, stop." This I heard loud and clear. Dino's authoritative voice could be heard two states away.

"Technically nearly perfect. But *purpose*. There is feeling, yes. But no purpose. You must have it. Without direction, you will drown. You may be young, but you don't need to hesitate. If you don't give everything to your playing, Ian, you will go hungry."

"I know."

"Hungry."

"All right."

"You know what I am talking about."

"Yes, I do."

Ian started to play again. The paintbrush stroked the canvas. I peeled that tangerine, broke off a sticky segment and popped it into my mouth. It was juicy and warm. The juice trickled into the tiny hammock between my fingers. I watched two old Italian women cross the street while arguing. One wore kneesocks that had given up on the job and gathered in clumps at her ankles. The other had a bad dye job—her hair was blacker than a briquette while her face was older than time. Everyone knew her hair hadn't seen that color since dinosaurs roamed the earth.

The music filled me with vivid-dream drowsiness. I watched two teenagers snitch a bicycle from the street, running like anything to the canal where they would toss it. Just like Dino's stories. When it was summer and the boys had too much time on their hands, the canal was filled with bicycles. A grandfather leaned down to speak to me. His breath smelled of a wine-soaked cork, his chin had a dent in it that split it right in half. . . .

I fell backward suddenly, jolting before my head hit the ground. Shit, I had fallen asleep, right there against the door, and Dino and Ian came out of the office and nearly stepped over my tumbling body. Oh, God, I could be such an idiot. I had fallen asleep, *right there,* and the first impression I left with Ian Waters was my body rolling into the room like the corpse in some Agatha Christie novel.

"What have we here?" Dino said. "Either a very bad Romanian gymnast or a spy."

Oh, the humiliation. I gave him the black-tongue curse again, added an essential part of the male anatomy.

"Guilty on the spy thing," I said. I hoped to sound casual, which is tough to do when you are reclining on one elbow and your face is hot enough to ignite a Bunsen burner. I struggled to stand. "Actually I was listening. I'm sorry. It was really beautiful. I must have fallen asleep."

"Rule one. Keep your audience awake," Dino said.

Ian grinned. I wondered if I should hate him for

colluding with Dino. Then he said, "Classical music can do that. Someone ought to put lyrics to it." He smiled.

"Ah!" Dino said in mock horror, and pretended to strangle Ian. "This is Cassie Morgan, astronomer. Ian Waters, talented, struggling musician. And heretic." All right. Since Dino attempted to restore some of my dignity, he could have his penis back.

"Astronomer," Ian said. "Wow." His eyes were a very gentle brown; his black hair threatened to swing over them. An angular face, long legs. He was tall and thin. In spite of performing before what must have been hundreds of people, he seemed shy, poetic.

"Still learning," I said.

"Tuesday, then?" Dino said.

"Tuesday," Ian said. "Thanks for listening," he said to me.

"Next time I'll stay awake," I said.

"No problem."

God, I was still kicking myself. That feeling of something being done wrongly, left unfinished, needing to be recaptured and played again, started churning inside as they headed out. Jesus, I should be put on some island for the terminally socially inept. Fuck-Up Island. It could be another perverse reality TV show. Mom came down the stairs, called a good-bye, and checked them both surreptitiously for blood and scratches.

Dino clapped Ian on the shoulder three times at the door before Ian left. Dino shut the door behind him, looked up at my mother, and smiled. "His mother is Italian," Dino beamed.

I went out to let Dog William back in. He was peering through the slats in the fence, no doubt watching as the figure of Rocket got smaller and smaller in the distance. I took a spot next to him, and through the narrow slat watched the black speck of Ian until he was gone. Dog William sighed through his nose as if saying farewell to the most interesting day of his life. I patted the top of his ugly head.

"I know it," I said to Dog William.

CHAPTER THREE

My father's house is also on Seabeck Island, and both of my parents live here to Minimize the Impact of Divorce. We all used to live together on a street not far from here, but Mom sold the place after she got together with Dino. Dad now lives in the house he grew up in, right on Outlook, one of the nicest streets in town, where a row of Victorians sit overlooking the waters of the Puget Sound. From his porch you can see the ferries gliding to and from Seattle, and he has a front-row seat every March, when some thirty-two thousand gray whales migrate down the coast and a gazillion tourists come to town to watch. Dad bought the house from Nannie, his mother, who now lives at Providence Point Community for Seniors. But Nannie comes over a lot and rearranges things back the way they were when she lived there. She's been forbidden to empty the dishwasher after she reorganized every kitchen cupboard when Dad was out mowing the lawn. He couldn't find the cheese grater for two weeks. Once we caught Nannie in the living room, trying to shove the couch back against the window where she'd had it for forty years. She did pretty well, too, for someone who must weigh about eighty pounds—she had it about halfway across the floor.

Mom and Dino bought the house we live in now on Mermaid Avenue (yes, it's really called that) shortly before they married. It's bigger than our old house, which was materialistic consolation for about a week or so, until real life set in. The divorce, the wedding, it all happened quickly. So quickly that you sometimes got the feeling that Dino was looking around with no small amount of resentment, wondering how he got from there to here. There being New York City, where he lived with his third wife, to here, a small island in Washington State, tucked far away from the center of the music world, married to a good but not great cellist, with a daughter who didn't appreciate what an astounding human being he was (i.e., hated his guts). How they got here was a tempestuous affair from what I have heard, although you don't want to think of your mother that way. It's okay to think of mothers in the same sentence as *lunch box* and *garden gloves,* but not in the same sentence as *passionate* and *tempestuous.* I will spare you the gory details of that time, the craziest, messiest kind of hell and chaos you never imagine for your life. Okay, one gory detail—my father, who takes insects outside when he finds them in the house, who rides them out on an envelope or some other handy airborne insect express material and gently lowers them to the ground, actually smashed his fist through his car window at the height of his anger and loss. Glass shards poked from the skin, sent blood down his Dockers.

Not that I blame my mother, not really. First, she's my mother and I love her and she's mostly a terrific person. But aside from that, it sounds like Dino chased after her with the determination of those dogs that travel thousands of miles to find their way back home after they tumble out of the back of a pickup. My mother, Daniella Morgan Cavalli, is, after all, a rather beautiful woman. Not in the sexy Barbie way, but like a medieval princess. Long, dark, curly hair. Dark eyes, a serenity that seems mysterious. People look at her, I know that. I have her eyes, I am told, but my hair is brown like my dad's, and is straight but not long enough to quite hit my shoulders. We both tend toward being full and curved and have to watch what we eat, but I distinctly lack that serenity people seem to find so alluring. She and Dino met when she was substituting for a cellist on maternity leave with the Seattle Symphony, and he appeared as a guest for three nights, performing *Amore Trovato* (Love Found), written for his third wife. In spite of this, my mother fell for him as if she had been kidnapped and brainwashed, and my father was sure this is what had actually happened. Dino's charm must have been intense, as prior to then my mother was a practical person who barely sniffed at a sad movie. My mother's charm mustn't have been too bad either—Dino stayed for three weeks, went back to New York only long enough to pack up his things. Lesson learned—charm is a one-way ticket to hell. Better to fall in love with a man who is dull as a pancake than one with *charm*.

Still, if I'm honest, I can't exactly blame Dino entirely either. Blame is so satisfying that you can forget it's actually useless. The truth is, there are a thousand reasons my parents aren't together anymore, and nine hundred ninety-nine of them I don't even know about or fully understand. I do know, though, that there are essential differences between them that I've noticed over the years: my father reads a map, while my mother doesn't mind getting lost; my father is consistently a believer, while my mother uses religion like some people use vitamins—when they feel an illness coming on. Before he paints a room my father tapes the edges and covers everything as thoroughly as an Egyptian mortician, while my mother's only preparation for the same job is to put on old jeans and take off her socks so she can tell if she's stepped in a paint drip. He cuts a peach; she bites it whole. The practicality I thought Mom had was maybe more an adaptive response to living with Dad, rather than her original, true self. Something like those fish that go blind after living in a dark cave.

Whatever the reasons for their split, I now go back and forth between locations, same as a letter with a bad address. I refuse, though, to be a messed up Product of Divorce, which some people think should be stamped on the side of you MADE IN MALAYSIA-style before they stick you

43

in a crate and pack you off to the Land of the Damaged. Broken home, remember? The message being that because a marriage is broken, everything in the home is broken too, including you.

But there is one thing that I would say about the going back and forth, and that is, you wonder if the adults would ever get divorced if they had to be the ones to change homes every week. This is all supposed to be all right, and we are required to be okay about it, but it's not okay. Not really. We can handle it, don't get me wrong. But the truth is, it's *not okay*. The truth is, you just start to get comfy, when suddenly you've got to pack up and remember to bring your book and your favorite earrings and your notes for your paper for Humanities. You've got to readjust to your surroundings—the parent, the pet, the step-siblings or lack of them, who has bagels, who runs out of milk, which drawer to reach for when you want a spoon. The truth is that you have a day on either side where it feels as if you've just come home from vacation. You've got to remember where things left off. Oh yeah, that's right—my room's a mess. Oh yeah, that's right—my CD player's batteries are dead and I haven't read my new magazine yet and I'd gotten in a fight with Mom before I left. And the truth is, as soon as you arrive "home" you are too often pulled into the perverse divorce game, Who Do You Love More. It begins with what looks like an innocent question: "How did it go at Mom's/Dad's?" It ends with this reverse *Sophie's Choice,* where instead of a mother choosing between children, you are asked to choose between parents. If anything, all this divorce stuff made you feel that if you were anywhere near love you ought to don one of those suits those people wear from the Centers for Disease Control.

That's why I was trying to get thoughts of Ian Waters out of my mind that day I went to my dad's for the weekend. Real simply, I didn't want to get hurt by the power of my own emotions. I wasn't doing a very good job of erasing him from my head. I'd stooped to the lowest depths of thoughts, pictured him kissing me deeply before leaving on a plane for Curtis, me sobbing miserably in an airport chair as his plane pulled away from the doorway. I mean, I knew how this story would have to end, if there was even to be a story at all. It was not an end I wanted to willingly walk toward.

Dad wasn't home when I got there, so I went out to the porch and sat in the swing and looked out toward the sound. At that time of year you had your occasional humpback, otters, and sea lions, and I watched for the odd shape in the waves, a break in the pattern that meant some creature was there. It was colder than hell outside, and everything was painted in the Northwest's favorite color, gray. The water was steely, and the sky a soft fuzz, but it was still beautiful out there. A kayaker with a death wish was bobbing around on the water, his boat a vivid red spot in a silver sea. For the millionth, compelling time, I saw those fingers stroke that violin case.

"Look who's here!" my father called out.

I went inside. My father had one arm around Nannie and the other around a fat bag of groceries.

"He thinks he's made of money," Nannie said.

"I bought her a *People* magazine," Dad said.

"That's hard-earned dollars you spent on that trash," Nannie said. I kissed her cheek, helped her off with her coat, which wasn't too necessary. She was flinging it off like an alligator wrestler in her eagerness to get to the bag Dad had set on the counter. She fished around inside with one thin arm, plucked out the magazine, squashing a loaf of bread with her elbow in the process.

"I don't even know who these trollops are," she said as she eased into a corner of the couch and stuck her nose in the pages.

"Hey, Cass. How about sweet-and-sour chicken?"

"Yum."

Cooking was one of Dad's post-divorce hobbies. Before that, his specialty was cornflakes with bananas on them. Now he was really into it. He cooked better than Mom ever had, which was probably the point. He has all of these fancy knives and pots, and various, curious utensils good for only one weird purpose—skinning a grape, say. I could have written a confessional *My Father Had a Spring-form Pan*. He built a shelf in the kitchen for all of his cookbooks, and Nannie kept bumping her head on it. *Who put this thing here?* she'd grouse, knowing full well who did it.

We had dinner and watched a movie, some PG thing about misfit boys who go to camp, which ended with the two parents who'd both lost their spouses deciding to marry. Of course there were two white kids (one good,

46

one evil), a black kid, an Asian kid, one fat kid, and one girl with glasses. It was worse than those movies where a dog wins a sports championship.

"Sex, sex, sex," Nannie said when the happy couple kissed at the end. "That's all you see in movies anymore." I guess that's why we weren't watching *The Rocky Horror Picture Show*. "I'm going to bed."

"Dishes await," Dad said after Nannie's flowered housecoat disappeared slowly up the stairs. "Would you go and check on her? I'm worried that by the time you get there Grandpa's photo will be up on my nightstand and her Poligrip will be in my medicine cabinet."

"No problem," I said.

I trotted upstairs, checked the guest room, but didn't find Nannie. I went to Dad's room to see if he was right. I was expecting to catch her red-handed, an unrepentant criminal of living in the past.

That's when I saw it—part of the cover of Dino's biography sticking out from under Dad's bed. It was splayed open to keep his place. I was sure he'd read it before, when all of the awful stuff was happening, but why was he reading it now, three years later? I walked over to his bed, looked underneath. There was a nest of papers, notes in Dad's handwriting, other books. *Composers Speak—Part 2 in the Young Musicians Series*, with that famous picture of Dino on the cover, looking sultry and young, during his days in Paris. And there was *Culinary History—Authentic Tuscan Recipes*. What was he doing, writing the Dino Cookbook? I wrestled with my conscience about sitting down right then and reading those notes. Guilt convinced me that Nannie would fall and break a hip or something if I did, so I left to find her. I saw the light on under the bathroom door.

"Are you okay in there?" I called through the door.

"Yes, thank you," Nannie said primly.

I waited until she came out and got settled into the guest room bed. She was propped on the pillows as if waiting for visitors when I kissed her cheek and turned off her light.

"What a day," she said.

"Good night, Nannie," I said.

"Good night, my special dear," she said. She was always a little sweeter at night. Maybe it was the nightgown with the bow.

I wanted to go right downstairs and confront Dad about his under-the-bed project, but when I got there he was drying a pan with a kitchen towel and whistling, having such a cheerful father moment, I couldn't stand the thought of breaking it. His T-shirt was loose over his jeans, and his hair had gone from polite to playful. He looked so happy I decided I didn't have the heart for a confrontation just yet. It would have to wait.

The next day I went to the movies with a couple of my friends, Sophie Birnbaum and Nat Frasier, Zebe and Brian Malo. Zebe's real name is Meggie Rawlinson, which sounds like some fifties cheerleader and doesn't fit her at all. We call her Zebe after her favorite zebra-stripe boots. We try to get together most weekends when there isn't a play, as everyone but me is in drama. Sophie and Brian usually are the leads and we give them crap because sometimes they have to kiss. They love each other like brother and sister, which apparently means they sometimes want to tear out each other's throats. Zebe does stage managing, and Nat is happy when he gets more than a couple of lines. Last year, every time we saw him, we'd say "This way, sir," after his Oscar-winning role as a waiter in *The Matchmaker.*

It was turning out to be Crappy Movie Weekend, as what we saw was basically one long boob joke. It was all girls in tight shirts with enormous buttlike cleavage and boys falling over their own tongues hanging out their mouths, the kind of thing that makes you wonder if there's any truth to evolution after all. Sophie got in a fight with Brian when he said that a little lighthearted movie with lots of tits was occasionally refreshing.

"We can help you hold him down," Zebe said.

"Hey, I don't want to touch him," I said. "Stupidity is a *disease.*"

"I'll wash my hands afterward," Zebe said.

When I went back to Dad's, the house was quiet. It was so quiet that the refrigerator humming was the only noise, and I got that has-a-mass-murderer-been-here-and-now-he's-in-the-closet-just-waiting-to-jump-out-at-me feeling. Instead, I found that Nannie's coat was gone, taken back with her to Providence Point, I guessed, and I noticed that a couple of pieces of toast had popped up from the toaster and had long ago grown cold. The coffeepot was on, with no coffee left in the pot, just a burning smear of brown. I always worried that this was how Dad really lived when I wasn't around, that the good cooking and orderly house were a show put on just for me and dropped the moment I left. I've come by unannounced before and saw unopened mail stacked six inches high, and egg yolk permanently wedded to the dishes it was on. That's the other prominent thing about divorce—you worry about your parents when they are supposed to be worrying about you.

I turned off the coffeepot and went upstairs. I found Dad on his bed, propped up not too differently than his mother the night before, with his glasses on and one toe trying to get a glimpse of the outside world from a hole in his sock. Those notes I had seen the night before were scattered all around him. Maybe it wasn't disinterest that had let the toast grow cold—maybe he was just excited to get back to his project.

"Knock, knock," I said.

"Oh, jeez." Dad startled, gathered up his papers. I'm surprised he didn't shove them under the pillow, stuff them in his mouth, and swallow them like they do in the spy movies.

"What time is it? You're early."

"Nope, right on time," I said.

"Wow," he said.

"So what're you doing?"

"Work."

"One, you look too guilty for work. Two, there's one of

Dino's books open in front of you. Unless you got a new job I don't know about, that's not work. What's going on?"

My father sighed. He looked out the window, as if hoping the answer to my question would form in the clouds. *I see a giraffe! I see a pirate ship! I see that I'm nosing around on my ex-wife's new husband to try to catch him doing something horrible!*

I moved closer to the bed to see.

"No!" he said. He actually put one arm over his notes, same as those kids who make sure you don't cheat off them.

"Dad, God."

"All right," he said. "Okay! I just had a little feeling about something and I wanted to check it out."

"What kind of little feeling?"

"About Dino Cavalli."

"No shit," I said.

"Cassie, watch your mouth. Is that necessary? I was just thumbing through this book recently and something caught my eye that didn't add up."

"You mean you were hunting through it line by line for something that didn't add up," I said.

He ignored me, which meant I was right. "I found something. I mean, I think I found something, and I was just checking it out."

"What did you find?"

"I don't know if I want to say."

"What? He's actually a woman," I guessed. "A killer. A killer woman."

51

"A liar," my father said.

I sighed. "You should get a girlfriend, Dad. I mean it. It's been three years, and you haven't had a date."

"I've had dates. This isn't about dates. This is important. Your mother's life. Your life. If he's lied about one thing, he's lied about others, mark my words."

"Marissa what's her name. She seemed nice. A little Career Barbie but . . ."

"All right, listen to this," Dad said. He adjusted his glasses and began to read. "'My mother would make a simple lunch, gougere, some bread, and then I would practice.'"[7]

"Goo-zhair. Is that edible? I think our neighbor's cat had one of those caught in his throat once," I said.

"It's a lie."

"There's no such food?"

"No, it's a real food, but it's a recipe from 1969. He's claiming he ate it when he was eight or nine, and the man is older than I am. The recipe first appeared in a Moldavi wine recipe book, and the wine itself used in the recipe wasn't even made until 1968."

"God, Dad."

"I know," he said.

"No! I'm talking about you! What are you doing? So maybe the food wasn't around. Maybe he made a mistake. Maybe they got his age wrong. Maybe a thousand things. What does this prove? You've already got plenty of reason

[7] Dino Cavalli—*The Early Years: An Oral History*. From Edward Reynolds, New York, N.Y. Aldine Press, 1999.

not to like him. Shit, in my opinion, *Mom* has plenty of reasons not to like him, and she still does."

Dad got up, gathered his papers. He looked pissed at me. "It just may prove what I've always known. He's a fraud. You just wait."

It's tough to lip-synch violin playing, but I didn't say this. I turned and left the room, as I didn't want to fight with Dad. Anything I said would sound like a defense of Dino, and the Civil War began on less.

"That snake was fucking *strong,* man," Zach Rogers said. "A reptile's muscles you can't exactly see, you know, through that skin and everything, but I had two encyclopedias on the lid. Two, and he still pushed open the lid and got out. Here's the psychic-phenomenon-ESPN-shit part. One encyclopedia? It fell open to a page on *dinosaurs.* Tyrannosaurus rex. Biggest badass dude of reptiles in history. Now, that's almost *creepy.* What are the odds?"

I was walking home from school with Courtney Powelson, my neighbor, and Zach, though I don't even think he lived near us. He was just sort of migrating along with us, and I had the feeling he was soon going to look up and wonder where the hell he was. He either had a thing for Courtney or he was so used to seeing me that he forgot we were separate individuals. I had every class period with him, even lunch. It was one of those annoying twists of fate in a supposedly random universe. I've noticed that this kind of scheduling cruelty never happens with anyone you actually would want to spend all day, every day, with. No, I got Zach. Zach was weird. Entertaining, okay, but weird. He made me believe in alien life forms who come to live among us to steal our souls and our Hostess Cupcake recipes.

"A dinosaur isn't a reptile, it's an amphibian," Courtney said.

Zach ignored her, which was a good thing, since she was wrong, anyway. Courtney and I walked to school together often, but she usually pretended she didn't know me when she got there. She was one of the Popular Group, which meant two things: one, she could outfit a small town in Lithuania with the amount of clothes she had (picture innocent Lithuanian children in glittery HOT BABE T-shirts) and two, she was destined to marry some jock, have a zillion kids, and thereby assure herself a spot in front of a television forever. Queen of the American Dream. She didn't often walk home with me, as she was usually doing some after-school activity—the Sexy Dancing in Front of Male Sports Team club or the I Could Play a Sport Myself but Then I'd Have to Get Sweaty club. *Her mother should have named her MasterCard,* Zebe said once. Courtney and her two brothers bugged the hell out of Dino. "They have the glazed eyes of too much technology," he said once. "You look in their eyes and see Gillian Island re-runs playing." *Gilligan,* he meant. Even though our houses were pretty far apart, you could often hear their TV blasting or the repetitive pounding of video game music. I still walked with her because, okay, I admit it, she was nice away from her friends, and because I was weak when it came to compromising my principles.

"I didn't even get to the best part yet," he said. "So the lamp I had shining on him? I stuck it down with duct tape. When this mother got out he climbed up the lamp, and when I found him, there was the snake, stuck on the duct tape, back of his head pinned like this." Zach threw back his head, did a really good stunned cobra impersonation.

"Hey, that was great," I said. "You could take that on the road."

"Eyuw," Courtney said. She shivered. I'm not kidding. Those kind of girls always shiver.

"I didn't even try to take it off. I was afraid I might skin him."

"Hey—perfect ad for the strength of duct tape," I said.

"Oh, my God," Courtney said.

"Had to take him to the vet. Luckily he was still alive," Zach said.

I pictured Zach putting his ear to the little chest to check for a heartbeat, a grateful tear coming to his eye. "How does a vet de-duct tape a snake?" I asked.

"Very carefully," he said. "Anyway, there's six encyclopedias on there now, to see if he can beat his record. He's my Bench-Press Baby."

"Well, here's our street."

I was right earlier, because Zach stopped and looked around. "Where the fuck am I?" he said. Then he shrugged his shoulders. "Cool."

Zach wandered off the direction we came, and I left

Courtney to an evening of video fulfillment. At home I let Dog William in, went back out front to get the mail. Up the road came Dino's car. He parked in the driveway and got out. He had his suit on but wasn't wearing any shoes. No socks, shoes, nothing. It was *October. Way* too cold for simple, barefooted pleasure.

"Dino?" I said. "Hey, did you forget something? Or is this a new bohemian phase?"

Now, Dino was usually a pretty distracted guy. But this struck me as a bit beyond his usual absentmindedness. We're talking *shoes.* Not exactly something that tends to slip your mind.

This, my friends, is how quickly life can change.

A little kernel of unease planted itself inside my gut. "It doesn't matter," Dino said.

He slammed the car door and went inside. Something more was going on here; something was *not right.* I could feel this *wrongness* coming off him, just like you feel someone's anger or joy. I followed him, saw him discard his tie on the floor. He paced into the kitchen, and a moment later paced back out again. I was getting a seriously eerie feeling. An uneasiness that didn't have a name. It was his agitation. And he had this weird look in his eyes, like he was watching something I couldn't see.

"He always knows where I am, doesn't he?" Dino said. "He can see me wherever I am, that bastard."

Okay, shit. Something freaky was definitely going on. My body tensed in high alert. I wanted Mom home. Creepiness was doing this dance inside my skin.

Dino strode into his office, shut the door with a click. The house was quiet except for Dog William *huh, huh, huh*ing beside me. I was glad for his presence—at least I wasn't completely alone. I had one of those inexplicable moments where I looked at Dog William and he looked at me, and I decided that dogs really had superior knowledge to humans, held the secrets to the universe, only they couldn't speak. It's an idea you quickly discard after you see them chew underwear, but right then I felt better thinking one of us understood what the hell was going on.

And then suddenly the silence was shattered. Sorry for the cliché, but that's what happened. Shattered, with the— sudden frenzy of the violin, the sound of someone sawing open a tree and finding all of life and death pouring out.

"Wow," I said aloud. "Jesus."

He didn't tune first. That was what I realized. Not tuning was like a surgeon not snapping on his gloves. Like, well, going out without first putting on your shoes.

It was the first time he'd played in months and months. But this wasn't just playing. This was unzipping your skin and spilling out your soul. I had a selfish thought then. Actually, it was kind of a prayer to anyone who might be listening and interested. Please, I begged. Don't let Dino be crazy when Ian Waters comes.

CHAPTER FOUR

Here's the thing about dealing with people who are beginning the process of losing it. Your most overwhelming urge is to make sense of something that doesn't make sense. You try to make it fit, even if it doesn't really. You look at their crazy world from your sane world, and try to make your logical rules apply. As I stood in the hall with Dog William, I decided that there was a plausible story for Dino's behavior. Something rational. I was having trouble coming up with a story, but hey, there was one somewhere because there had to be. Maybe he got a letter from an old friend he wasn't so happy to hear from. And Italy—Italy was hot, right? How many times had I heard *that*? So you know, maybe he was homesick for his shoeless days in Italy. And what about Einstein? A genius, yeah, but he couldn't match his socks, so he gave up wearing them.

Maybe this was something like Einstein. A shoeless, paranoid-ish genius thing. Of course, the deep inside piece of you that knows everything was saying this had nothing to do with Italy or Einstein or an old friend. That inside piece of you knows that your life is veering in a direction you have no desire to go. Basically, downhill.

That night I heard yelling. Dino just really going at it downstairs in his office. I'd heard him yell before, usually at his managers, but I couldn't imagine who he'd be yelling at now. Mom had gone to bed already, and the house had been silent. A moment later I heard Mom come out from their bedroom, her hurried steps down the stairs. The front door opened, slammed shut. I slipped out of bed, peeked out my front shades. Dino was on the front lawn in his bathrobe, his skin looking white in the moonlight. He stalked around a bit as if trying to decide what to do, then went behind the hydrangea bushes in the direction of the shed. I lost sight of him, then waited a while to see if he would reappear. Nothing. Finally I got back in bed, stayed on high alert. The house was quiet. I tried to go back to sleep, but when I finally started to doze I heard their voices downstairs. I couldn't make out their actual words, and though a part of me wanted to hear, a bigger part didn't. The uneasiness I felt that afternoon was appearing again, adding a new piece, and I wanted it *away*. But I could tell that my mother's voice was calm, a little pleading, and that Dino's was insistent.

The next morning I went down to get breakfast. I was exhausted from the night, feeling like shit and wondering how to define all the oddities of the day before. Mom sat at the kitchen table, drinking coffee. She looked tired too. She looked more than tired. She looked like someone had crumpled her up into a ball, thrown her in the trash, removed her, and tried to smooth her out again. I confess I had a Child of Divorce Reunion Fantasy Number One Thousand, where I for a moment imagined my father finding out that Dino really was a killer woman and that my parents would have to get back together. I saw them running through a meadow, hand in hand. Okay, maybe not a meadow. But I saw me having only one Christmas and one phone number and only my own father's shaved bristles in the bathroom sink. Having both of my own sane, well-rested parents in the kitchen in the morning. I didn't have these moments often, but the only time Mom ever seemed even mildly tired with Dad was when he had a bad bout of marathon snoring. Why she had brought Dino into our lives I'd never understand. I'd give her some excuse, but three years was a little long for temporary insanity.

"Well, that was fun," I said.

"You heard," she said. Mom pushed her bangs from her forehead, rubbed her temples. The gesture made me pissed off at Dino, at what he caused.

"I heard yelling. I didn't hear actual words. What was going on?"

"Dino was trying to write last night, and he swore he could hear the Powelson's television. It was bugging him. His ears—you know he can hear a leaf drop off a tree."

"I heard the door slam. I saw him outside."

"He went over there. To their house. He cut their cable wire with a pair of hedge clippers."

I almost laughed. I did. I mean, think of it—Dino creeping down the street in his bathrobe, aiming toward the glow of light in Courtney and gang's living room window. I could just picture him hunting around in the junipers for the cable, his gleeful discovery of the thick wire, the satisfactory snap. Then, the sudden extinguishing of the light to a pinpoint. The whole Powelson house with its television IV yanked. "It's almost kind of funny," I said.

"It's not funny, Cassie. Okay, it's a little funny. Oh, shit." She chuckled to herself. She shook her head, held her coffee mug in both hands.

I wanted to crack up, but the joke felt like a sick one, slightly morbid. If it had just been this, another Dino tantrum, I could have laughed. But there was also his shoeless display of weirdness yesterday. This wire cutting—it was more than excessive frustration. I knew that. "Something strange happened yesterday," I said.

"Oh?"

I told Mom about Dino. The shoes. His paranoia that someone always knew where he was. The way he played that violin. She just looked at me for a while. "He's off his medicine," she said finally.

"What do you mean, 'He's off his medicine'?"

"He's trying to write. He says it makes him too foggy. That he can't create when he takes it."

"I didn't even know he had medicine."

61

"For his depression."

Mom had first explained to me about Dino's depression early on in their marriage. No one I knew before had ever tromped off to see a psychiatrist every week. This seemed more than a tad over-dramatic, and I said so to Mom. She went into this big discussion about what clinical depression was, as if I'd never heard those ads on the radio ("Do you have any of these symptoms? Change in eating or sleeping habits? Loss of interest in things that used to give you pleasure? Being critical and nasty to the people you live with?"). It apparently was not I'm-having-a bad-day, but I'm-having-a-bad-life, with complications ranging from not being able to get out of bed to feeling like the world was out to get him. All things you want in a second husband.

Obviously, this depression also made him incapable of seeing that he was luckier than 99 percent of the world's population. Okay, I know it sounds unsympathetic, and I know most of the time it's a chemical thing that happens to good people and can't be helped. But in Dino's case, so much of it sounded like a spoiled child who needed to be sent to his room. Really, did people who lived in third world countries with no running water or indoor toilets and that had to sew thousands of faux leather jackets in zillion-degree heat in order to eat get depressed and stay in bed? Could they not function without their psychiatrist connected to them like those sicko parents who put their kids on a leash? Call me cold, but his depression seemed like a luxury. I mean, I was depressed myself at having to live with the guy.

"Can't you make him take his medicine?" I said.

"Oh, sure," she said. She was right. It was a stupid thing to say. No one could make Dino do anything he didn't want to.

"I don't get this. What's going to happen here? Is he just going to keep getting worse? He's going to start thinking he's Jesus?"

She didn't answer. I guess she didn't know either. Great. Terrific. What did this *mean*? "Cassie?" she said finally. "There's one more thing. I didn't want to tell you, but you'd probably see the truck." She was quiet for a moment.

"What?" I meant, *What now?*

"He cut our cable, too."

"Are you kidding me? Why?" I didn't know what to think or feel. None of this seemed real. I guess I felt a little panicked. My voice was high and shrill.

"He said . . . he said he did it so no one could listen in on his work in progress."

"Oh, my God."

"I've got a call in to the doctor."

I felt a gathering in my chest, an on-alert tightness. Then, I knew what I felt. I was afraid.

That day at school, I looked at the people in my classes and thought about how different my yesterday must have been from any of theirs. No one in those rooms would have guessed what happened in my house last night. There was

63

something about it that made me ashamed. And it was big. Too big to hold all by myself, even if it was embarrassing as hell. Zebe is the best listener in the world, even patiently hearing about your dreams in boring detail (*And then I turned into a fern. A talking fern, and then I got onto a bus heading to Miami, only it wasn't really Miami. It looked like the living room, and my second-grade teacher Mr. Bazinski, was wearing a kilt and sitting on an ottoman teaching long division . . .*), so at lunch I tried a little of what happened on her. Not all of it. Just enough so I could handle the rest on my own. She had all of the basic facts—we'd been friends for a couple of years, and she knew my family.

"Dino's going nuts," I said.

"What? That cuddly, cutesy-wootsy teddy bear? I think you should write an essay and nominate him for Stepfather of the Year."

"Don't even call him that. My mother's husband. Okay? I don't even want *father* in the same sentence as Dino."

"I noticed you weren't acting like yourself," Zebe said. "Here. Have some Cheetos. Nothing like overly orange food to give you comfort. Think about it. Orange sherbert. Orange Jell-O. I'm going to dye my hair orange."

"Don't you dare." Zebe had this long, jet-black hair that was so shiny you could practically see your reflection in it. That day she was wearing fishnet stockings and a plaid skirt. She could wear anything and make it look cool.

"So what's Senōr Loco done now?" she asked.

"Dino's paranoid that someone can hear the new stuff he's writing," I said. "Through the television cable." I used my can-you-believe-how-stupid-he-is? voice. It was Zebe and I loved her, but this was as far as I was willing to go. I couldn't speak about how afraid it had made me. This craziness happening in *my family,* for God's sake. People might think it was catching.

Zebe twirled her finger by her head. "Oh, my God, what a freak! My dad got real paranoid when my parents got divorced. He climbed in a window of my mom's to steal her journals. He was sure she was going to post nasty stuff about him on the Web. She was even going to press charges, but decided it wasn't worth the hassle."

Zebe and I ate Cheetos. I thought about what she said. Really thought about what it must have meant to her. A ladder against a window. Your parent rooting around like an intruder. A police car in front of your house as the neighbors looked on. Maybe I was wrong when I thought no one at my school would believe what had happened to me. I looked around the cafeteria, the rows of tables jammed with people, scattered lunches, noise, crap on the floor. John Jorgenson grabbed some sophomore's baseball cap and threw it to his friend, and Danielle Rhone was trying to find something she dropped under a table, and three freshmen were huddled together over open books, doing their homework. Reese Lin shoved what looked like a full lunch bag in the garbage, and Todd Fleming brought three small pizza boxes to his table. Angela Aris and James what's-his-name leaned against the wall, making out. I wondered what went on behind the closed doors of these people's houses. A mother that drank too much, a father that hit. Parents that fought, or tried unsuccessfully to hide an affair, or who couldn't leave the house out of fear.

Maybe we all had our secrets.

I walked home alone from school that day, no Siang or Courtney. Zach and I had apparently had a successful operation to separate Siamese twins, at least for the moment. I was coming down our road, trying to ignore the fact that it was Tuesday, the day of Ian Waters's next lesson, and so of course was consumed by thoughts of nothing else. *Please let Dino act normal,* I said over and over in my head. *Please, please.* I had decided under no uncertain terms not to fall for Ian Waters, but I still didn't want him to think I lived in a nuthouse. Here was the thing—Ian was going to go away to school, and that was that. Letting myself fall for him was only going to lead to pain. I, for one, didn't need to jump headfirst into some overwhelming feeling that would lead to disaster. I could make a rational decision about where I was going to put my heart, or if I was going to put my heart anywhere at all.

I was what you would call Steeled with Resolve when this old Datsun, a horrible shade of banana yellow, drove up behind me on our road. It stopped in front of our house as I walked up, and this beefy, motorcycle type got out of the passenger's side, flipping up the seat to let Ian Waters and his violin out of the back. Rocket leaped out after him.

"Hey," Ian said when he saw me.

God, he had beautiful eyes. Gentle brown. Like deer fur, or those elbow patches on the jackets of college professors. A soft, comforting brown. I'd forgotten what effect the sight of him had on me. Goddamn it.

"Hey," I said eloquently.

"You've got to meet my brother and his best friend. Chuck, this is Cassie. Dino's daughter." I didn't bother to correct him with the real version of our twisted family tree right then, as huge Chuck was holding out this bear paw for me to shake, and the driver of the Datsun, a twin of the other guy, was turning around to see me. "And that's my brother, Bunny."

"Howdy," Bunny gave a wave.

Either Ian or his brother must have been conceived in a petri dish, because they were the unlikeliest brother combo you'd ever seen. Bunny was outfitted in a motorcyclist's black leather pants and a vest with a T-shirt underneath. He was older than Ian, by maybe seven or eight years. He had a wild bunch of dark brown hair, and was solid as the side of a mountain. You wouldn't dare point out the fact that he had the name of a cute fluffy animal. He looked like he could kill with his bare hands.

"Be good," Bunny said as Chuck got in and shut the door. Boy, I'd be good if he said that to me. I'd sit and embroider Bible verses, I'd be so good.

The car pulled away. I saw something that surprised me. They had a bumper sticker: TRUST THE PROCESS.

"We're twins," Ian said, and grinned.

"I could tell by your matching outfits," I said. Rocket had curled up on the lawn. I could hear Dog William whining on the other side of the fence.

"He's my stepbrother. He moved us out here when my stepfather died. He thinks it's his personal responsibility to look after us. He comes over and makes, like, six boxes of macaroni and cheese."

"Wow," I said. "I like his bumper sticker."

"Oh, man. Don't ever get him started on that stuff. I'm serious." We headed into the house. "Chuck and Bunny are into the whole metaphysical thing. They've been friends since they were, like, two. They go around to their motorcycle groups giving talks on The Wisdom of Your Inner Voice."

"Okay, this time you are kidding."

"I wish I was."

"That's hilarious. Metaphysical motorcyclists."

"It's worse. Neither of them has a motorcycle. Jeez." He shook his head and laughed. Okay, great. Ian Waters was nice, too. Beautiful, talented, *nice*.

"Shall we get started?" Dino said when we came in. I tried to check him out for any sign of irrational paranoia. His shoes were on. His eyes looked normal. I allowed myself the thought that maybe we'd all overreacted about yesterday. Or maybe Mom got Dino to take his medicine. This super-fast-acting medicine.

Dino grasped Ian's shoulder and squeezed it in warm greeting. It looked like the lesson was going to go okay, and I went upstairs. After a while I heard the music starting. God, if I could only explain it. You wanted to let it take up residence inside you. Let it flourish there, like a garden of wildflowers. You wanted to possess it, hold it, become a part of it. It wrapped around you like the cape of a wizard, full of magic color.

I wanted it. That music, him. I put my pillow over my head. That boy and his violin scared the crap out of me. My heart was beating so hard it felt like it was trying to make an escape attempt.

An eternity and an hour later, I heard the front door close as Ian left. Mom came home shortly after, and we shouted greetings to each other from different floors, something that never failed to piss off Dino. Soon, dinner smells rose up the stairs.

Dino's face was tight at the table, stern and rocky. The favorite game of temperamental people is Try to Guess Why I'm Ticked Off. (*Contestant number one, Why do YOU think he's pissed off? Why, I'm not sure, Bob, but I'm going to go with 'Because I Left the Faucet Dripping. BEEP. I'm sorry, that's incorrect. The correct answer is: 'Because You Happen to Exist.'*) Even if I'm determined not to play, I get sucked in. My brain just does what it wants anyway, same as when I'm sitting in calculus, wondering if Mr. Firtz could possibly have a sex life, even though the thought is revolting. The brain can be a sicko, out-of-control thing sometimes, and at dinner I started wondering who did what wrong this time. Likely Dino was doing a Mount Rushmore imitation because we'd shouted at each other across the house. I put my money down on that one.

"How did the lesson go?" my mother asked Dino. She seemed more relaxed than she did that morning, in spite of Dino's obvious attitude. Like me, she was probably relieved to find Dino more "normal" again. Which meant, back to his old asshole-ish self.

"A beautiful lesson with the boy. Except for the fact that he was late. Cassie was entertaining him."

I never thought Dino was very attractive—if you've never seen a picture of him, his nose is chunky and his forehead is broad, and he's got full lips. He's pretty short, too, just a little taller than Mom unless she wears heels. His crowning glory was his headful of curly gray-black hair, but it's like the game you can play with the blond girls at school—imagine them without the hair and there's not much there. I'm not sure why women liked him so much. But right then, he was downright ugly. That's the thing with mean people. Eventually their spirit shows through like mold on cheese.

"Entertaining him? I talked to the guy for maybe a minute and a half," I said. I let the irritation show in my voice. I didn't care. I plunked a dollop of guacamole on my taco salad, took a forceful bite.

"The lesson started late."

So that's what his problem was. In forty years when he got Alzheimer's, he might forgive me.

"He needs to focus on his music. Nothing else."

"I said hello. He introduced me to his brother."

"Sounds harmless to me," Mom said. "She's not having

70

a love affair with the guy, Dino. *Hello* won't kill his focus."
She speared a tomato.

"This is not some high school boy, Daniella. We are attempting to train a genius. He has no room for kissy face."

"Darn, and I thought you didn't see my tongue down his throat," I said. I got up. Shoved back my chair. I wasn't hungry anymore. If there is something that can make you as angry as being unjustly accused, tell me. Or being disproportionately accused. You do well in school and you don't do drugs or have sex, but they get mad at you for not making your bed.

I went outside to the shed, got out my telescope. Swore under my breath at the psycho creep. It was late October and cold out, and I'd wished I'd interrupted my anger by getting a sweatshirt. Too late now. The clouds were doing this manic fleeing, in a hurry to get somewhere, and as they whipped past, they'd reveal these bursts of brilliantly clear sky. I hauled out my equipment and set up in the open grassy patch by the front of the house. It was the perfect viewing place—open sky, the garden ringed with hydrangeas and a view of the sound. The water smelled cold and deep and swampy in the darkness, the smell of thousands of years of whale secrets.

I sprang out the tripod legs of my telescope, swore at the fact that I only wore socks, which were now wet from dewy grass. Hey, cool. Now I could take them off and be a lunatic like Dino. Dog William whined for my company from behind the fence. If I was lucky I'd see Mars in between cloudbursts. It was more work than it seemed, looking through a telescope, as the Earth was continually moving and you had to move along with it. You don't realize how fast this actually happens, and it's kind of both creepy and wonderful when you stop to think about it. And it makes you realize there is absolutely no way to avoid change. You can sit there and cross your arms and refuse it, but underneath you, things are still spinning away.

Anyway, the telescope always made me feel better. I could go to a different place and didn't need chemicals or airfare to do it. I started hunting around for Mars when I heard tires on gravel. Bike tires. Oh, my God, bike tires. It was inky black out there, so all I could see was the white of his T-shirt underneath his black coat until he got closer. Ian Waters put his feet on the ground, balanced his bike with his hands. God, there he was, all of a sudden. Ian Waters.

"Hi," he said. His breath came out in a puff. That's how cold it was getting.

"Hi," I said. "What are you doing here?" I tried to breathe. My heart was doing this charming maraca number.

"Performance tape." He pulled a cassette from his pocket, lifted it up. "Mr. Cavalli wanted to hear one of my concerts. Can you see anything tonight?"

"Mars." I was trying to ignore the fact that his presence was charging up the night like an approaching lightning storm. I swear, my insides felt this surge of energy, a hyperawareness. I could smell his shampoo. I tried to breathe deeply. I mean, this was stupid. This was no big deal. I forced myself to sound casual. "Want to look? You've got to be quick, before a cloud comes."

Ian set his bike down on the grass, climbed over it. His coat was apparently a conductor of electricity, because when his sleeve touched my arm as he bent over beside me, I felt a jolt of current. I shivered.

"Cold?" he said, as he looked into the telescope where I had pointed it.

"I'm okay." Which was a lie. Some cruel person had invaded my body and was squeezing my lungs. I could barely breathe, so I'm not quite sure why I was suddenly worrying about my guacamole breath.

"No way," he said. "Is that it? Mars?"

"Big white ball? Yeah." Casual. No big deal.

"That's amazing. That's *Mars*? That's an actual planet? Man, that's hard to believe." He stood straight again. His eyes were shiny and happy. "We're looking at a *planet*."

"I know it. That's how I feel about it too."

"I've never seen inside a telescope before."

"Never?"

"No. You know, this is my usual method." He leaned his head back, looked up. "Wow. This isn't bad either."

He was right. I looked up with him and saw that the sky was showing off. The clouds had moved aside for a moment, and the blackness was deep, deep. The stars were both simple and magical, thousands of pinpoints of light. It was one of those moments you wonder how we could ever forget what was up there. There is that majesty, you are overcome by the wonder, and then the next day you're worrying about your math homework.

We just stared up there for a while, and then Ian sat down on the grass, on the tails of his coat. It occurred to me briefly to worry that Dino might see us, and about the trouble I'd be in then. I sat down on the grass beside Ian. Right there next to him, and I started imagining his arms around me. Eight months, I reminded myself. Eight months and he'd be gone and not looking back. I remembered how much it had hurt when I broke up with that asshole Adam Peterson, even when that had been my choice and he was a creep. I remembered my father's arm through the glass of his car when his heart was destroyed. I leaned down on my elbows. "This is the best way to see the stars this time of year, anyway," I said. "The telescope gets impossible. Shaky images. The atmosphere is more . . ." I looked for the word. Moved my hand in the air.

"Unstable?" he guessed.

"Turbulent."

I was sitting very close to him and he looked over at me, laid down on his side and propped on one elbow. He looked at me and I looked back, and he held my eyes for a while. I looked deeply inside of him, and he saw me, too. Something passed between us right then. Some force, some connection, and, God, I wanted it so badly, him seeing me that way, me seeing him. I wanted more and more and more of it. I granted myself a concession. Friends. That's what I would do. I'd be Ian Waters's friend, and I could still have some piece of this without getting my heart broken. I could do that. I was in charge of my feelings; they weren't in charge of me.

Ian looked away from me, back toward the sky. "Wow," he said. He shook his head. Stood up. "Whew."

"Are you all right?"

"I've got to go."

"Okay."

He went to his bike, set it upright again. "You know, I'm jealous. You here, doing what you love."

"You do what you love," I said.

"I don't love the violin," he said.

"You're kidding."

"Sometimes I hate it."

"You do?"

"It runs my whole life. Then I try to remember that I'm lucky to have a talent for it."

"Talent?" I said. "You've got more than a *talent*."

"Mr. Cavalli thinks my playing lacks *passion*."

"Well, he's got too much of it. Way too much."

"That's what it takes to be great, he says."

"Then maybe it isn't such a good deal to be that great," I said. Passion—you had Dino on one side with way too much, and the Powelsons on the other with absolutely none. The cable truck had come and gone, and now their house glowed blue again from television light. There had to be a happy medium somewhere.

I was standing next to Ian and his bike. He picked up one of my cold hands. He rubbed it between his own to warm it. He let it go again. Friends could do that. Friends could wish that he didn't let go.

"Bye," he said. He smiled, pushed off hard on the pedals

and set off down the road. I watched the back of him dis-appear.

I heard one of our upstairs windows slam shut. Angrily. Dino had been watching us, I realized. And then I realized something else—Ian had ridden off with the performance tape still in his pocket. Maybe the reason Ian came over had nothing to do with the tape after all.

"Ian Waters." I said his name into the darkness.

I rubbed my arms against the cold. The feeling I had gotten when our eyes met—I tried to shake it. Anyway, it was no big deal. Really. Because I had it all under control.

CHAPTER FIVE

People don't crack up in a linear, orderly fashion. A person on the brink can do something really wacky—believing he can be heard through his cable, for example—but then return to his regular old self for days afterward. It's a great way for you to convince yourself that things are okay enough. Then something happens again. And again. Until the creepy things are coming closer and closer together, and *regular* is farther and farther apart. It's an elevator ride—down, up. Down two floors again, and up seven. Up again to the highest floor, where the cable will snap and the car will drop in fast, mind-blowing destruction.

Dino was okay for most of the week after he cut our cable. Then on Friday night, Dino, Mom, and I decided to go out to dinner before I went over to Sophie Birnbaum's. During football season my friends and I sometimes go over to Sophie's in an informal ban of the display of caveman hormones going on at our school stadium. We play marathon Monopoly with our own system of money using M&M's, our reward for having to put up with cheerleaders flashing their asses at us during the afternoon assembly, and for being forced to clap for the football players with their D-plus grade averages.

We had dinner, and Dino was driving back. Mom and I were discussing whether I needed a ride home after Sophie's or not, when Dino spoke.

"I've ruined him, I'll guess," Dino said. "That's why he's stalking me."

Just like that, out of nowhere. The air in the car went cold.

"No one is stalking you," Mom said. "Quit that."

"He's jealous that I'm succeeding without him."

"Who?" I asked.

"You know who," Dino said.

Mom caught my eyes in the rearview mirror. Her eyes said, *I know. I heard the same thing you did.* They said, *Please, Cassie. Keep your mouth shut.*

"He's probably driving one of those outhouse trucks. What are they called. Porthole potties." Dino chuckled to himself. Porta-Potti, he meant, and it might have been funny. I might have laughed, imagining the poor sailor who would look out of a porthole potty. I might have cracked up at Dino being so hilarious about some guy stalking him, because of course it was a joke. But I didn't laugh. I was scared.

Insanity, see—it's hilarious until it's deadly serious.

Mom was scrambling eggs the next morning and talking on the phone. She wasn't paying attention to them the way she should have. They were getting brown on the bottom. "I've got to go, Alice." Alice was Alice Easton. Mom's good friend and a clarinet player in their orchestra. They often carpooled together. Alice was the warm kind of person who baked a lot. We were always getting things from her like banana bread and cookies and muffins. Good kind of friend to have. "I'll try. Okay. Bye," Mom said, and hung up. One of those kind of hang-ups that happen because you are suddenly in the room.

"I thought you were going to make him take his medicine," I said. Here was my message: *Fix this*, I was saying.

"I never said that. I said I was going to talk to the doctor. Which I've done. No one can *make* him, Cassie. The doctor says we'll just have to wait and see what happens."

"Terrific. What's next? The CIA is going to talk to him through the television? Who does he think is stalking him?"

"William Tiero. Look, it's pointless to try to make sense of this."

"William Tiero? Why William Tiero?"

"I don't know, Cassie. They've had a long history together. One of those love-hate things. Epic drama of good intentions and bad blood. I don't want to talk about this now, okay? I'm exhausted. Just . . . I can handle him. Try not to worry."

"I don't really see how that's possible."

"Let me worry. The good thing is . . . well, he's writing," she said. "He'll finish his writing, and things will get better. I promise."

When you think of Hemingway and William Styron and Virginia Woolf and Robert Lowell and Mozart, think too of the people around them. The brothers and friends and wives and nieces and daughters. Think of all of the people who had to be normal in crazy conditions. Who had to pay bills and figure out what to have for dinner. Who worried, and tried to understand, and called doctors, and placated in their attempt to define and control what wasn't even of this world. Who acted as the stabilizing force, the pull of the moon on a wobbly earth, calming its own natural impulse to spin out of control. And think of those who couldn't hold on to their own sanity while being pulled down by others. Liszt, who went mad himself dealing with his crazy family, including his daughter with three kids out of wedlock with Wagner; and poor Robert Frost, with his nervous breakdown after trying to pay for all of his family members in insane asylums. And Theo van Gogh, devoted caretaker, who died six months after his mad brother. Sometimes, the job would have been too much.

I decided to get out of there. It wasn't just the night sky that was tumultuous, filled with smashing air currents and forces of nature at their most raw and untamed. My house felt that way too. Depression is a force, paranoia is a force, huge moving masses that affect everything in their way, same as continents colliding. And just like looking through a telescope when the weather gets cold, the instability in the air makes the images blurred and confused. I wanted to be in a place where I could count on things being calm and making sense.

I walked to Dad's. I had to pass Ian Waters's house, the small cottage near town that now had a new coat of paint and some flowers out front since he'd moved in. I felt a little surge of glee seeing his tennis shoes on the front porch. I admit, I walked past kind of slowly, hoping he'd see me and come out, but the house looked quiet. It was probably a good thing. All week I'd been working hard to keep the thoughts of my new friend where they should be. I tried not to keep meeting his eyes in my mind. Eight months, I reminded myself, and he'd be off with his violin. I'd be lucky if he had time for a letter after he went to Curtis.

When I got to Dad's, I just hung out with him and helped him change the oil in his car. Afterward we drove over and picked up Nannie from Providence Point, and Dad made us all dinner. I didn't want to talk to him about what was happening at home—God knows how he'd take that and run with it. I just wanted to be with him. He made this great buttery pasta that probably had a gazillion calories, and then we played Crazy Eights and Nannie cheated. She beamed with victory and rode home with the most smug look you ever saw. It reminded me exactly of Zach Rogers earlier that day when we got back our math tests. He waved it over his head like an Olympic flag, in spite of the fact that he mysteriously got every one wrong that I did, and that during the test I could feel his eyes rolling around my paper, sure as marbles on tilted glass. Dad and I drove Nannie back home, and learned that we'd only gotten a glimpse of what was apparently a full-blown immersion into a life of crime. I dropped her purse on the way out to the car, and about five thousand restaurant sugar packets spilled out, along with two thousand little squares of jam and another several thousand tiny cream containers.

"Mom. What's this?" my father asked.

"What's what?" she said, scooping them back in with knobby fingers. "I don't see anything."

"Why do you need to do this? You take your coffee black. If you want jam, I can get you jam."

"I can't hear you," she said.

"The *jam*."

"I can't hear a thing he's saying." Which was a pretty great problem-solving technique, if you ask me.

"You got good taste," I said to Nannie. "They're all blackberry. My favorite."

"Don't encourage her," Dad said.

Before she went inside Providence Point, Nannie squeezed a five-dollar bill into my palm and a couple of jam packets. I kissed her cheek. "Go easy, Nannie," I said. "We don't want you convicted for condiment theft. You go to that prison, you'll meet big-time operators. Maple syrup stealers."

"I got catsup in my brown purse," she said.

On the way back home, Dad turned on the radio, hit his palm against the steering wheel to the rhythm of some eighties station. All eighties, all the time, lucky us. I was praying he wouldn't sing along, then wondered if God would punish me for only checking in with him during times of convenience: 1) when something monumentally awful was about to happen, 2) before a test, 3) when hoping something embarrassing would happen to the homecoming princesses riding around the school track up on the backseat of a convertible, and 4) when I sensed a parent was about to act in a manner that would make me wish for those paper bags they give you on airplanes.

"You're awfully happy tonight," I said. "Have you been drinking Optimism in a Cup?" That's what he called coffee.

"Nope. It's a natural high. Life is good."

"Hey, you're in love," I said. I pictured a female accountant version of Dad, and hoped she didn't have kids I'd have to deal with. Poor Zebe has a stepsister who actually goes to our school and is in her chemistry class. *She sits and files her nails and studies her split ends like they're about to discover a cure for cancer,* Zebe told me. *She carries a pink purse with her initials in rhinestones.*

"No, I'm not in love." It began to rain and Dad turned on the wipers. His eyes were as shiny as the wet pavement under the streetlights. "I'm just close to finding out something important."

"Oh yeah? The meaning of life? Why dogs roll around on dirty towels?"

"Better."

"If it's about Dino, Dad, I really don't want to know."

"Fine. I won't tell you."

"I think it's wacky you're snooping on him."

"I don't have to tell you a thing."

"Okay, fine. Tell me."

"Hand me an Altoid."

"Jesus, Dad, okay, I said tell me."

It started to really pour, the way it can in the Northwest. Dump, is more like it. It's the kind of rain that makes you wonder if a monsoon could really be much worse. The kind of rain that can make even a gas station minimart with a creepy cashier look cozy and inviting. Dad switched his wipers to manic mode.

"'Bermuda, Bahamas, come on, pretty Mama,'" Dad sang. "'Key Largo, Montego, ooh, I want to take you . . .'"

I folded my arms, stared out the window. Some poor dweeb got stuck walking his dog in the rain—if he lifted his head, he might drown like a turkey. "You know, for a parent, you're really pretty childish."

"Okay, okay," Dad said. "I'm having a little trouble locating Mr. Cavalli's birth certificate." Dad raised his eyebrows and smiled. His teeth looked really white in the darkness.

"So what. The guy's old. Foreign country. Some ancient hill town, for God's sake. People with no teeth. Women with mustaches."

"We'll see." He looked smug. Right then he looked just like his mother after she won at Crazy Eights.

Here's what I thought then. I was surrounded by lunatics. Dad was as bad as Dino. Okay, maybe not, but you know what I mean. It occurred to me then that there was very little in the world that wasn't ridiculous to the point that it made no sense. Putting on neckties was pretty weird, when you came to think of it. Ditto nylon stockings, and grown men using sticks to knock little white balls into cups, and government-access television stations. What the hell was normal, anyway? I mean, my God, something is strange with the world when pom-poms are a status symbol. Aliens would someday look at us with completely baffled expressions. Dogs already do.

I'd let my father have his lunacy, mostly because there wasn't anything I could do about it anyway. Control is easier to relinquish when you have no choice. Besides, I told myself, what he was doing was harmless, wasn't it?

Here was another funny but not funny thing. Remember the poor dweeb walking his dog in the rain? That poor dweeb was Dino, and that was Dog William, made unrecognizable by hair glued to his body with water and by his miserable expression. When I came home that night, Dino's wet wool coat was hung over the stair rail, smelling like a barn animal. His soaking socks were curled up in something that resembled embarrassment on the hall floor. He was walking around the kitchen in his bathrobe, his curly hair straight as a pencil, nothing like the simmering photo of him on the cover of his Paris journals. It struck me that Dino had aged. Maybe since the day before. Mom was drying Dog William in a towel. He looked cute for the first time in his life.

"Jeez. What happened here?" I said.

"Dino felt like a snack. Got caught in the rain," Mom said. She didn't seemed concerned. In fact, she seemed content, just drying off poor old Dog William.

"Hey," I said. "I saw you. I didn't know it was you."

"You could have given him a ride," Mom said. Yeah, I could have just invited him right on in the car with Dad. It'd be a nice, calm ride. Like when they transport violent criminals across state lines.

"I don't mind the rain," Dino said. "Good for the skin." He pinched one of his cheeks. He was pretty cheerful for someone who appeared recently shipwrecked. It must have been a good day—the weirdness of the car ride the night before had disappeared as quickly as it had come.

"He looks sweet," I said, pointing my chin toward Dog William.

Dino batted his eyelashes.

"Not you," I said. "The dog."

"My heart is broken," he said.

"How's this?" Mom put the towel around Dog William's face. It hung down his back, nun-style. "Sister Mary William."

"Dog with a bad habit," I said.

Dog William had enough of religion and took off like he was late for his bus. He was probably rolling around on the carpet, fluffing up and getting dog hair everywhere.

"I got us something," Dino said. He opened the brown

bag that was on the counter. Really, it did this soggy tear, as the bag, too, was drenched. Dino held up a package of Hostess Cupcakes and a packet of Corn Nuts. Hey, good taste. Usually he won't put anything near his mouth that doesn't have some hyperculinary aspect to it. Sun-dried gorgonzola, rosemary cilantro crepes with raspberry sauce, that kind of crap.

He opened the cupcakes, even approached them the right way, by peeling off the icing and eating that first. I had a little surge of positive feeling. One of those maybe-everything-will-be-okay rushes of hope that usually only comes to me after a big swig of Zebe's espresso. Dino put his arms around Mom. He lifted up her hair, kissed her neck. She leaned into him, and I could see the chemistry between them. I hated to see it, but I did. I knew it explained some things about why Mom was with him.

Dino left the kitchen and went into his office in his bathrobe. I heard him tuning and then the brief fits and starts of playing, which meant that Dino was writing. Mom made a cup of tea, sat down at the kitchen table, and warmed her hands around the mug. I had some too, even though it was the kind of tea that tasted like licking a grass welcome mat. Mom tilted her head and we both listened to Dino create, as Mom's own cello leaned in the corner like a bad drunk. She looked pretty. She took a barrette from her pocket, pulled her hair back. Her face was peaceful. She smiled. "He had a good day of writing. An awesome day," she said.

"He seems really happy," I said. She did too.

"He said that for the first time in his life, it's coming easily. Maybe I was worried for nothing."

"That's great, Mom."

"We may make it to March after all," she said.

"You don't have to lurk back there," I said to Siang Chibo the next day after we got to my house. "Just walk with us, for God's sake. The stalking has got to go. You make me feel like I'm in one of those horror movies where you know something awful's gonna happen and the girl's car never starts."

"I can't walk with her. She makes me nervous."

"Who, Courtney? Just pretend you're watching bad TV. That's how I get through most of the school day."

"She makes me feel like a loser."

"Don't ever feel that way. You are not a loser. You are so smart. Courtney could only fantasize about being so smart. You know how some people laugh at their own jokes? Courtney can't. She doesn't *get* her own jokes."

Siang smiled. "Is Mr. Cavalli here today?"

"No. He's at the dentist getting his teeth cleaned. Gingivitis." Lie. But I tried to toss Siang some reality every now and then. Just to keep the adoration at manageable levels.

Disgusting gum disease didn't dampen Siang's enthusiasm one bit. "Let's go in his office."

"Ooh, okay. That'll be a memory I can put in my scrapbook. You can't touch anything, though, because he's been writing. If you mess anything up in there, I'm dead."

I knew I'd made a mistake the second I opened the door. At first I only saw the mess of papers, empty pages, all empty white sheets strewn around on the desk and the chair and the floor and around by the windows. It was easy for your eye to be drawn to the one page that wasn't blank, the one that was smeared with blood. It was crumpled up, as if it had been used as a towel to clean up some bleeding, and that's probably just what had happened. It lay among some shards of glass, a pile of crystally chunks, the remnants of the frame that had held William Tiero's picture that had obviously been thrown against the wall, same as that wineglass. The force had knocked the print that hung above his desk, those yellowy flowers, askew. It was barely hanging there, threatening to crash to the floor.

Siang gasped.

I tried to take in what I was seeing, but it didn't seem real. Some awful feeling filled my heart—horror, shock. I felt like the ground was suddenly pulled from underneath me, and that things were falling, falling. He was writing, so everything was going to be okay. And here it was. All of those empty pages. All of that frightening white.

"I'm not sure what's happened," I said.

"Oh, my God," Siang whispered.

I wanted to shut the door. I wanted this out of my sight. Those pages, that gash of blood, sucked the air right from me. I felt a wave of shame, too, a sense of letting Siang down in an important way. I reached for the knob, but Siang put her hand on my arm.

"Wait," she said. Siang stepped into the office, did

something I would respect her for forever. She walked over to that painting above his desk and she straightened it. She made sure it wouldn't fall.

Tears gathered tight and hot in my throat. I just kept seeing Mom the other night with her tea and her happiness. I kept thinking about our hope.

"It's okay," Siang said. She actually put her thin arm around my shoulders. "Come on."

I closed the door behind Siang and me. The latch clicked. I felt like I was trying to shut a monster into a room. A monster that would not be held back for long by something so simple as a lock.

I brought Mom to Dino's office when she came home. I had to confess to her that I'd gone in there with Siang. Mom just stood in the doorway where I had, held her hand to her mouth. *Oh, dear God,* she had said. *No.*

That night, I didn't know where Dino was. His car was gone. I knew where Mom was, though. I found her in their bathroom, the pills from Dino's medicine bottles laid out along the counter so that she could count them. The white pages sat in a stack on their bed. What you learn is, stability is a moving target. What you learn is, destroyed hope is the most profound loss of all.

I went outside, took out my telescope. I was out there a long time, and I was looking at the moon. Thinking how many people looked at that very same moon. Wondering if maybe Ian was looking at that same moon now, too. And it was like I had almost called him to me, when I heard those bike tires. I thought I imagined them. I actually walked to the edge of the lawn, because I couldn't believe my own hearing. But there it was—the sound was coming closer. It was him, all right, and suddenly all of the bad things just lifted up. They just rose and made room for Ian Waters as he rode, a bit wobbly, down that gravel street, as he laid his bike down on the grass. I needed something to take the place of the scary things in my life right then, and my heart surged with this ridiculous giddiness, went from bad to good with the simple sight of his coat.

Bright orange maple leaves from our trees had begun to cover the lawn over the last few days. When Ian walked toward me, his shoes and pant legs *shish-shish*ed through them.

"This is so weird. I was *just* thinking about you," I said. My heart filled with wonderful-fantastic.

"You were?"

"Just this minute."

"What were you thinking?" He stood close. Put his hands on my arms.

I forgot what friends could say and what friends couldn't. I forgot all about his leaving in eight months. It was so good to shove aside what was happening in that house behind me and have something else take that space. I would take five minutes of wonderful-fantastic, if that's all I could have. "I was thinking that maybe you were looking at the moon, too."

"Can I?" He nodded toward the telescope.

"Sure."

He dropped his hands, moved to the telescope, and peered in. The wind blew in a gust, picked up an armful of the leaves, and tossed them around. A few made a run for it down the road, turning mad circles. Ian's hair blew around too. There was something about smelling his shampoo that made everything feel it was right where it should be.

"It looks like . . . the moon," he laughed. "It really looks like the moon."

"I know it."

Ian shoved his hands in his pockets. "Are you all right out here? It's getting cold," he said, and he was right. October had done that sneaky October thing, changed a season on you without you noticing it. Fall always came with a sudden realization.

"I'm great," I said. I had a nice little cozy bonfire going on inside. Warm, toasty happiness. His care made everything just fine. "I like the cold. It smells good out here. Can you believe it's almost Halloween already?" I said.

Ian looked up, surveyed the sky with those eyes of his. He didn't want to talk about Halloween. "Cassie," he said to the sky, and then looked at me. "I've been thinking a lot about you lately."

My heart avalanched. Raced my stomach to my feet.

"Me too," I said.

"I've never met anyone like you before. You're . . . real. I like that."

Ian reached up to my face, tucked a strand of my hair behind my ear.

"So pretty," he said. I closed my eyes. Listened to the leaves scratching along paved driveways and the road. I felt Ian's warm breath near my cheek, knew we were about to kiss. I felt as if I were being sucked in, taken captive. He could have asked anything of me and I would have followed, led along by this joy in his presence. I leaned into him. His coat smelled as good as the night—like coldness and fall and burning leaves.

We kissed. Soft lips, night breeze, drowning. Dangerous, willing drowning.

We had already pulled away from each other when the headlights shined up the street. Headlights, oh, shit—Dino. Instant fear reaction. Instant guilt at being caught, and the sudden remembrance that there were way too many reasons not to be doing what I was just doing.

I stepped away from Ian, and real life filled the space between us as Dino parked his car in the drive and just sat there in the driver's seat, watching us. This, Ian and me, it was something I couldn't do. I just couldn't. Not only because Dino would be pissed, and he certainly already seemed pissed, not only because our lives were fucked up enough already, but because of what would happen to me if I let myself feel this much, this deeply, this good. Ian was leaving, and when he did I would feel this much, this deeply, this destroyed. I'd already seen what happened when you let your passions have their way. There were plenty of images to choose from—take your pick. My mother counting pills lined up along the bathroom counter, round yellow pills like dress buttons. My Dad's haunted post-divorce eyes, the chaos in my mother's post-divorce house, bills and dishes and laundry, all the evidence of a life out of control. My father with the Cavalli books spread out over his bed. Broken and destroyed hearts. I was only seventeen. It was too soon to be part of a train wreck.

I broke away, ran into the house before Dino got out of his car. I left Ian Waters standing alone on the lawn. I saw his face, enough of it, anyway, to see that he was surprised and hurt, but I didn't care. I told myself I didn't care. What mattered was avoiding the train wreck. I ran upstairs to my room, shut the door. I shut it all out behind me. Shutting doors was the solution of the day. I tried not to imagine Ian standing there outside, making his way home to that house by the ferry terminal. I just said to myself *No*. I held that snow globe with the bear in it, turned him upside down. He was the more sensible one of us. Sure, he was floating aimlessly, but he would never leave that glass dome. He would stay inside that place, even if it snowed and snowed.

CHAPTER SIX

"Cassie? I need to talk to you about something," Mom said to me in the morning. What a surprise. After last night I knew we would be having this conversation. She sure hadn't wasted any time—I was in the bathroom getting ready for school. I had just brushed my teeth and was doing a quick toothpaste survey, seeing if I'd ended up with a white toothpaste drip. I swear, every day I end up with a spot of toothpaste in a different location. It's like a game of Where's Waldo.

"What?" I said. I knew what.

"It's about Ian."

"What about him?" Defensiveness crept up my spine, settled somewhere in my throat.

"Look, I don't know what the situation is. . . ."

"There is no situation," I interrupted. Which was

mostly true. There wasn't going to be a situation anymore.

"Okay, fine. If that's the case, great. There are just things you don't understand here, about this. If you were to get involved . . . okay, Cassie, stop with the face. Let's just say you were. It's not a simple thing. Not even for you."

"I know that. That's why I'm making my own decision about it. You don't have to tell me that." I was angry. I didn't feel like I was the prime concern here. "Tell me, though, because, you know, I just don't get it. I don't get why Dino should have such a problem with me and Ian, anyway. Can't Ian have friends? What, he'll be contaminated like the kid who lives in the bubble? Or does Dino just not want me to be happy?"

"Come on, quit it. It has nothing to do with Dino not wanting your happiness. He's got a responsibility to Ian. Ian's got to stay focused. Dino's got to stay focused too. It complicates things unnecessarily."

"For Dino."

"For Dino, for Ian. For Ian's family. Ian is coming here for training. Professional training. This is his life course we're talking about. He needs this scholarship. Think about him, too. Dino had to have a talk with him last night."

"Oh, great. Just great." Humiliation. Like we were a couple of kids caught playing doctor. Shit.

"He can't be coming over here with you on his mind when he needs to be dedicated to that violin right now. There's a lot at stake here. Yes, for Dino, too. The structure, the chance to help this kid succeed—it's a stabilizing force. It means a lot to him to have the chance to help Ian make it. Cassie, let's just . . . if we keep things . . . uncomplicated . . ."

"I already told you, I'm not going to get involved with him. You can tell Dino to relax. Ian's going away, I know that. It'd be stupid."

"Exactly. I don't want to see you get your heart broken, either."

"It'd be stupid," I said again. "Nobody has to talk to anybody anymore."

"Dino's record deal, this concert—it's all final. His three pieces have got to be finished by March. He's got to write. Ian's audition is right before that. Let's just get through those two things. Remember what's best for Ian, if you care about him. Help me out here."

"Mom, *okay*." Jesus. I got it. It was over. Finished. I'd decided that before she even opened her mouth. Before Dino ever opened his to Ian.

"Things will calm down after March."

"All right," I said.

"I love you, and I'm sorry things are crazy right now."

"I love you, too," I said.

"You got toothpaste there by your collar," she said.

I walked past their open bedroom door and could see Dino's figure in bed, the hunch of his bare shoulders. Even as he slept there you could feel the unease in his form. I resented the lack of peace he had brought my mother and me, resented the fact that you could look at that sleeping back and see a possible eruption, a mountain of problems rather than the quiet security that sleeping shoulders should make you feel. I wanted the safety of someone folding warm laundry, or plunking down a bag of capably chosen groceries, or fixing a broken lawn mower. But in that bed was the meteor we lived with instead, who brought unshaven torment and sheets of notes written in almost clichéd fury and shoved in the kitchen garbage along with the coffee grounds and crushed Cap'n Crunch box. It occurred to me then that all we want a good part of the time is to feel in safe hands.

If you've ever made a decision not to have something you really want, you'll know how I felt over the next few days. Sure, there were these moments of resolve, of Zen-like peace that lasted all of a few seconds. But mostly I was pissed off. At my mother and at Dino and at the world that didn't arrange things in a better way. At my own chickenshit self.

It wasn't the kind of pissed off that was raging and full of energy, but the variety that was flat and snappish and lethargic. I was going through life in a fog, an expression that was true in every sense. I felt like I was watching and not really participating, like my life source had called in sick and was wrapped up in a quilt somewhere, zonked on cold medicine. And the fog was a literal truth, too—for those days it lay around in wispy streams, around the water and on the lawn in the morning, as if the clouds had pushed the wrong elevator button. That's what fog is anyway—lazy clouds. Clouds without ambition. The fog was eerie and beautiful, soft and thoughtful, and it usually lifted in the afternoon to an annoying display of sun that made the October orange colors so bright that they hurt your eyes. Everything glistened with dew, and it was vibrantly cold out. I didn't want that, the cold that made you want to put on a big coat and do something useful and happy, like rake leaves. I wanted the rain again, or just the fog, looking miserable and spooky.

I went through the motions at school, caring even less than usual about the fact that Kileigh Jensen highlighted her hair or that rumors were flying about what Courtney did with Trevor Woodhouse, which everyone knew anyway by taking one look at them. The things that I might have laughed at, the fact that Sarah Frazier wore enough makeup for her and two of her closest friends, for example, or the coincidence that Hailey Barton's bra size doubled right about the same time that two Chihuahuas disappeared from the area, didn't even seem very funny.

My emotions were manic-hormonal, and when Jeremy Libitski got up and turned in his math test after, I swear, five minutes, I started to get all panicky. By this time you *know* better. You *know* there's some kid who always turns in his test after five minutes and you have that oh-shit moment of realization that you're still on the second question. You know to tell yourself that he's either some super-smug genius or just went along answering *B* to everything. But I panicked, and even the easy stuff seemed suddenly complex to the point of total confusion—

Name:, for example. This is how messed up I was.

On Friday it was Halloween, and I decided to go to Brian Malo's party even if I wasn't really in the mood. I thought that maybe being with my friends would help me remember where I was before I even met Ian Waters, and remember that I existed fine without him before. It's strange, but you can feel excitement in the air on Halloween night, even if you're staying home, as if all the energy of those little kids too jazzed to eat dinner is just zipping around the atmosphere. We carved pumpkins the night before, and I Just Said No to those intricate designs that take three days without food or sleep to carve—haunted houses and cat faces and Leonardo da Vinci's *The Last Supper* done in gourd. I did two triangle eyes and a frown and tried to put a tooth in there, but it fell out and I had to stick it back in with a toothpick. Mom, who for the last few days had been talking to her friend Alice a lot on the phone and walking around Dino as if she were carrying a feather in cupped hands, carved the same thing she did every year, a music note. Dino came out of his study and watched us light the candles and sat there in the dark with us, which is probably a metaphor, come to think of it. Since Mom confronted him with the blank pages, he'd been defensive, then well behaved. It reminded me of Mom (a leadfoot) when she gets a speeding ticket. First, she's ticked off at the cop. Then, for three days running, she won't go a notch over the speed limit. After that, she's back to her old extreme and dangerous ways.

When I left, Mom and Dino were doing something

they never did—just sitting on the couch and watching a movie. Very regular couple. Very non-genius of Dino. His arm was around my mother, sucking up. This was what his illness was like. A crash. Then enough quiet to make you think it might be getting better. Then an earthquake. And Mom would just buy into it. That's how bad she wanted things to be okay.

I walked to Brian's, because I liked to see the little kids with their costumes flowing out behind them as they ran, their parents calling *Thank you!* to open doorways, the miniature ghouls and power guys and gypsy girls. I remembered sweating like a sumo under rubber masks, and as a kindergartener, parading around the classes of big kids. I remember pouring out my candy on the floor when I got home from trick-or-treating, picking out the Butterfingers and separating similar things into piles. I remember my Mom wearing a witch hat to answer the door, and my Dad holding my hand when we crossed the street, and me sleeping in my bride costume when I was six. Yes, okay, I had a bride costume, so don't give me any crap about it. That night, the streets were full of the sound of tennis shoes running on pavement and of the spooky music some people played when they answered their doors. The air smelled like singed pumpkin lids and the beams of flashlights bounced around the darkness, and for some reason it all made me want to burst into tears.

Brian's party was noncostume, but a few people were there anyway in bloody and gory wounds and cat ears and the like. Michael Worthman, who I had a crush on last year, came as Minnie Mouse, which doused any lingering sexual chemistry. Beth Atkins, a girl who made costumes for drama, came dressed as a cow, demonstrating that it takes guts to wear an udder. Jeff Payley wore a dog costume, and went around shaking his butt and saying, "Look, I can wag my tail!" I ate pumpkin seeds and wondered why, as the experience is vaguely like munching on toenails. I talked to Zebe, who was wearing fishnet stockings and glow-in-the-dark fangs that she had to take out in a rather drooly fashion whenever it was her turn to answer.

"Michael Worthman's been checking you out all night," Zebe said.

"He's wearing a dress. With polka dots," I said.

"Hey, his legs look great in it," she said, raised her eyebrows up and down, and popped in her fangs again.

I left after a couple of hours, telling everyone I had a sore throat and wanted to go home to bed. I didn't talk to Zebe about Ian and me, because for starters, nothing existed between us. I was still out of sorts, and all of the cheer around me was just making me feel crappier. Only a few boys who were too big for trick-or-treating were still on the street, and Mom had blown out the pumpkin candles. When I came in, Mom and Dino had already gone to bed and there were only a handful of Sweet Tarts packs and boxes of Dots left in the candy bowl. Mom's taste in candy stank—she always went for the low-fat stuff in case we had any left and she was tempted to eat it. Dots were as far down on the evolutionary candy scale as you go, but I took a few anyway, which only goes to show the level of my general dissatisfaction. I went upstairs and got in bed, ate Sweet Tarts and disgusting cherry Dots in the dark. I tried to fend off images of Ian coming down my street that first time I saw him, of his face when I left him that night. That kiss. God, that kiss. I tried to get rid of overly sentimental pictures of my mother handing my father a cup of hot cider after we would come back home with our candy on Halloween nights. It occurred to me that if you loved it sucked, and if you didn't love it sucked, so either way you were screwed. Maybe love was better. At least sometimes you got chocolates.

My resolve was weak, so I was glad I didn't know Ian's phone number. I reminded myself for the zillionth time that I had to do what was best for Ian, too. I felt on the edge of tears, as if I could have cried at the sight of a drooping plant. Some kind of grieving was working around inside of me, and I didn't want any part of it. I got up to pee, and went downstairs for more candy or a glass of milk or a miracle cure. For some reason, I can't even tell you why, I went into Dino's study and pulled the Cavalli biography from the shelf. I sat right there on the floor, with the open book on my lap.

Lutitia Bissola, neighbor: The boy had his first concert for us, in the piazza. Anyone doing their shopping stopped to watch. His mother and father held hands and listened, and Mrs. Mueller, I think it was Mrs. Mueller who started it, put the bouquet of flowers at the child's feet when he was finished.

Francesca Bissola, neighbor: It wasn't Mrs. Mueller. It was Honoria Maretta. But after she put the flowers down, everyone else began laying down objects.

103

Honoria Maretta, grade-school teacher: I put the flowers down, yes. He was my student, my boy. He was like a son to me. He would come to my house to see my cat sometimes, and I would give him books and pizzelles. They were his favorite. I would bake them on a Sunday, when he might come over. My only little child, among all my students.

Francesca Bissola: Alberto what's-his-name put a loaf of French bread by the flowers.

Lutitia Bissola: Alberto Terreto. He put the bread down. And then there were other things. A zucchini. A melon. A lemon branch. Little offerings, laid at the boy's feet. Even Father Minelli had opened the doors of the church with the sound of the playing and stood there listening, his face turning red from the sun.

Francesca Bissola: His face was red from too much wine. The sun had nothing to do with it. He was a boozer, God rest his soul.[8]

I smiled. In spite of myself, and in spite of the Dino-hero-worship, those people from Sabbotino Grappa could get to you. The words brought you to another time and place. Escapism was a nice thing sometimes. Personally, I don't see the problem with escapism and denial, those friendly twin coping mechanisms. I carried the book back to my room, read some more until the hot sun of Italy made me sleepy enough to turn out the light.

The next time Ian came for a lesson, I waited in my room until he was safely inside Dino's office, then I hightailed it

---

[8] Dino Cavalli—*The Early Years: An Oral History.* From Edward Reynolds, New York, N.Y. Aldine Press, 1999.

out of there before they even started tuning. In my current state, I didn't even dare listen to Ian play. I didn't trust myself not to do something humiliating and out of control, same as you fear shouting out some swear word while you're at a church service. I could just see myself flinging open the door and throwing myself in his arms or something ridiculously schlocky. Or else I'd start weeping at the sound of that violin, picturing the notes drifting all the way to Italy, winding their way among the leaves of the olive trees.

Getting out, that was the main thing. Fall was still doing the cold, crispy thing, so I put on Mom's navy peacoat and borrowed Dino's lambskin gloves and hat that made him look like a bank robber. I stepped out the front door. Dog William had fallen firmly and steadfastly in love, and was looking happier than he'd ever looked in his life, lying on the grass with Rocket. His lips were curled up and his teeth showed, and anyone who says dogs don't smile is dead wrong. At least someone had their relationship life sorted out. He even looked kind of cute again. Rocket was sprawled out, looking serene and sphinxlike, and you could already tell who was the boss of the couple. I kicked through the leaves on our road, passed old Mr. and Mrs. Billings' house. Their pumpkins, out on their porch, now looked a bit caved in, same as Mr. Billings's mouth without his dentures.

Something about Dog William's happiness pissed me off, and I took my sour mood down the road and kicked at leaves. Goddamn, I mean, even a dog handled his life better than I did. I looked up, and saw that banana yellow

105

Datsun stuck in the road. There was Bunny, Ian's brother, and Chuck, Bunny's friend—the metaphysical nonmotorcyclists—standing there beside it.

"Get the jack," Bunny said.

"What jack? Monterey Jack?" Chuck chuckled. "Jack-in-the-box?"

"You don't know jack shit," Bunny said. "In the trunk. And the lug wrench."

"What's it look like?" Chuck was as big as a dump truck and was wearing a fringe vest with beads. He had a lovely braid, I don't know, maybe two inches long.

"You know what it looks like. A big cross. With knobs. Quit stalling. Jesus."

"Do you guys need some help?" I asked. "I'm about two seconds from a phone."

"Hey. The teacher's kid," Chuck said.

"Ian's friend," Bunny said.

"Whoo hoo. You saved me." Chuck raised one arm, did a little victory dance. It reminded me of when you set a big bowl of Jell-O on a hard surface. "Rescue chick."

"No problem," I said. "Should I call a tow truck?"

"Tow truck, my ass," Bunny said. "It's a flat tire. Get back there and find the jack," he said to Chuck. Bunny shook his head. "Sheesh. He's never changed a flat before. We could be here all day."

"You know, my house is right there. I could call someone for you."

"I've changed thousands of tires," Bunny said. "It's him that hasn't. This is a learning experience."

"I hate learning experiences," Chuck said.

"Learning experiences suck," I agreed. "Anything that's called a learning experience, you know, run for your life."

"What a couple of whiners," Bunny said.

Chuck had the trunk open and was fishing around inside. "Is this the lug wrench?" He held up a hat with ear flaps.

"I hope neither of you has worn that thing," I said. "Very Elmer Fudd." Chuck tossed it to me and I yanked off Dino's burglar hat, put it on. "Cozy," I said.

"Oh, man, you two are a handful," Bunny said. I was starting to have a really good time. "You two will try my abundant patience."

"Okay, okay. The lug wrench," Chuck said. He took it out, held it up in one hand as if it had the weight of a toothpick.

"You blocked the tires already? Good. Now loosen the bolts while the car's still on the ground." Bunny folded his arms, watched Chuck sit down on the asphalt.

"Cold ass," Chuck rubbed his huge butt. He stuck the lug wrench on one of the bolts. "Knee bone connected to the shinbone." He gave it a crank. It freed easily, a knife through warm butter. "Big friggin' deal," Chuck said. He sure looked pleased with himself.

"Don't congratulate yourself until the job is done. You can't change a tire and pat yourself on the back at the same time. Not enough hands," Bunny said.

Chuck whipped through the second bolt, but the third stuck. I learned a whole bunch of cool new swear words, in inventive combinations. Sweat gathered at his temple and in the nooks and crannies of his shirt. I could smell the sour odor of underarms under stress.

"Never count your chickens before they hatch," Bunny said.

"Shut the F up, Bun," Chuck said, and let loose a stream-of-consciousness array of nasty terms in Bunny's direction.

"So why are you letting him make you do this?" I asked. Maybe it wasn't such a good time to bring it up. Chuck was grunting like a pig stuck under a fence.

"Learning. Experience," he exhaled. "Personal. Growth."

I wanted to laugh. Picture again what I was seeing. This motorcycle guy in a fringe vest with a two-inch braid, wrestling a tire and sweating bullets and gasping about personal growth as his buddy watched over him with the folded arms of a sadistic PE teacher.

"You got to do what you fear," Bunny said. "Embrace the unknown. You keep yourself sheltered, you over-protect yourself, you might as well stay home and become an agraphobic."

"Agoraphobic," Chuck grunted.

"Agraphobic probably means you fear farmland," I said.

Bunny ignored us. "Growth is in the feared places."

"Did you steal that from a *Star Trek* movie?" I said. "It sounds slightly ominous."

"There!" Chuck said. "Hot damn."

"Excellent. Step two."

"Shit, there's more?"

I watched Bunny instruct Chuck to jack up the car and remove the tire. Kyle and Derek, Courtney's two little brothers, got off the school bus and came over, slung their backpacks to the ground and watched.

"I saw this guy get crushed by his own car on *True Traffic Tragedies*," Kyle said. Kyle was twelve and wore slouchy pants. Derek was a year younger, but was bigger than his brother.

"Gee, thanks for sharing," I said.

"If we had our video camera, we could film this and win a thousand bucks."

"I saw this other guy get his leg pinned on *Road Rescuers*."

"That looked so fake," Derek said.

"No blood," Kyle agreed.

"Hey, guys, there's back-to-back episodes of *Fat People on Bikes* this afternoon." Bunny looked at his watch. "Starting now."

"Oh, cool," Derek said.

They picked up their backpacks, headed off. *"Fat People on Bikes?"* Chuck said.

"Hey, they believed me, that's all I care. Little television monsters." I guess he and Dino had one thing in common, which would have made Dino shudder.

"That's all they do. All day, every day," I said.

"I hate it when kids don't *participate*," Bunny said. "They could be outside playing ball. Collecting bugs."

"Hanging out at ye old swimmin' hole," Chuck said.

"Shut the F up, Chuck. If you don't participate, you're just taking up oxygen."

"Life is a banquet. Approach it with hunger," Chuck said. "Hey, I'm done, right?"

"Wow, it looks great. I just hope it doesn't fall off when you're driving," I said.

"I saw that on *Terrible Traffic Traumas,*" Chuck said. I smiled. I really liked those guys.

"Now you've had your learning experience," I said.

"Congratulations, Chuck, you big idiot," Bunny said.

"Thanks, man," Chuck said. "Sorry about all the things I called you back at the lug nuts."

"No problem. I'll consider us equal for what I said to you when you made me call Sonja for a date."

"You should've heard him," Chuck said to me.

"I hope this Sonja said yes," I said.

"With my good looks? What do you expect."

"He was trembling like a baby bird," Chuck said.

"Anyway," Bunny said, in a lame effort to change the subject. "We better get going. Hey, Lassie, thanks for your help. It was great hanging out with you."

I laughed. "Cassie," I said.

"Cassie? Man, I could've sworn he said Lassie."

"Woof," I said. *"Lassie?"*

"I don't know. I thought maybe your folks were real animal lovers."

"Bunny, you F-ing fool," Chuck said.

"You thought it was Lassie, too," Bunny said.

They climbed into the car. The small spare tire looked shy and inadequate on the Datsun.

"Jesus, you stink," Bunny said to Chuck.

Chuck yanked the paper Christmas tree deodorizer off of the rearview mirror, thrust it under his shirt, and gave it a swipe under each arm. "Smellin' like a rose," he said. Then he started the engine, gave a wave, and drove off.

After Mom confronted Dino about the blank pages and his lies, Dino did appear to get down to real work. Supposedly this was what we were wanting, but I didn't know why. The pressure of having to create and the creation itself were what led him to a disturbing restlessness and increasingly odd acts. Several times I heard him awake in the night, creaking down the stairs, performing in his office, and then clapping for himself when it was over. During the day his usual perfectionism was in high gear—he would remake a bed Mom made, rewash the dishes, pour out coffee that was made for him and make it again "properly." His testiness increased. He would turn every innocent remark into a perceived criticism of him. *It's a nice day,* you would say. And he would snap in reply, *Did I say it wasn't a nice day? Just because it's a nice day and I don't remark upon it doesn't mean I'm a pessimist.* He bit Mom's head off for giving him the wrong size spoon, yelled at me for walking too heavily down the stairs, leading me to have Brief Fantasy Number One Thousand and Twelve, whereby I borrowed Nannie's old bowling ball and sent it crashing down two flights.

I was living with a bolt of lightning, never knowing

when or where he might strike. I spent a lot of time in my room, ate dinner as fast as possible. Headphones are great when you live in a disturbed home—I started wearing them at night, so I could pretend a peace that didn't exist. Worst of all, though, Dino started up his freaky obsession with William Tiero again.

The newspaper is gone, Dino said one morning.

Probably late, my mother replied.

Maybe he wants my paper, Dino said. *He wants me to wonder where it went, to wonder if he has been here to take it. He is messing with me.*

God, it gave me the creeps. There was this feeling of horrible anticipation, of knowing that things would not keep going this wrongly and suddenly right themselves. No, wrong like that would keep building. Wrong always seemed to double and grow like cells under a microscope. Right could be steady, but wrong fed upon itself. Sometimes I wished "it" would just go ahead and happen, whatever "it" was.

Mom looked like she was losing weight, in spite of the fact that Alice's loaves of banana bread were increasing. Dino's working, the writing—it seemed to pour a life-giving liquid onto old, sleeping torments of his. He started smoking, too, a habit he'd given up years ago. One cigarette after the other he smoked, horrible bursts of nicotine poison filling not only his lungs but mine and Mom's and Dog William's, getting into the strands of our clothing and even making the bread left out on the counter taste bad. You'd find snakey bits of ash all over—

in coffee cups and saucers, and once in Mom's potted ficus plant. I hated those cigarettes. They were a visual reminder of a growing disease.

"I don't understand something," I said to my mother one afternoon. We were having a domestic mother-daughter moment, folding laundry together, which was a rarity in our house. When you've got a working mother, I've noticed, you learn to live with dirty clothes, talking yourself into the fact that no one will really notice the blotch of yogurt spilled on the leg of your jeans, or you learn to do laundry yourself, or else you learn to root through stacks of clean/nonclean clothes for a pair of socks, with the skill and speed of a pig hunting for truffles. Zebe's mother is a graphic designer, and Zebe has used adaptation number two. She is so good at the laundry she could do the presidential underwear. Everything in her closet is folded and organized by color, but I still love her anyway. At our house we usually do the root-and-find method, although Dino's clothes always manage to get done. Something about seeing my mother iron his shirts really pisses me off. I know she hates to iron. I know she would rather go out in sweats than get the wrinkles out of cotton, yet there she is, starching and pressing Dino's clothes. Fast forward to Brief Fantasy Number One Thousand Five Hundred—two big steaming iron-shaped holes over the boobs of each of Dino's shirts.

Anyway, we were folding clothes. "I don't understand something," I said, which I think I already mentioned. "If composing causes Dino this much pain, why doesn't he quit? Why doesn't he take up fishing or something? Embroidery? A low-stress occupation like forest ranger?"

Mom held one matchless sock in her hand. She thought about this. "Because quitting would cause him more pain," she said finally.

"I don't get that. If something causes pain, then bam, get rid of it," I said. I was thinking of Ian. Okay, I thought about him endlessly. Okay, I had daily arguments with myself over my desire to just give in to my feelings and to say to hell with what Dino might think. But I was mostly holding all of that at bay. Fear can give you more strength and resolve than anything else I can think of.

"Oh, Cassie, nothing's that simple. Very few things are that black-and-white. I wish they were. Nothing's a hundred percent good. Nothing's a hundred percent bad."

"Okay, eighty-nine percent. If it's that bad, get rid of it. Eighty-nine percent is enough."

"You're talking like a scientist," she said. "Some things can't be measured. Let's say you love astronomy. But let's say it causes you some problems. Back pain, eye strain, I don't know."

"We're talking mental anguish. Astronomy doesn't cause that."

"What if it did? What if, say, I don't know. Maybe this isn't a good comparison. Say you couldn't get into a school to study it. Say your math skills weren't good enough. Say you really had to struggle or something. What would you do?"

"Give it up."

"But you *love* it."

"It depends how much I love it versus how much pain," I said.

"Love is not something that can be measured, Cassie. Sometimes love just *is*. Sometimes it's a force with its own reasons. Reasons we don't necessarily understand, but with a power that is undeniable."

"You sound like an After School Special."

Mom sighed. "Fine. Never mind. Sometimes you can cattle rope your heart and sometimes you can't, is all."

"Now you sound like a country-western song."

"I'm shutting up with my motherly wisdom. You're on your own."

"He's giving us all cancer. He's giving the *ficus* cancer."

"I'm going to make him smoke outside," she said, though we had already agreed about her ability to make him do anything.

"I think he should become a bank manager," I said.

"Without his music, Dino wouldn't know who to be."

Two nights later I went to a school music concert. I usually didn't go to these things, but Siang had told me that she was doing a solo and hinted around that she'd like me to come. I wanted to do something nice for her after her kindness that day in Dino's office. Usually once I got home on a cold night, any good plan I made didn't seem as good as staying inside and warm, especially a plan like listening to classical music, which I got more than enough of anyway.

But I didn't change my mind—I went out into the cold night and fought the cars jamming the parking lot, and found a seat with Sophie Birnbaum and her parents. Sophie's little brother played the viola and was in the concert too. His group played first, and Sophie and I grimaced at each other at the squeaky parts and made fun of some of the names in the program, like Harry Chin.

I was having a grand old cultural time when Siang's group came on. She looked so thin and scared when she walked up to the microphone in her long black skirt and white blouse, her hair straight and shiny black, almost blue, under the lights. I could see her hands shake, and all I could think of was the time Marna Pines puked right on stage during the second-grade play and how no one ever forgot it. Poor Marna would always be remembered as the girl who threw up right during her solo, stopping the show cold until the janitor could come out and deal with the whole matter with his mop and sawdust. Forever after she would be Pukey Pines, or one notch up on the cruelty ladder, Upchuck Woodchuck, due to her slight overbite. I didn't want anything like that for Siang. Sure, her Dino hero worship drove me nuts, but there was something more than fandom at work in the way she tilted Dino's painting straight again. Siang was a good person.

The orchestra had a false start, causing some of the audience to snicker. Then the orchestra began again, and Siang came in with a forceful stroke of bow against violin, her chin down, her fingers flying. Jesus, there was Siang with her little *Indiana Jones* Boy Sidekick voice and her annoying habits, just taking control of the whole situation and kicking the shit out of that violin, which I know isn't exactly an appropriate musical critique but true anyway. The audience didn't move. She just had them there right with her. My heart just got all full. I was so proud of her.

After the concert I waited for Siang and told her how great she was. Her parents told me about eight times that it was good to meet me, beaming at me as if I had just given them one of those huge Publisher's Clearinghouse checks for a million dollars. I found the frosted sugar cookies at the cookie table and brought back one on a napkin for Siang and then headed back outside, feeling satisfied and happy and hopeful, though I'm not exactly sure why. I got out of the school parking lot, and instead of going home, I was overcome with a strange urge, which was to drive down to the ferry terminal, near the little house on the corner where Ian now lived.

Maybe it was Siang's bravery that made me do it, frail and breakable Siang showing so much power in front of that audience, or maybe what was really knocking around inside my brain was what the metaphysical motorcyclists without motorcycles had been saying about fear. Mom's voice was there too, I think (although she would not have been happy to be a motivating factor), talking about love as a force with its own reasons. Maybe all three things collided together and formed something new, some philosophical Big Bang in my brain, I don't know. What I do know is that I parked across the street from Ian's house. My body was cruising along without my permission—it got right out of the car and walked to the door, and it was only after I knocked that my brain caught up and I realized what the hell I had actually just done. The optimistic energy I'd been infused with after the concert had evaporated instantly, reminding me of my other failed surges of *Yes!* like the time I decided to redecorate my room with some leftover paint we had in the garage and got as far as the door frame before I realized I was tired, far from finished, making a mess, and running out of orange.

Now I just stood by Ian's door, looking at this mosquito with its dangly legs all caught up in this spider's web by their porch light, and thinking a panicky *Shit! Oh, shit!* I heard footsteps and a dog barking, Rocket, no doubt, and I had the urge to jump into the huge juniper plant, the same way as when we used to play Ding Dong Ditch when we were kids.

The door opened. Ian's mom stood in the doorway, with Rocket peering around her legs like a shy toddler, and I wished I had something to hand her—one of those peanut butter cookies I was going to stick in my pocket back at the cookie table, a pamphlet about a politician, or a trick-or-treat bag (weeks late, but still).

"Mrs. Waters?"

"Yes?"

She had Ian's eyes, but they looked different on her, wrinkled at the edges, like they knew things that had made her tired. She was wearing a T-shirt with some metal rock group on it, which surprised me. Golden wings spread out with a skull between them, and pictures of scary-looking guys. She was holding a towel, drying her hands, and I could smell something warm and buttery cooking inside.

She opened the screen door and held it open with her foot. Her hair was pulled back, and her forehead was broad and sturdy. Ian's *mother*. The one who taught him how to be in the world and who told him to clean his room and to get in the car because they were late.

"Can I help you?"

"I'm . . ." Okay, real functioning words were required, and if it says anything about my character, the first ones that sprang to mind were a lie. A bad one, too. The name that first popped into my consciousness was not my own but *Harriet Chin*. "Cassie Morgan. A friend of Ian's." I put my hand out for Rocket to sniff. She put her black nose against my palm and licked my fingers.

"Oh!" Ian's mom said.

"Ian studies with my stepfather, Dino Cavalli." What a shameless name-dropper I was.

"Cassie. Come in! I'm Janet. Ian's mom. Ian's not here, but please. I know this sounds very fifties housewife, but I was just making cookies. I had this incredible craving for fat and sugar."

I liked her already. Her toenail polish was chipped. And anyone who has a craving for fat and sugar and gives in to it is okay by me. "No, thanks. I better get home. I just stopped by to say hi because I hadn't seen him in a while. I'm always gone when he's around lately." I peered around her, into the house. Ian's home. It was very sparsely furnished; well, pretty empty, actually. Trés minimalist.

"Well, I'll tell him you came by. Are you sure about coming in? I gorged on dough, and now there are warm

119

cookies. I'm going to make myself sick if someone doesn't stop me. Hormonal chocolate frenzy."

"What is it with that?"

"I have no idea, but I'm worse than the lions with the zebra carcass on Animal Planet."

"Well, good luck. I wish you cold milk and the ability to fit in your jeans tomorrow."

"Amen. I'll tell Ian you came by."

I crossed back over the street, got in the car that had already grown cold. Okay, so his mother was cool, too. I turned the key, just watched the dashboard lights glow for a minute. I looked over at Ian's house, at the yellow light in the windows, at the lawn growing frosty-tipped in the cold night, sparkly by streetlamp. Small house, with a porch that needed painting, same as his mom's toenails, and what I guessed was one of Rocket's tennis balls in the driveway gutter. This didn't have to be as large as I was making it out to be, or as scary. This was a houseful of normal, faulty people leading normal, faulty lives, and Ian was one of them. I liked the people in his world. And he did not, I realized, hold the secrets of the universe or the power to destroy. He was just himself, with a spirit and a talent who also lied to the dental hygienist about flossing every day, just like the rest of us.

I sat there, and my heart opened up, just a little. Go where you fear, Chuck and Bunny said. Participate. I could hear my heart make room. *Maybe,* is what it said.

CHAPTER SEVEN

It is one of those Murphy's Law things that if you have a group project at school, the more important it is to your grade, the more likely you are to get stuck with partners whose safest contribution is to color the map. Even that makes you nervous. The project in question was a report on the economic system of a Pacific Rim country.

Partner number one, Jason Menyard, studied the list of choices. "Let's do Honduras," he said. "My parents went there on vacation."

"Honolulu. They went to Honolulu, you idiot." Partner number two, Nicole Hower. Nickname, Whore, because if you said her last name fast, this is what it sounded like for one, and for two, because her clothes gave the impression that she wanted to share her boobs with mankind, some goodwill mission like those people who go to third world countries to spread knowledge of how to keep their drinking water clean and improve their educational systems. Jason's eyes were already so glued to her exposed chest you would have thought a good movie was playing there. Pass the popcorn.

"How do you know?" Jason said to Nicole's boobs.

"Your parents brought mine back a present. Macadamia nuts. You don't even know where your own parents went. God," she said.

"Show some respect," Jason said. "'R-E-S-P-E-C-T,'" he sang. "'That is what you mean to me. Ooh, just a little bit.'" Jason snapped his fingers.

"Hey, he actually does a good Urethra Franklin," Nicole said to me.

Right about this time I was working on dual theories: that Nicole's parents were first cousins, and that Jason's brain and a jockstrap had much in common. Basically made of holes and not holding anything too important. I was also coming to the quick realization that I'd have to go to the library after school that day, since I'd basically be doing all the work here. This meant I'd miss the chance to see Ian before his lesson. I'd been holding on to that little open feeling, preparing myself to take a step in his direction whether Dino liked it or not, and I was going to do it that day. I, for one, would let Ian decide what was good for him. This glitch in the plan filled me with the low-level annoyance that is actually rageful, crazed fury held in a straitjacket.

At the library I grabbed everything I could on

Honduras and bolted out of there. Finally, I headed home. I breathed a grateful sigh of relief when I saw Rocket on the front lawn entertaining a gloriously happy Dog William. Call me a pessimist, but I started having the creeping fear that now that I had finally gotten the courage to make a move, Ian would not be there that day, so I was glad to see that I was wrong. I dropped fifty pounds' worth of Honduras books on the table and looked in the fridge for something to quench my weight-lifting thirst. I could hear the rumblings of Dino's voice in his office, intense, making a point.

I closed the fridge door, stepped back into the hall to eavesdrop. I would have put my ear to the door, just like they do in the movies, had it been necessary, but it wasn't. In fact, Dino's voice got louder and louder over Ian's playing.

"Bam, bam, bam. You need to hit it." I could hear something being smacked against a table, a book maybe. Ian continued to play. "Again," Dino barked.

Ian stopped, started again. I don't know what he was playing, something frenzied and fast.

"Bam, bam, bam," Dino said again. The book cracked against the table three more times. The sound made me flinch. "Don't you hear me?"

"I'm sorry," Ian said.

"Don't stop. Pick it up and do it again. It is forceful. Fast. One-two-three. Not one. Two. Three. You have no command."

"I'm sorry," Ian said again.

"What is sorry? Sorry has nothing to do with any-thing. I don't give a fuck about sorry. I give a fuck about you doing it right. What is the matter with you?"

"I don't know," Ian said.

Something crawled up along my backbone. Shame. I'm not sure why—shame at Dino's behavior, shame for Ian. I felt sick.

"I thought you were supposed to be such a talent."

"I'm sorry," Ian said again.

"Do it again. Show me that what everyone says about you is true, because it is not what I see."

I held my breath. Prayed that my feet would stay where they were and not burst in to interrupt this cruelty. The prayers were unnecessary, though, if I were telling the truth. I knew I couldn't go in there. It was nowhere I belonged, and something I didn't understand.

"Maybe it's not true," Ian said. "Maybe I wasn't born with some gift."

"Nobody is born with that gift. It's not about *gift*. It's about *need*. A deep, ugly seed of need," Dino said. "What is your need, Ian? In what need does greatness lie?"

"I don't have a need. I play because I choose to."

Dino laughed. Mocking. "What bullshit."

"And when I choose not to, I'll stop."

"You know that's a lie. Choice has nothing to do with it. There is no choice."

"Maybe not for you."

"Need. Ugly need. You're no different."

"How do you know?"

"You have no choice. You must save your mama, Ian. You must save her from despair. That is your need. You are the savior." What the hell was he talking about?

"You don't know anything about it," Ian said. His voice was angry, full of tears.

"I know all about it. Play to save your mama, boy."

"No."

"Play! Bam, bam, bam. Play it."

Silence.

"You think I'm hateful, don't you? You think I'm a bastard. But you also think I'm right. I know you."

"You don't know anything about me."

"I *know* you. Play, God damn it. The need will speak."

More silence.

"Stupid boy."

And then, the beginning notes of the song. So tender, you pictured them floating in midair and then breaking in two. The music rose, gathered intensity. I recognized the part they had been practicing. It came, forceful. Building. Bam, bam, bam. I heard it; I knew nothing about this shit, but I heard it. One, two, three—driving into me, hard, so hard.

He stopped then, and the silence was abrupt. The kind of sudden, sharp silence that comes after a slap. And then Dino began to applaud. "Bravo!" he said. "Bravo, boy!"

I stood there, stunned. My heart hurt. My soul and insides felt wrung out, perched on the desire to sob. Oh, how I hated Dino right then. The office door opened and

125

Ian ran from it. His coat was over his arm, and he shoved past me. He slammed out the front door, hard enough to rattle the windows.

Dino came out from the office. He looked at the shut door, shook his head.

"Bastard isn't the half of it," I said to him.

"You're a child," he said to me. "Silly child."

Erik Satie, contemporary composer, wouldn't wash with soap, and became so suspiciously obsessed with umbrellas (yep, I said umbrellas) that he had more than two hundred of them when he died. Tchaikovsky, of *Nutcracker* fame, killed himself with arsenic, and Schumann spent the last years of his life in an asylum. Beethoven was a Peeping Tom. When he was arrested, it is said that he yelled, "You can't arrest me, for I am the immortal Beethoven!" Police later found that he had spread feces over a wall of his house. Crappy taste in decorating, if you ask me.

And since what happened next happened on Thanksgiving, let me tell you a few food-related wacky-genius stories. Poet Elizabeth Barrett Browning was an anorexic, due to her brother's death and her father's inability to let his children leave the nest (he disinherited any of them who dared to marry). Lord Byron was a bulimic, dieting and exercising down to the skeletal, and believed that if you ate a cow, you'd endanger the appetite of all cows. Charlotte Brontë basically threw up to death while she was pregnant because she was too whacked out to handle it. Vincent van Gogh ate his own paints. Yum.

Let's also not forget that more people commit violent crimes on Thanksgiving than on any other day of the year. This is not just by people forced to eat Brussels sprouts, which would make the statistic understandable. Thanksgiving can be torture, and I don't just mean the times when some well-intentioned person suggests, "Let's all say something we're thankful for," and you want to drop through a hole in the floor. I mean that for some people life is already stressful enough without multiplying human relationships by five or ten or by however many napkin rings you happen to have.

Every year for the past three, my mother and Dino hosted a Thanksgiving party for certain members of the Seattle Symphony board of trustees, high-end givers, major players in the music arena, and Dino's associates— his manager and agents and anyone from his recording companies and publishers who wanted to travel in for the occasion. I believe that he chose Thanksgiving in the hopes that most people would be with their own fami- lies—he'd be able to extend an invitation and get social credit for that, without having to have total follow- through. A good plan, really, but it never ended up that way. A gazillion people answered the formal invitations, mailing back tiny envelopes of RSVP.

Mom had the event catered, thank God. She can get flustered when the phone rings and she's making a grilled cheese sandwich. This year it seemed like there were more people than ever in our kitchen, more trays of food, more waiters carrying hors d'oeuvres and canapés. The house looked beautiful and different than our regular house with the cereal box left out on the counter. You wouldn't believe how good it looked. We're not talking decorations of turkeys with accordion-paper stomachs like we used to have when Mom and Dad were married and had Nannie and Aunt Nancy and Uncle Greg over. No, we're talking cinnamon-smelling candles in hurricane glass on every surface, and evergreen boughs, and cranberry-colored vases of white roses. Linen napkins, and china with boughs of fruit around the edges. We're talking a turkey the size of a brown bear, and the dining room draped with gauzy curtains and burgundy ribbons. There was enough food to feed a small town, all of it steaming and glossy and colorful. Mom wore velvet and I wore my beaded vintage dress, and Dino's dark suit and restrained curls made him look like the man on the *Paris Diaries* cover, whose sex life was the talk of the town when he was younger.

I was glad my dad couldn't see us now. This was the good news, the everything-is-working-out-beautifully that you want to hide from the other parent. Their worst nightmare of their former spouse having a better life after all, as they passed the yams back at home. We all smelled soapy and perfumed, and the doorbell kept ringing and ringing, and the house got so stuffed, people went outside to cool off. You wondered if all of these people didn't have family to be with, or if the chance to be with a world-famous composer and violinist was enough to make them ditch their own grannies.

Andrew Wilkowski, Dino's new agent, had apparently

solved this conflict by bringing the whole gang along. He had brought his quiet wife, thin as a file folder, and his twin seven-year-old boys, who wore ties and ran around like crazed, midget businessmen, popping olives and caviar. I don't know why they liked the stuff—fish eggs as a delicacy was always a hard one to understand—but I swear they ate half of the mountain of it, in spite of the fact that their mother told them repeatedly to stop. I caught her grasping each of their arms fiercely and hissing in their ears, showing her less passive side. Andrew Wilkowski also brought his aging parents, who looked at the thin wife and caviar-sucking children as if they were characters in a horror flick. Meanwhile, Andrew himself was glued to Dino, filling his plate and wineglass and doing the most shameless ass kissing I'd seen since Katie Simpson brought our sixth-grade teacher a dozen roses and a box of chocolates on her birthday.

I played good daughter at the party, and tried not to miss the old days of Dad's overcooked turkey and Mom's pies and watching the Macy's parade on television. I talked to lots of old people with white hair who probably each had a gazillion dollars, ate way too many little chocolate tarts, and tried to figure out if there was something going on in the romance department between these two waiters. I saw that Dino had broken free from Andrew, and for a moment I was sincerely happy for him that he managed to cut loose from the weasely brownnoser.

But then I noticed that Dino was striding with a sense of purpose to the dining room windows. He peeled back

129

the curtains, cupped his hand to the glass, and looked out. There was something about the way he walked—too much purpose, obsession, fury—that I recognized from that night I saw him on the lawn when he cut the cable. Oh, God. Not now. No.

I immediately scanned the room and looked for Mom. Instead of chatting amiably with the orchestra creative director or with one of the donors, I saw that Andrew Wilkowski had taken her elbow and was heading out of the room, as if to talk to her in private. Great. Terrific. Something was definitely wrong.

Dino apparently had not found what he was looking for. He moved toward the hallway and the front door. I thought I'd better follow him, though what the hell I'd do if he freaked out while I was with him I hadn't quite figured out yet. Dino opened the door and I stepped out after him. I did not want to step out after him. I wanted to go someplace else, where I was completely alone and where no one could find me. I wanted to tuck my quilt around my head, disappear. I did not want right here and right now.

Outside, the night was amazingly quiet, with the noise of the party behind us, inside the house. It was November cold, and the air was dewy and full of rain not yet fallen. Thick, wet clouds filled the sky. A couple of people were standing and talking by the long line of parked cars. I heard a trunk slam, and a man and a woman with instrument cases walked back up the street to our house. Dino looked up and down the street, and headed toward the box hedge at the perimeter of the yard.

"Dino?" I said.

"William," he called. "Wil-yum."

A bit of hope. "Did we lose the dog?" I asked.

"No, not the *dog*. William Tiero, the leach. I know you're here."

Shit, I thought. *Oh, shit!* I wanted to call for Mom, to find her, but I didn't think I should leave him. I didn't know what to do. I just had no idea.

Dino crouched over, looked under the hedge. I was glad that the people with the instrument cases had gone inside. I decided to be calm. If I used a really calm voice, then he'd be calm, and I could go and find Mom.

"You're getting your pants all wet," I said. "Let's go in."

"I knew he couldn't stay away."

"William Tiero is not here, Dino," I said. My voice sounded high, like it might break. I was fighting a weird sense of unreality. I didn't even feel like me, talking calmly to this man I lived with, who was looking in the hedge for someone who wasn't there. I felt like I had gone into someplace past fear. Someplace way farther than that, where you cut off from what's happening in order to function. I was watching this poor girl with this crouched-over man who was losing it. I looked down and saw my own hands, and they seemed familiar but not.

"You don't know what you're talking about. That prick will never let me out of his life."

"No one's in the hedge, Dino," I said.

131

"You're right."

Dino came out of the hedge, hair messed, bits of leaves on the arms of his jacket. I don't know how to describe his eyes except to say that they were not unfocused or bleary like someone who's been drinking. In fact, they were the opposite—hyper focused. He stood still, listening. It was as if his senses were broken open—his hearing more acute, his gaze taking in things no one else could see.

"Why don't we go inside now," I said.

"He's not in the hedge. I'll check the back. You check the cars," he said.

"Please, Dino." I wasn't doing well with calm. My voice was pleading and anxious. I was climbing the slope of panic right alongside of him. Where was my mother? Where was someone who knew what to do?

"Check the cars before he drives off. He called and hung up just now. He can't stand it, that this is happening without him."

"William Tiero isn't here, Dino." Okay, the calm was gone completely. *I don't want to do this! I can't!* I felt like crying.

"Of course he's here. I know he's here." He pulled his cell phone from his jacket pocket, showed me the display. It was true that someone had called. The ID read UNIDEN-TIFIED CALLER. The letters glowed in the gathering darkness. The two people who were talking by the car were carrying large instruments into the house now, also. A bass and a cello, by the looks of it.

"Is everything all right?" one man asked.

I wanted to cry out. *Help me,* I wanted to say, but I didn't. "Fine," I said. "The dog is missing."

"Pets," the man said. He hauled his instrument through the door, a loud gust of party sounds escaping as he went through.

"Dino," I said. "Unidentified caller. That could be anyone. William Tiero is not out here in the bushes. Or anywhere." *Please,* I begged him with my voice. But you can't reason with insanity, or plead with it. It's the frightening tyrant, the boss, the kidnapper.

"He did this last year. I smelled his cologne. I saw him looking in the window. I'm going to catch the dirty little bastard. I'm going to check the back."

I changed my tactics. "Let me check the back. I'll make sure I find the dirty little bastard," I said. "You go inside."

"He couldn't let me free. Obsessed."

"Come on."

"He'd rather have me dead than free of him."

I took Dino's arm. His unreason made him seem capable of anything, and I didn't even want to touch him. But I did—I pointed him toward the house. I tried to keep from letting the tears come, from letting out my own desperation. I looked around for Mom. Inside, people were gathering in the living room. The quartet of musicians had set up an impromptu concert, began to tune for the crowd. I wondered if they were expecting Dino to join them. Some woman was ushering everyone out of the dining room for the concert—they were squeezing out of the doorway and packing into the living room. Dino stalked into the dining room, empty of people now. He looked back out through the drapes again.

"I see movement," he said. "Turn off the lights so that I can see."

"Dino, no. He's not there." I felt the tears working away at my throat. Where the hell was Mom?

"Turn out the lights!"

His voice was loud, and I flinched. I knew that my job right then was to hide the mess, make sure none of these people noticed anything. To keep the secret. So I went to the switch and turned off the lights to keep him quiet. Thankfully, everyone was either jammed in the other room or overflowing out into the hall, happy to be in an important house of an important man, spilling drinks and talking and eating tiny, fancy desserts on glass plates.

Only the candles flickered in the room. I could see their flames reflected in the glass that Dino was peering through. "Shh," he said, even though I wasn't saying anything. "Come here."

I went. I hated standing beside him. His breath was fogging up the glass. His coat was hanging dangerously over the candles on the table under the window.

"Be careful, Dino," I said. I watched his sleeve dangle by the flame. "Jesus."

"Holy shit, look!" Dino said.

I looked outside, where he was pointing. "Oh, God," I breathed.

He was right.

He was right, there was a figure outside, a dark figure in a big coat.

I jumped my ship of sanity, got into Dino's boat, because he was right. And if Dino was right about this, maybe William Tiero really did have evil plans for us. Maybe Dino really was in danger. The quartet began playing in the other room. All four instruments, a sudden, thunderous sound of frantic motion.

"Get the gun," Dino hissed.

"Don't be crazy," I said, which is a rather stupid thing to say to a crazy person, but my own thoughts were out of control. My heart was thumping like mad, my hands shaking. A man in the bushes . . . "We don't have a gun."

"I said, get the gun!"

Right then, the figure came close to the glass, toward us. I let out a little scream at the same moment that I realized it was my mother standing before us, Andrew Wilkowski's navy wool coat draped over her shoulders. It was also at that same moment that Dino's elbow knocked over the glass hurricane candle and the flame began to lick up the fabric of the curtain.

Here is what I saw in my mind. The flame, gathering speed up the curtain, bursting into a ball of fire. Catching onto the other draperies, moving with the fury of some mythological god to the adjoining room full of people. I heard screams in my mind, the panic of sequined and silked guests, someone tripping on a velvety hem. Smoke suddenly everywhere, one doorway, glass breaking.

Flames spinning up the stairwell, surprising a couple who were upstairs, looking for their coats. Fire trucks with twirling, dizzying lights on the dark street, and charred remnants of furniture and bodies, people crying on the front lawn, the house consumed and then disappearing under gusts of water from the hoses.

I watched as already the flame was beginning to lick its way up the curtain. I could see my mother through the glass, her mouth frozen in an O.

I grabbed the curtain with my hands. My bare hands, I just grabbed it and crumpled it up. It was the only thing I could think to do. No, let me say that again. I did not think at all, I just acted. I gathered up the fabric in a ball and extinguished the flame. The quartet kept playing in the other room.

Before I knew it, my mother was beside me. She was holding my hands in hers. There was ice in a towel. I didn't know what happened to Dino, but I guess Andrew Wilkowski had brought him to his room and calmed him down, telling guests he wasn't feeling well, implying he had had too much to drink, which was a sin forgiven with an amused smile. I couldn't stop shaking. My body just shook and trembled until I threw up. There was a call to a doctor, but my hands were okay. I was okay finally, and I stopped shaking after I was wrapped tightly in my blanket. The only thing that remained of the night was a small scar, which I still have. It sits in the curve between my thumb and forefinger, the place that looks like a small boat if you hold your hand up in the air.

I will never forget that night. The mark reminds me what fear can do to you, how fear can distort what is real to the point that the damage is permanent.

It was the same shape, come to think of it, as the scar on Dino's neck.

CHAPTER EIGHT

Zebe called the next morning, asking if I wanted to hang out with her and Sophie, but I told her I was going shopping with Mom. I didn't think I could stand acting normal and pretending that things were fine, and my other option, letting myself fall apart with them, sounded like it would take more energy than I could stand. I wanted to be *away*. It didn't matter where away was. The air was low on my own bike tires and I didn't want to stop and pump them up, so I grabbed Dino's bike, the one with the basket on the handlebars, and started to ride out to the ferry docks. The burned curtain lay in a heap on the floor after Mom took it down, and the whole house looked hungover from the party. On top of everything else, the caterers had done a crappy job of cleaning up and there were cups set in odd places—the potted plant, behind the toilet—and bits of food on napkins. Two people had forgotten their coats. Dino had still been sleeping when I got up, but Mom looked haunted and stressed and she snapped first at me when I dropped my toast on the floor and then at Dog William when he lunged at it with greedy opportunism. God knows what she'd be like when Dino woke up, or what would happen then.

My hands were freezing on the handlebars and my legs were cold even through my jeans, but I didn't care. The fresh air felt good. The atmosphere inside that house felt doomed. It felt fatal.

It's mostly downhill to the water, and the ferry dock is the end point of the bay. I had Brief Fantasy Number Four Thousand Twelve, of sailing straight down that hill and flying off the end of the dock, destructo-movie style. I like those kinds of movies. Things blowing up and strong, definite action. Zebe and I go together because we can't stand the frilly-ass movies of girls fighting their way to the big cheerleading final, or some such dance-movie-drama crap. We both like the certainty of action movies.

I sped past the bakery, warm smells catching up to me a block later, and the haircutting place and the bookstore. I passed the new Thai restaurant, with the surprising name of Phuket. We couldn't believe it when they put the sign up. Even Dino laughed. Brian Malo told us he called the place a few times, just to hear them answer the phone. I have no idea if this was bold humor on the restaurant owners' part, or if these poor people had no idea they're telling the nice folks of Seabeck to Fuck It.

I set the bike down on its side. I was so cold my nose felt like it could break off, making me one of those Roman statues you see in the museum. I sat on one of the benches on the dock, shoved my hands into my pockets. There were a few fishing boats tied up, though what you'd fish for that time of year, I have no idea. My fish knowledge is on the slim side. It smelled like *green* out there, murky. The smell of fish/seaweed/cold depths. Seagulls were walking around with the aimless air of those with nothing better to do, or were perched on pilings, wearing the cool, unaffected looks of those secretly sure they are being admired. Kind of like the jocks in the cafeteria at lunch.

I watched a ferryboat come in, knocking into the dock, reminding me of my stint during driver's ed when I backed into the side of the garage. The boat unloaded and reloaded, glided away again. There was something about watching the ferryboats come and go that was calming—the rhythm of the departure and arrival. I was wondering how many people on that boat led simple lives where they ate meatloaf and worried about their lawn having weeds and their bathrooms being shiny. That's how it was *supposed to be,* wasn't it? But maybe *supposed to be* was what was wrong. Maybe *supposed to be* was like a child's drawing of a night sky—stars all alike, a yellow moon—simple and pretty and nothing to do with reality. It seemed cruel to feel all this shame because we had more than weeds to worry about.

I was deep in my own profound (ha) line of thought when I saw Rocket trotting down the dock. I was surprised

and so glad to see her. I was just so happy to see a creature who was so nice and simple and cheerful. I patted my
leg, and she came to me. She set her chin on my knee, and
I gave her a good scruffing under her ears, all the while
looking around for Ian. My stomach was lurching around
like crazy with sudden nerves-slash-excitement. I couldn't
see him anywhere, though, and wondered if Rocket just
regularly went off on these small, independent adventures.

I was already planning my return of Rocket to her
home—*I thought she might be lost*—when I saw Ian walking
up the dock. I almost didn't recognize him—he wasn't
wearing his long black coat, but instead had some puffy
ski jacket on. It was good to see him. God, it was so good.
Happiness was spilling over.

"I saw you ride down here," Ian said.

"Fly down here," I said. It was so freezing out there
that when I spoke I felt like a member of those African
tribes you see in *National Geographic,* with the discs in
their lips. I sounded the way you do when you get back
from the dentist.

"You can see this whole area from the bedrooms
upstairs," Ian said.

"Wow."

"It makes up for the fact that the rooms are midget-
size. I heard you came by."

"I just . . . I don't know. Something possessed me."

"Hey, I'm glad. I'm glad you didn't go in too."

"Why? Your mom seemed great."

"She is great. The house, you know, we're still moving in."

"Trés Zen. Feng shui."

"We might've had that for dinner last night," he said. God, I liked him.

"My lips are so cold I can barely talk," I said.

Ian reached out his fingertips, set them on my mouth, the way you would shush someone you loved. That gentle. Then he moved his hand to the tip of my nose. "Your nose is cold, too."

I took hold of his fingers, held them in my hand. We were just standing there on the dock, me holding Ian's hand, and Rocket looking on to see what might happen next. We were both smiling away at each other.

"I haven't seen you in a while," I said. I hadn't really *seen* him since we kissed. Except for when he was at my house last, when he left in a rush after that horrible, humiliating lesson.

"I'm quitting."

"What? What do you mean? Don't let him do that to you. If this is what you want, don't give in because he's an asshole. . . ."

"He's an amazing player. Amazing, God," Ian shook his head. He settled his hand more comfortably in mine. "Amazing doesn't even touch how he plays."

"But he sucks as a human being."

"I don't know how you take it. I don't think I can. Is he always like that?"

"Domineering?" I asked. "Critical? Mean?" I didn't say

crazy. The other things were bad enough. "Yeah, pretty much. He's got a few really likeable moments, and that's about it. I don't know how I take it. I've been thinking about moving in with my Dad." I didn't know I'd been thinking that—it just came out. One of those times the subconscious is clicking along doing its own thing, like when you're walking home and realize you're there but don't even remember the trip.

"What about your mom? She needs you."

"Maybe." I thought about the lesson I'd overheard. *You must save your mama, Ian. . . .* What had Dino meant? There was something about this comment that seemed unapproachable, but I wanted to approach it anyway. I decided to tread carefully, to give Ian an open door in case he wanted to go in. "My mom can take care of herself, though. I mean, doesn't yours?"

"Sure, she does," he said. He ignored my open door. Maybe the comment was more of Dino's usual craziness. "I just thought you'd worry about hurting your mom's feelings by moving out."

"You're right. It's the only thing that's keeping me from getting out of there." I cared about Mom. Too much to let her think she failed me.

"Rocket!" Ian yelled. The dog had trotted off and was smelling a net that a fisherman had thrown onto the dock. "Come on, girl."

Rocket looked up to see if Ian was sure, and when he clapped his hands, letting mine go, Rocket came reluctantly back. Ian sat down on the bench, and I sat beside him. He told me about Thanksgiving, how Chuck and Bunny made lasagna and garlic bread. Bunny had brought over some incense and it stank so bad Ian's mom had to open the windows and they all had to wear their coats as they ate. I told him about mine, but left off everything about Dino's behavior. I only told him about the food, and the guests, and the two waiters on the brink of a passionate affair.

"See everything you'll miss if you quit?" I said. I don't know why I was encouraging him. His continuing meant one thing—that Dino would do whatever he could to help get him into Curtis. That Ian would move a zillion miles away. Still, I'd rather have him go away than quit what he loved because of Dino.

"Everything I'll miss? Everything I'll be free of, is more like it," Ian said. "Pretentious people."

"Endless practicing?" I offered.

"Nothing but music. I'm so goddamned sick of it. I want other things in my life." He looked at me then, and a jolt passed between us. At least, I felt it. He took a strand of my hair, wound it around one finger. My hair had never been so happy.

"Free of Dino's nastiness," I said.

"That accent." Ian shook his head. "I hear it in my sleep."

"And all of the endless stories about Italy. God, I get sick of that."

"He tells me them too."

"His mother teaching him to play the piano, which he

144

couldn't do, but when they brought out his father's old violin . . ."

"He played some song like he learned it in the womb," Ian interrupted.

"I hate when he gets to the 'in the womb' part. *Womb* is a creepy word anyway, but when he says it . . ."

"Wuuum," Ian tried out an Italian accent.

"And the bicycles," I said.

"In the canals," Ian said.

"I've heard it five thousand times."

"I never understood why they threw them in," Ian said.

"'We were hooligans.'" I tried out my Italian accent. Mine was better.

At that moment, that very second, we both looked at Dino's bike, lying on its side there on the dock.

"That's his bike, isn't it?" Ian asked.

"Mmm hmmm."

"It had to be."

I turned to Ian. "Are you thinking what I'm thinking?"

"Are *you* thinking what *I'm* thinking?"

"Let's do it."

"Ve are zuch hooligans," Ian said. He sounded kind of German.

I picked up my end of the bike by the handlebars; Ian lifted the back tire. I was giggling away like mad. "Ze bicycles in ze canal," Ian said. "Is ze serious matter." He was more German by the second.

We lugged the bike to the end of the dock. Rocket was

looking on, giving us the *Those wacky humans* dog look.

"Hold ze bicycle in ze air," Ian said. His hair was in his eyes.

"A moment of victory," I said.

I tried my best, but it was heavy. My end was drooping during that part of the ceremony. We counted. One, two, three. We heaved it as far as we could, which was maybe a few feet. It landed in the water with a splat more than a splash, and lay on the top for a minute before the back wheel started heading down. We started to clap. I was filled with a surge of joy. Water rushed through the wire basket.

"We are ze king and ze queen of bicycle tossing," Ian said.

"Conquerors and champions," I said.

Ian took a pinch of my sleeve, brought me in to him in a hug. I could smell his coat, nylon left outside; his hair, some kind of clean vanilla.

"I'm quitting lessons, Cassie," Ian said.

"Don't do it if it's just because of Dino. Don't let him have that kind of power."

"It's not just Dino. Cassie? I don't want the violin running my life. I want more."

"Okay, then. All right," I said.

"And I don't want to go away to Curtis," he said. I set my cheek against him, let the hope fill me. I could hear his heart, even through his puffy coat. It was beating pretty wildly in there.

"Then you won't go," I said.

We pulled apart. Here's what I felt—our eyes, they made a pact. To be away from the music, the all-encompassing enemy, to be safe with each other. It was settled. No more violin, no more frenzied, singular visions. Ian would be the place where everything was okay.

Ian leaned in, kissed me. Warm, so warm, soft. A long, slow kiss. I didn't pull away, and I didn't run. He swallowed me up and brought me in.

When we pulled apart again, we just looked at each other. Because of course, everything had changed.

I started seeing Ian every day after school. He hadn't told his mom that he'd stopped going to lessons, so he'd pretend to leave at the same time each day and we'd meet somewhere. Sometimes we'd go to the ferry dock, and sometimes we'd go to the planetarium, because Dave, the guy that works there, always lets me in for free. We'd sit in the plush seats, and I'd point things out to Ian and he'd interrupt me with questions. Every now and then Ian would have Bunny's car, and we'd park somewhere and kiss and steam up the windows and go to the edge of want. Or we'd sit in the chairs in the back part of the library and talk, and once we listened to classical music on the big, puffy library headphones, those old kind from when headphones were first invented. He explained to me the difference between legato and staccato, and for the first time in my life I actually cared. About the music, about someone else. Cared—love. My God, love. Here it was, and it was fantastic. Everything felt larger. I felt like things made sense. I was myself, and more than I ever knew I could be. I wanted to be so close to him that I was *of* him. I wanted to be in his mind, in his arms. I loved the way his hair fell in his eyes, his gangly limbs, the way I had to stand on my toes to reach him. I loved his sudden laugh, the way he thought about things, his intelligence. I started wearing his coat around when we were together. I would have worn it when we were apart, if I could. And Ian was a harbor. A place to hide from what was happening at home. A gazebo to run to and take shelter in during a thunderstorm. If you think that all of this is corny, tough shit. That's the way it was.

I explained away my absences with my handy Honduras project. It was the biggest project in the history of projects. It was the longest, too, even though we'd given the oral report on it weeks ago, Nicole holding and gesturing to the visual aids like a game show hostess, and Jason sulking and not saying anything because we'd rejected his idea of playing music in the background while we spoke. He'd brought in a tape recorder and a compilation of Hawaiian favorites. He perked up when we let him pass out the information sheets to the class, though. Of course, all three of us got an A, even though the only thing those two really contributed to was my understanding of homicidal behavior.

I kept different pieces of my life in different places. I was overcome with this bizarre need to talk about Ian, to bring him to me with words, but I only gave in and did this with my bonded twin, Zach Rogers, the talented duct-taped snake impersonator. I chose Zach to mention Ian to because one, he had every class with me, and two, because he had the memory of a goldfish. I didn't tell any of my friends about Ian, even Zebe.

"What is with you?" she asked me at lunch one day. "You aren't yourself. I feel like I'm talking to my Coke can. No, wait. It's more responsive." She held the can up to her ear. "Yeah, uh huh, I know," she said to the can. "God, Cassie. You've been acting weird for over a week now."

"No, I haven't. I'm fine."

"Shit, you know? I thought I was your friend."

"I'm sorry. There's really nothing . . ." I thought quickly. "Things are messed up at home. More than usual. I'm thinking of moving in with my dad. It's just really been on my mind a lot."

"You can't talk to me about that?" Zebe said. "Man, oh, man, you gotta share this stuff or it kills you. I was going to tell the counselor you had an eating disorder just so she'd call you into her office."

I still got together with everyone on most weekends, but inside I was rushing through those times and others. I had an ever-present inner *hurry up!* until I could be with Ian again. So that I could be free in the afternoons with the ease of one all-encompassing lie, I told my friends and even Siang that Mom got me a job helping with symphony correspondence.

I'm not sure why it felt so necessary to keep Ian a secret. I guess I wanted what we had all for myself, to protect it. I didn't want what was happening between Ian and me to become the usual thing, where you date for a few weeks and everyone talks about it like it's a ridiculously moronic soap opera, and your friends call his friends and his friends call you and it all becomes stupid and shallow. It was too special to have as the news of the day. It was too deep to be about other people.

I also didn't tell my parents about Ian for obvious reasons, and though I did tell Ian about my parents, I didn't talk about Dino. I didn't tell him that since Thanksgiving, Dino was up and down and paranoid and rational. I was sure it was too bizarre for him to handle. It was too bizarre for *me* to handle. Let's face it. Mental illness is embarrassing. In a perfect world, we wouldn't look down on people too ill to hold it together, who cry while looking out the window and don't bother getting fully dressed before going out. We'd be patient and understanding, instead of letting out our fear and uneasiness with the same kind of jokes we make about funeral directors. But it does make you uneasy. You do want to hold it away from you by saying his tie would match his straitjacket, even if that's not nice. This is not me, this is not mine. My mom makes cookies, too.

I couldn't show Ian that part of my life. It was something I wanted to run from, so why wouldn't he? And there was another thing, too. Ian was a part of the situation in a way a stranger wouldn't be. I can honestly say that I lost track of who I was protecting, and why.

"He didn't show up for his lesson again," Dino said one night as we were all in the car going out for dinner. "Two times, now. Two times!"

"I told you, just let him sort it out on his own. He's obviously struggling with the music just now."

"I'm going to call his mother. You want me to wait until it happens a third time?"

"Third, fourth. Let him have a rest. You know how the pressure can get to you," Mom said. "Let him decide he wants this. Be calm, Dino."

"We're losing precious time, Daniella," Dino said. "Don't you see? We've only got three and a half months before his tape must be in."

"Why is this so important to you anyway?" I asked. I never did get that. I mean, why not let Ian *be*?

"How can you understand? I can make a difference in his life. I can save him the struggle I had," Dino said. His eyes in the rearview mirror looked disgusted at my question.

"You see yourself in him," Mom said.

"Youth, need, talent . . ." Dino said. "But how can I help him if he doesn't help himself? It's a waste, and I detest waste. He will lose his chance if he doesn't stop these foolish games."

"Maybe he quit," I said. I couldn't help myself. I was a little smug at having the inside information. I also wanted to help Ian out. He was so happy about not playing anymore that the sooner Dino got it through his head, the better. Dino's pride at not having succeeded with his first student would just have to hurt a little. Or a lot. The Curtis School a zillion miles away would just have to do without Ian. If you're thinking here that my motivations

151

were selfish, you're right about that too. Sure, I was glad he quit. If it meant he wouldn't leave, I'd have been happy if he decided to become a ferryboat driver and live here forever.

"Ha," Dino said. "He'll never quit."

A little flame of anger rose up. "What makes you so sure?"

"I know. He will never quit. He'll be back."

"You can't know," I said. "You can't know for sure what someone will or won't do." I hated the look of the back of his neck, that curly hair he was so proud of. What I'd have given for a pair of scissors.

"Don't be ridiculous. He'll be back. I'll call his mother in the morning," Dino said.

"No, Dino. It will be better if he comes back here on his own," my mother said. "You know how it gets sometimes. You think you never want to see a sheet of music again."

We pulled up to the restaurant. I didn't feel like eating. I didn't want to sit across from Dino and see him get salad dressing in the corners of his mouth. Hatred and nourishment didn't go together.

"His mother will do what I tell her to do. They always do. That idiot Andrew Wilkowski would jump off a bridge if I told him to," Dino said.

"Wearing his music-note tie," my mother said.

"Tacky man. William Tiero, that prick. He was the only one who wouldn't. He told me what to do, and I hated it. How many years, I followed like a lamb."

"All right, love. Let's not think about that now," Mom said. She opened her car door.

"They would all jump off a bridge if I told them to." Dino snapped his fingers in the air. *Just like that,* those fingers said.

Christmas came. A big tree was brought into the house, delivered already decorated, a present from Andrew Wilkowski, who probably had just gotten his first commission check for the deal he set up for Dino, the CD currently titled, *Then and Now,* a mix of his old stuff and the new pieces, a way of putting out a new album without a full set of fresh material. You should have seen this tree—it was the kind of thing that you see in department stores, with miniature packages wrapped in gold paper and gaudy, huge ornaments and sparkly pears and doves. It was either gorgeous or horrid. Either way it didn't exactly give you what you would call a warm, Chestnuts Over the Open Fire kind of feeling. More, Nordstrom's Holiday Home Sale. When it was being delivered, Courtney and her media-monster brothers practically wet themselves with excitement. They stood in the street and watched the tree—and the two delivery guys it took to carry it—disappear into the house. Mom said Courtney actually brought her parents by later to gawk. This wasn't hard to do. You could be three miles away from the front window and still see it. Thank God there were no lights on it, or the Coast Guard would think there was a ship in distress.

In spite of the tree, there were bits of evidence of the

way Christmas used to be too, when it was just Mom and Dad and me. There was this decrepit gingerbread house we'd made years ago, the candy so ancient that it was pale and drippy and would kill you if you ate it, and our old Nativity scene. Mom and I still liked to have fun with it by moving the figures around in what you could politely call "nontraditional positions." Mom's not very religious in any regular way. She called the Nativity "Christmas Town," as in *What's happening in Christmas Town today?* I'd wake up to find the camel in the manger, say, with Joseph chipping in with parenting duties out front, and then I'd move them around to surprise her the next day with everyone standing in a circle around the donkey. Several years ago, the scene acquired a large plastic dinosaur, and later, a miniature replica of the Statue of Liberty that Mom got when she played a festival in New York. The poor folks of Christmas Town ran from Godzilla one day, and the Statue of Liberty got to be a fourth wise man. I remember that my dad used to get a little ticked at us for this, as Christmas Town had been a gift from Nannie, and he disapproved of our sacrilege. I remember Mom sticking out her tongue at him, and him swatting her butt. I don't think Dino even noticed Christmas Town. I'm not sure Dino even noticed the Christmas tree that had invaded the living room.

I spent Christmas Eve with my dad. There was no talk of his Dino detective work right then, thankfully, but I saw that the books and notepads were still in his room, stacked neatly beside his bed. Dad had brought Nannie and two other old ladies home with him for the holiday, and he made a fantastic dinner that all the old ladies loved. One of them, Helen, drank too much wine and fell asleep before we had dessert, snoring away in Dad's favorite chair. We opened presents, and Nannie and the other old lady, Mary, got rambunctious.

"That would look lovely on Helen," Nannie said when she opened the nightgown from Dad. She placed it on top of the snoozing old lady.

"Put the necktie on her too," said Mary. So Helen got decorated with Dad's new tie, a car-washing mitt, and my new hat. Mary and Nannie were laughing so hard I thought we'd have to call the medics. Dad was trying to get Helen to hold the hand mixer I'd given him, when she snorted and flinched kind of violently, sending the car-washing mitt sailing and landing on the coffee table in a half-empty bowl of Dad's clam dip. Nannie was holding her stomach with laughter, and had to hurry off to the bathroom. I'd never seen her this loose.

"Jeez, what was in that wine?" I said to Dad. He was happy and relaxed, having a grand time, too. When we got everyone packed in the car to go, Nannie had to come back in because she'd forgotten the slippers I'd given her. She was in there so long that it shouldn't have been a surprise that when we came home, we saw that her own Nativity scene had been moved to the dining room table, and the Christmas cards had been set upright along the mantel, just as they used to be when she'd lived there with Grandpa.

Christmas day I spent at home with Mom and Dino. If your parents are divorced, you know this is one of the side benefits of the whole deal, the time when all of the crap and the moving from house to house actually starts to pay off a little. Two or more Christmases, two or more birthdays. Zebe won the holiday lottery. She has five Christmases and one Chanukah. She has Christmases with her Mom, Dad, Grandpa, Grandma (they're divorced, too), and her other set of grandparents. Her stepmother is Jewish, so she gets Chanukah with them, too. Handing her the keys to a department store would be easier. Everyone wants to give you the holiday they remembered. You actually start to feel sorry for those kids whose parents are married to each other, poor deprived souls. Your social calendar becomes busier than the president's during election year, and keeping track of everything becomes akin to solving those annoying puzzles where you slide around the numbers and try to get them back in order. You never want to see another Christmas cookie or a turkey again in your life. You realize there are many stuffing variations, all pretty gross. You realize how truly *different* Mom's family is from Dad's family. But you've got a stocking in every house, and candy and love and presents rain down upon you, like the Red Cross flying overhead, dropping packages. All this because your parents sucked at being married to each other.

Dino had apparently done his shopping in no less than fifteen seconds total, and in the gift section of the men's department. He gave Mom a six-in-one flashlight, a gold pen, and a box of handkerchiefs. He gave me an executive desk dartboard and an executive stress-buster ball to squeeze in your hand. I was glad he passed on the golf ball-care kit and the six-pack of holiday boxers. The day was nice but uneventful, and after dinner, Dino went into his office to work. There were only three months left until the concert. Mom and I sat in the kitchen and ate a piece of apple pie, then took thin slices of what was left in the dish until we were thoroughly disgusted with ourselves. Dino emerged, his hair disheveled and tired-looking, his eyes with dark circles. Mom made him tea, rubbed his neck.

"We would have a pomegranate, this time of year," Dino said. "In Italy. No, a pomegranate every day."

"You must be exhausted," Mom said.

"Unspeakably."

Dino went to bed, and after I let Dog William outside for a last holiday pee, I headed for bed, too.

Mom must have been feeling sentimental. She'd come in my room to kiss me good night. "Merry Christmas," I said to her.

"You too, my girl," she said. Her braid had swung over my face. Her own face looked thin and tired.

"I hope it's a really good year," I said.

Mom paused a beat. "I want that too," she said.

I woke up really early and happy the next morning, knowing that Ian and I were going to meet. Something about the morning seemed oddly still, too quiet, and when I peeked through my blind I saw why—it had snowed during the night, and it was a beautiful soft white everywhere. Snow is magical, and if you don't think so, you won't see magic anywhere. I got that excited feeling, like there'd be school closures, even though we were off school already. I went in Mom and Dino's room, shook Mom awake so she could see. She crept up so as not to disturb Dino, went out in the backyard in her nightgown and made a snowball to put in the freezer, like we always did. *I told you I thought it was going to snow. I could smell it in the air,* she said. She was always proud of her weather-predicting abilities, especially after no one believed her. There was no practice that day, so she went back to bed, and I got showered and dressed. I was too excited to go back to sleep.

I was hunting around the back of my closet for warm stuff when I heard a big *bamp* at my window. I swore at first, thinking it was Courtney's brothers, but when I looked out I saw Ian standing right outside, and bits of a snowball dribbling down my window. The street was still sleeping, and Ian's boots had made a path down the road. God, it was pretty out, and Ian had on his dark coat and held a slim white box. He was standing there in full view, really dangerous, and I urged him down the street with my hands, held up one finger to indicate I'd be right there.

I grabbed the slim white box in my own room, shoved on my mittens and my old boots, but got this in reverse order, since I couldn't work the laces. I flung off my mittens

158

and tried again, pulled on my new snow hat from Nannie, and was happy/unhappy about it. Unhappy because it was scratchy, happy because the scratchiness reminded me of really great snowy days in uncomfortable hats. I tried not to clump down the stairs, and when I stepped outside, the only thing the cold hit was my face. I had on layers of clothes and so I could barely move, just the way it should be. Ian was down the street, clapping his mittened hands for me to hurry.

I clomped and sloshed down the street. I picked a clean patch so that I could make my own footprints. Something about marring smooth sand or snow and making our mark must go back to our caveman days, because it is such a satisfying feeling. I was hot already and pulled off my hat, making my hair look superb, I'm sure. Otis, the neighbor's cat, was picking his way across the snow with tenderly raised paws and a great deal of caution.

I tossed a snowball in Ian's direction. "That's for the one at my window," I said. My aim sucked and I hit the Fredericis' mailbox.

"You better watch it," he warned. If my hair had gone all undersea creature on me, Ian didn't seem to care. He grabbed me up in his arms and lifted me up and set me down again.

"Snow," he said. His breath came out in a puff.

"I love it," I said. "This is the best."

"Let's go to the riding trail, then we can do the presents," he said.

"Okay."

We walked hand in hand, or rather, mitten in mitten, which is about the coziest and Everything All Right with the World feeling you can get. We walked toward the school, the center part of the island, where there is a perimeter of forested riding and walking trails. We walked past the trail marker, and I slid the snow off its top into a heap. The trail didn't look real. It was a postcard day. The branches of the trees were heavy and drooping with white thickness, and the ground was a soft and sparkly carpet.

"So beautiful," I said.

"You too," Ian said. He took hold of one strand of my hair, looked at the color of it against his mitten. He looked at my face. "Brown hair, dark eyes, white snow."

We walked a bit, just listening to silence. Snowy quiet is more quiet than regular quiet. It's like the world is holding its breath.

After a while, Ian stopped. "Presents?"

"Sure," I said.

We both knew what we were getting each other. We agreed to get each other the same thing, only we'd choose which kind. Eliminate all gift-giving hassle and anxiety. We swapped boxes. I bit the fingertips of my mittens and pulled them off, tossed them to the ground so that I could open the package.

"Ready?" I said, and we both pulled the scarves from the boxes. Mine was red, amazingly soft, fuzzy. The one I'd chosen for Ian was blue, with thick, wide stitches.

"Let me," Ian said. He wrapped the scarf around my neck.

"I love it," I said, and wrapped his around his neck, tucking the ends inside his coat.

"Me too," he said.

We hugged for a while, stood together, and I had that feeling you get in nature that you are small against its grandness, same as when you used to see the tiny figure of a person against the Latitude Drive-In Movie screen, before they tore it down to put a strip mall there. Ian put my mittens back on my hands, and we walked a little, boots crunching.

"Fir, cedar, evergreens," Ian pointed. "Spruce. Poplar. Deciduous. Water can go up hundreds of feet, to the tiniest branches up there. Just travels up, molecule by molecule."

"I didn't know you knew about these things."

"I like to study trees." He looked upward, and his dark hair fell away from his eyes. "They're quiet. They're solid. Sure of where they are."

"You must get tired of sound."

"God, really."

"You could study trees instead."

Ian laughed.

"You could."

"I'd love that. I would so love that."

He stopped on the trail then, and we kissed in the snow, in our new scarves. It was one of life's perfect moments, where you look around and think *I want to remember this*. You try to etch it in your brain so that when you are Nannie's age and are living at Providence Point, you will look out the window and see red and blue scarves against a white background, Ian's breath against the backdrop of trees, new snow beginning to fall; at first, small diamonds, and then huge fat flakes that sat on the shoulders of Ian's dark coat and fell upon his hair. You will remember the soft flakes against your upturned face, the way they fell upon your tongue, and Ian telling you he loved you into your hair. You would remember all of it, and feel that sense that you had everything you ever wanted in the world.

We walked back home, stopped at the beginning of my street. The media-monster boys didn't even have their sleds out, and there were no forts or snowball fights or snowmen and women, but the blue light from the television shone from the living room windows. Mr. Frederici was shoveling his walk, even though the snow would likely turn to rain by night, and the snow would be mostly gone except for a few lingering patches by tomorrow. That's how the snow was around here. A day or two of thrill and traffic all messed up, and then you had to wait another year for it to happen again.

Ian put his mittened hands against my cheeks and kissed me, his mouth cold, and then warm again. His dark hair was wet from the snow. I'm sure I had mascara all over my face, but he looked at me like he loved me. Then Ian gazed down my street, at our house.

"My mother was playing one of his recordings yesterday," Ian said.

I was silent. We both just stood and looked at my

house. Unease was starting at my toes, creeping up. The day had been so perfect.

"What his music does to you—there aren't even words."

Perfect, and fleeting.

Ian returned to his lessons, of course.

He didn't even tell me. I just heard his voice in the house a few days later and I knew what had happened. God damn it, it made me mad. I wasn't sure who I was so mad at. Dino, for being right. Ian, for giving himself up. He had broken our pact. It was *settled*. At least that's how I saw it.

"Ian!" I called, after he left on his bike. He put on his brakes, had his head down. Like Dog William when he peed on the carpet. I ran to catch up to him. Fury, confusion, and hurt all mixed together so I didn't know which was which.

"You didn't tell me."

"I'm sorry. I don't know. I couldn't."

"Why? And why are you doing this? You don't even want this. Why? Please. I just don't get it."

"Look at you. I knew you'd be hurt. I didn't want to hurt you. I just couldn't do it." He reached over, picked up my hand. He rubbed the top of it with his thumb.

"What happened, Ian?"

"My Mom found out I quit lessons, and flipped. I told her about us. She doesn't even want me to see you anymore. Cassie, I don't want that."

Great. Nice Janet with the chipped toenail polish. Anger bubbled up. Love meant nothing, I guess. Not compared to what that violin meant. I turned my head away. I stared at the Fredericis' house. I didn't even want to look at him.

"I don't want that," he said. "Do you hear me? Cassie."

"I don't see what the point is. You're going away. You're going away, right?" I said to the Fredericis' house. I didn't understand. I didn't get how things could change from that perfect day in the woods to where they were now.

"Cassie, look at me." He took my chin. Brought my eyes to his. "You know I love you."

"You sold yourself out. You're going away, right?"

His eyes were wet, from cold maybe. Maybe he was about to cry. "Yes."

"Leave me alone," I said. I broke away from him. Hurt, the winning emotion, was rushing forward, gathering up my insides and holding them too tight. Hurt squeezed my heart, and I ran. He betrayed himself, so he'd betrayed me.

CHAPTER NINE

I knew Ian came early to lessons to see me. I knew he stayed late, hanging around the front lawn. He even threw something at my window once, which I ignored.

"The boy is back," Dino had said that first day, with this horrible glee in his voice. How I didn't throw my water glass at him, I'll never know.

"So it all works out," my mother said.

I hated everyone. Dino. Even Mom sometimes. Dog William for being happier than ever, having Rocket back in his life. I fantasized about funding my father's sabotaging-Dino efforts, the way one government secretly funds the destruction of another. Okay, the way *our* government does that. I hated school and almost everyone in it. They changed the seating chart in World History, and I ended up sitting next to these two girls who I always thought looked like those monkeys from *Planet of the Apes*. In science we started labs. My partners were Orlando, who didn't yet know he was gay, and this girl, Julia, who already knew she was. So during one class it was the Bad Primate Movie film-fest, and the next it was the Rainbow Pride Hour, with Orlando using words like *exquisite,* and Julia showing us pictures of her and Allison Lorey at homecoming. Zach, of duct-taped-snake fame, had suddenly moved after his dad got a new job. I felt a sadness and inexplicable loss. Twins separated, phantom-limb stuff. I actually missed him. Worse, we were into that long spell where there were no vacations until Spring Break, unless you count that perennial holiday favorite, President's Day. Such a time of revelry and celebration, where the whole country stops in joyful remembrance of William Howard Taft and Grover Cleveland. Party on.

The next time Ian had a lesson, I stayed in my room. Chuck and Bunny had given him a ride; I heard their car and Bunny's deep voice calling out a good-bye. No Rocket that day—Dog William would have his heart broken. Good.

I held the snow globe, turned it upside down enough times to make the bear truly pissed off, if he could get pissed off. I thought maybe I should name him. I wondered what a good name for an unanchored bear would be. Bingo? Dave? Timmy? I ignored the goddamn beautiful sounds coming from downstairs. I wondered how Sabbotino Grappa, full of lemon trees and curved, cobbled streets could produce a man with a stone heart.

"Cassie!"

A knock at my door. Shit, a knock. I dropped the bear on my bed. I guess the music downstairs had stopped some time ago. It was Ian. At my bedroom door.

"Are you crazy?" I said to the door. "Dino will kill you."

"Open up. Come on. Cassie, come *on*!"

"Ian, what are you doing?" I said through the closed door. "He's right downstairs."

"I don't care."

"Go away."

"I'm not leaving until you talk to me."

"Jesus," I said. I opened the door. "Get in here before he sees you." I yanked his sleeve, shut the door behind him. "What are you thinking?"

"I'm thinking I'm in love with you. I'm thinking I miss you and I'm sorry you feel I've let you down."

His brown eyes were soft. I wanted to put my hands in his hair, inside his coat, around his waist. *Pain versus happiness,* I'd told my mother. There must be a simple mathematical solution to figure it out.

Some strange memory came to me then. A story from when I was little, told again and again by my parents. I was climbing the attic stairs as my mother stood behind me. *Are you afraid of the stairs?* My mother had asked. *No,* I had said. *I'm just afraid of falling.*

"Hey," Ian said. "I'm in your room. I've never seen your room."

He looked around at my lamps and my hula dancer

dashboard guy, and at my Einstein Action Figure. He picked up the tiny plastic television on my dresser, looked inside the peephole and clicked through the pictures of Dogs on TV—tacky dogs in tacky costumes. He stared at the star chart on the back of my door.

"You've got to get out of here," I said.

"Not yet." Ian took his sweet time looking around. He read the quotes stuck up along near my bed, picked up my snow globe, which I'd ditched quickly on the mattress. He gave the bear a spin, watched him swirl.

"I've had him since I was a kid," I said. "He used to be glued down."

"I like him like this," Ian said. "He looks happy. Free. He's just cruising around." Ian gave him another spin.

"He's totally unanchored. Lost in space."

"He's *smiling*. Look, miniature painted lips. Smiling." He held the globe above us, pointed out the tiny red line on the bear's face. "Cassie, what are you so afraid of?" Ian said. He handed the globe back to me.

"It's obvious."

"No."

"Losing you. Having you go away. Feeling too much. It doesn't seem to lead to good things."

"It's like . . . you're on vacation. But instead of enjoying the sun and the palm trees, you're worrying the plane's gonna crash on the way home."

"You *are* leaving. I *will* lose you."

"I'm here right now. We don't know what the future will bring. Why don't we let that take care of itself."

I didn't say anything. Ian resumed his survey of my room. He saw my scarf, draped over my desk chair, ran it between his fingers. He picked up my pillow, held it to his face to smell my scent.

"I love the way you smell."

"Ian." I could barely speak.

"Cassie, *let go.*"

I felt my throat close up with tears. Sometimes you build up these walls, you build and you build and you think they're so strong, but then someone can come along and tip them over with only his fingers, or the weight of his breath. I started to cry. Ian came and put his arms around me, and I tried to think tough things because I hate to cry. I told myself not to act like I'd been abducted and brainwashed by evil Hallmark robots, but it was no good. He held me, and I tried not to think about what was really on my mind—all the times that people came together and really loved each other, all the times that meant they'd have to lose each other, too.

"I'm sorry," I said.

"What are you sorry for? Don't be sorry."

"Just, how I handled things."

"I've hated disappointing you," Ian said.

I got myself together. Unburied my face from his shirt. I probably got makeup on his dark coat. I'm sure my eyes looked trés Ringling Brothers.

"God, Ian. What are we thinking? You've got to get out of here. Dino's going to know you're here. He's like a hawk. A hawk with ESP. He notices everything. He catches every *thought* someone has that's against him. He catches every thought about maybe having a thought someone has that's against him."

"I don't care. I'll do the audition, but I want a life, too. I told my mother the same thing. Dino's going to have to accept it too."

"It's supposed to affect your focus. Spending time with me means you're not giving everything to your music the way you need to. You only have two more months until your audition."

"I can handle it fine. There's no reason I can't do both," Ian said. "I don't care if Dino knows. I don't want to hide anymore."

I felt a surge of brave glee. It felt good. No, it felt *great*. "I hope you know what you're doing," I said.

"I've never been more sure."

"Oh, God. He's going to kill me." More glee in this, the anticipation of good conquering evil. Some sicko part of me was thrilled at the idea of the shit hitting the fan. It was very Romeo and Juliet, only we know what happened to them.

"Kiss me. Then walk me down."

"Man, you are asking for it."

"He's going to have to understand."

I knew when he said this that he didn't understand Dino very well. We stepped out my door, walked down the stairs. Of course, Dino was coming out of his office when we reached the landing. I'm sure he knew where Ian was the entire time, and was keeping track of the passing minutes on his watch.

"Ian needs a ride home," I said. "He came to ask me." So much for conquering evil. I was already descending into fear-induced excuses and barely concealed panic. I realized that I'd have to make good on my quick thinking, was relieved to remember that Mom carpooled that morning, as she often did to save on ferry passage.

"Thanks for the lesson, Mr. Cavalli," Ian said. And then he picked up my hand, laced my fingers in his.

"Good-bye, Boy Wonder," Dino said.

I drove Ian home, my heart leaping around with Oh, Shit, What Have We Done jubilation and anxiety. And at just plain happiness at being with Ian again. You know what I'd missed? The smell of him, how he always smelled like he'd just come in from the cold, and like that vanilla shampoo. And now I could smell him there in the car beside me and it made me so happy. I felt like I could just drive around for the next twenty years and be perfectly content, there in Mom's Subaru, with her half-eaten roll of butterscotch Life Savers in the ashtray, paper coffee cup crinkled on the floor, and Seattle Weekly in tossed disarray on the backseat.

I turned the radio up loud. Some old rock song. Something very un-classical. I guess even Mom needed a break from it too, while she was driving. Ian patted his thigh with his palm to the beat. We arrived at his house and kissed in the car for a while. Man, did I like kissing Ian Waters.

We steamed up the windows until Ian had to go. I hated to see him leave. Kissing him in the car made me want to never have to see the back of his coat going away from me. He walked up the steps to his house, and I watched him. He turned and waved good-bye.

It wasn't until I'd gotten home that I realized he'd forgotten all about his violin in the backseat.

The bizarre thing was, Dino didn't say a word about Ian and me all that night, or the next day even. He was only his usual depressed self, this morose person who was becoming our usual household companion, this man on a constant hunt for the ways he was sure he was being harmed. I wondered if he'd given up on the theory that he could feel more in control of his own life by controlling someone else's, or if he just didn't care anymore. What I really thought, though, was that it was all building up inside of him—his anger, his disease. The vicious mix was simmering.

Dino must not have even told Mom about Ian and me. She didn't mention anything, or even seem annoyed with me. Dino stayed holed up in his office, then went to bed early. He just stayed disconnected from me. But then again, he'd never truly connected with me in the first place. I was like the dishwasher, or the coffee pot, and always had been. I just came with the package, and as long as I was doing what I was supposed to do and kept quiet, fine. Sometimes, in a step-situation you've got all the pieces, but it just doesn't make a family. Everyone is trying to make believe that it is, but you can tell the difference. No divorce book is going to help, no "new traditions" are

172

going to help, and God, no family vacations are going to help (unless purposely staying behind at the rest stop and making a new life there fixes things), because it just doesn't feel right. Your parent makes a choice, based on who knows what, and you're forced to live with that choice. That's the reality. "Family" is not the reality. Zebe had a stepsister who's supposed to be a sister, and I had a stepfather who's supposed to be a father, and we're all just faking it, and not very well, either. There's an aversion to the Required Relationship, same as I have an aversion to those miniature, creepy corns. They look unnatural to me, but I'll eat them if I have to. Let's just be honest. Sometimes there's love there, and it all works great. But sometimes there isn't. A lot of times there isn't. These people are just strangers who live with you and take on assumed family-like names. And even the tolerance that usually comes with blood relatives isn't there. It's all painfully staged. It's a bad play, that you sit in your seat and squirm during with awkward anxiety; it's a pair of shoes that *just don't fit* that you jam your feet into anyway. It's not home. It's people in a house.

Anyway, he didn't say anything. I called Ian for the first time.

"Check it out," I said. "I'm calling you at home."

"Say something more so I can hear how you sound on the phone," he said. "Just talk."

"Four score and seven years ago," I orated. "This country brought forth a new nation. Really important things started happening, and men who weren't even gay started wearing white wigs and frilly coats. They looked lovely, but even more importantly they . . ."

"I like your voice on the phone," Ian interrupted. I was just getting warmed up, too.

"I better not stay on long. I just wanted to tell you that he's been silent. No screams. This is actually me talking, and not my murdered ghost."

"See? We didn't need to worry. He probably just accepts that there's nothing he can do."

"Ha. Calm before the storm," I said.

And I was right. The next day I felt the tension, more than saw actual evidence of it. The air was thin and nervous, electric. Being in the same room with him was unbearable—you could feel that pebble that had just snapped into the windshield, the breakage line snaking up, the knowledge of an inevitable shatter. We bumped elbows in the kitchen the next day, as Dino went for the refrigerator and I went for the cereal bowls, and I could actually feel him flinch. Mom was making coffee and obviously talking Chinese, because I couldn't understand anything she was saying. I got the hell out of there, fast. I thought maybe I should live at school. I could borrow the janitor's room, that snug, weird place of mops in buckets and detergents, and a calendar with sports cars on it that was still showing September. I even made small talk with Courtney on the walk home, even though every talk with Courtney is small talk, if you know what I mean. We talked about nail polish, for God's sake. She told me about a hair removal kit she got on the Home Shopping Network with her mother's credit card. I fed her more topics—hairstyles, breast implants, the love life of Toby Glassar, this muscle-choked senior guy all the blond girls liked—until she looked at me as if we had really bonded. *Thanks for the great talk,* she said, and then told me she had to leave to go watch the soap *All My Sex Partners.* Okay, it wasn't really called that, but you get my drift.

I stayed in my room until Mom came home and it was dinnertime. If there's ever a time you feel the stepfamily disconnect, it's at the dinner table. You've got to sit there and look at your differences until you've downed your lasagna as fast as possible. You learn that every planet teaches manners differently, and the one your new alien family members came from probably either didn't teach them at all (making dinner a revolting nightly replay of a pie-eating contest), or taught them too well (making dinner a new Olympic sport called Every Food Has a Rule). That night, the tension was lying between us, sharp and thread-like. No one was talking, and the sounds of silverware on glass plates were painfully loud, seemingly capable of breaking apart what was holding us all together. You could hear Dino's chewing (you could always hear Dino's chewing), and he was drinking wine. Too much wine, I could tell, from the way my mother kept eyeing his glass as he refilled it. She was obviously on the wrong page; her own tension stemmed from the surplus Burgundy and not from what was going on between Dino and me right under her nose.

"My bike is gone," Dino said finally.

I swallowed hard. It was either that, or blast out a mouthful of lasagna. I practically burst out laughing from nerves and surprise. His bike. Thrown in ze "canal" by ze two hooligans. I'd almost forgotten about it.

"What do you mean?" my Mom said.

"Gone. Stolen."

"Who would steal *that* bike?" Mom said. She actually laughed. I felt like busting up too. I took a drink of milk. Trained my thoughts—*death, destruction, devastation*—so that I wouldn't bust up and explode it out my nose.

"It's gone," he said. He chewed a chunk of bread. You saw it in there, being swirled and mashed to death. "I wonder if you know anything about this?" he asked me. "You are the one who rides it."

"I don't know what happened to it." Lie. "I haven't ridden it in weeks." Truth. *Couldn't* ride it since it was at the bottom of the sound.

"I went into the garage and noticed it wasn't there."

"I wonder who might have done something like that," I said. "You never know." I mean, where was his paranoia now? Why couldn't William Tiero have done *this*? He'd supposedly followed us, tried to ruin Dino's career, sent us annoying junk mail, called repeatedly, and done a thousand other things. He should have at least been in the lineup.

"I spoke with Ian's mother," Dino said. "This afternoon."

"Why?" Mom asked.

176

"About the budding lovers," Dino said.

There it was. The beginning, and I was already lost. I was already gone to anger; he'd already won.

"We're not lovers," I said.

"Shall we count our blessings for that?" he said.

"Not yet, anyway," I said. I wanted to put the knife in. I wanted to twist.

"You are such a silly child. Your immaturity is astounding."

"I'm supposed to be immature. I'm the kid. What's your excuse?"

"Wait a minute. What is going on?" Mom said. Her face was flushing red.

"You have no idea what you're doing. No idea of the harm you can cause."

"You have no idea what *you're* doing," I said to him. "You're going to kill any desire he has to play that stupid fucking violin."

"Listen to this tramp, Daniella," Dino said to my mother. "Look at her. Listen to her mouth."

"Hold on a moment here," my mother said. "You just hold on. I don't want to hear that kind of talk from you, Dino. Or you, Cassie."

"She is ruining everything. Don't you understand that?"

"What is going on?" my mother asked.

"Ian," was all I could say. "Ian and me."

"He's got less than two months. Seven weeks, and he's not ready. Even the *Chaconne* is rough. How can I help

177

him? How can I make it turn out all right for him when he is running around in airy-fairy land with her? This child could destroy everything he's worked for."

"Ian has some say in this too. I am not some evil sorceress making him do things against his will."

"Jesus, Cassie! What's been going on? I thought we agreed. . . ."

"The boy must be managed. His career must be handled. He's not to be trusted to know what he needs," Dino said.

"Sometimes love just *is*," I threw her words back at her. "Sometimes it's a force with its own reasons."

"Where did you get such idiocy?" Dino said. "This is a practical matter. Someone's life is in your hands. He fucks up this audition, and his future is shit."

"Maybe he doesn't want to play. Maybe you should let him be. His life has nothing to do with you." I pushed my plate away.

"Cassie," Mom said.

"I'm his teacher. He is my responsibility. I can change his life. I have a chance to make things go right for him. You think you understand him? You don't. You don't know the first thing about him."

"Oh, you don't think so," I said. I hated him saying that, I really did.

"*I* understand him."

"Come on, you guys. Let's all just calm . . ."

"You can't possibly understand him. You're making him do things he doesn't want to."

"I know him. I know his life."

"Maybe he doesn't want to turn out like you. Maybe he doesn't want your life." I couldn't help the words falling from my mouth. They had a will of their own, the same as thunder does. The same as some storm that needs to be released. "Maybe he doesn't want to be depressed and crazed and making everyone unhappy because his beloved music has made him nuts."

"God damn it, Cassie, that's enough," Mom said.

"Maybe the tortured-genius thing just doesn't look too appealing."

"You've raised an imbecile, Daniella," Dino said.

Mom stood up. "I said that's enough. Both of you."

"I have that book by my bed. I've read it. All about Sabbotino Grappa, all about your beautiful parents. I feel sorry for them. Your mother must have been ashamed that she raised such a nasty person."

Dino shoved out from the table, knocking over his wineglass. His hands were flat on the table, and I could see them shaking. "Shut this child up," he said through his clenched teeth.

"People . . ." Mom said.

"Shut this child up about my mother!"

I had gone too far. I knew it even before he picked up the chair with one hand and threw it. It crashed to the ground, a horrendous clatter. I shut my eyes against the sound, against the scene. When I opened them again, I could see that Dino was leaving the room, and that my mother had covered her face with her hands and just held her head there, as if trying to hold the pieces of herself together.

179

"Mom?" I was afraid to talk. I had already done too much of that. "Mom, I'm sorry."

My mother raised her head. She sighed. "You know, Cassie, I'm sorry too."

"I hope you're okay," I said.

"And I hope you're okay."

We sat in silence.

"I guess none of this is all right," she said finally.

You know what I was most sorry for then? I was sorry for her. That things had turned out like this for her. That she had made a leap and ended up crashing onto concrete.

"Probably not."

"Life's messed up at the moment."

"Yeah," I said.

"If you're fine just now, I'm going to go talk to Dino."

I nodded.

Every circus needs a ringmaster, and ours gave my shoulders a squeeze and disappeared out of the room.

Dino found a way to solve his problem with Ian, which was that he would allow Ian to have a private life, only he would give him no time in which to have it. His requirements for continuing to help Ian were that Ian must commit to daily lessons with him and to evening practice at home. Dino and Ian's mother had had a meeting. *They'd jump off a bridge if I told them to,* Dino had said. Ian's mother had a talk with Ian. He had no choice, Ian told me. Curtis was the single scholarship-only college in the country. Affording even a small part of a partial scholarship was out of the question, paying living expenses was out of the question, and a degree from Curtis would ensure his best shot at a job and performance contracts.

What about trees? I had asked.

I can't do trees, Ian had said. *I just . . . I can't explain. I've got to make his happen.*

I don't get it. It's your life.

It's an opportunity I can't pass up.

I had the sick feeling that Dino had been right about one thing. He understood Ian in this way that I didn't. There were things I couldn't see or know. I didn't realize then that everyone had their secrets.

I didn't see much of Ian, which was obviously part of the plan. He studied in the morning at home to finish his requirements for school, came over in the afternoons for lessons, and had to leave quickly in order to get his practice time in. We only had a moment for a quick hello and good-bye, and the times I saw him he was tired and strung out. The only real piece I had of Ian was his music, traveling up the stairs during his practices, or coming through the door as I sat my back down against it and listened to what was happening inside that office. I savored what I had. I'd close my eyes and let the music lift me up and hold me. *Yes, yes, good. Very good,* Dino would say. I would imagine lemon trees and cobbled streets made warm by the sun, orange-colored buildings and baskets of figs. I would imagine us sharing a cup of coffee at a small iron table, sneaking into an old church to gulp cool air. A life together of simple, good things. I imagined bicycles in canals, Sabbotino Grappa at sunset.

After practices, Dino himself would disappear into his office and his own place of creation. If he was paranoid then, I didn't know it. I never saw him. But my mother was dealing with things I had no idea about. I heard her on the phone a lot with Alice, and Mom would hang up quickly when I came in. I would hear her crying, and when I would investigate, she'd wipe her face and lie and say she wasn't.

It was as if Dino and Ian had both descended into some other dark world, where all thoughts and all moments were music, music, music. Frenzied playing, lost men. Italian phrases—*sforzando, con calore, adagietto,* a land with its own language, even. The repetition of passages; frustration at not getting it right, try again. Try again until it is perfect, the perfect translation of all of love and sorrow, of struggle and triumph. It wasn't notes they were playing, not really. It was not songs. They were playing all the passion and drama of life, nothing less. Expressing the questions, searching for the answers. At least they were able to do this through their music. I had questions, questions that seemed to multiply like bad news multiplies. Even the vastness of the universe, looking through my telescope, did not put those questions into perspective.

Siang came over one afternoon, when they were at their height of joint possession, Dino with his composing, Ian with his practicing. I was worried about her being there, tried to get her to go home, as I was afraid of what she might see. The day before I'd experienced the first sign in a while that Dino was still in the throws of his illness. I had come home to the stereo blasting, and when I turned it down Dino stormed from his office. *What are you doing?* he had said. *I need that on. If that prick is listening somehow, he won't hear a thing.*

Siang had practically begged to come in. When we finally went inside, I wished right away I had held my ground. The kitchen was a mess—filled with clutter and disgusting cigarette butts. Their snakey stink was everywhere—in coffee cups, on the newspaper, in the sink. I cleaned up as Siang either didn't notice or pretended not to. She had slung her backpack to our kitchen floor, unzipped it and rifled through.

"I want to show you something," she had said. "Something I found out."

"I don't want to hear obscure facts of Dino's life, okay? I don't give a shit how old he was when he first rolled over." I clanked a coffee cup against the side of the garbage can to dump the ashes, saved it from getting cancer.

"It's not that," she said into her open backpack.

"I don't give a shit when he first said goo goo."

"Just wait," she said.

"He got his first chest hair at sixteen. Whoopee."

Finally, Siang pulled a folded sheet of paper from her backpack. She carefully flattened it out, smoothed out the creases with her palm. "That painting. In his office. The one over his desk."

I looked at the image. Sure enough, it was the painting of the flowers that Dino had there, the one Siang had straightened so carefully that day we had seen the blank pages.

"So?" I said.

"And this," Siang said. She fished around in her backpack some more, pulled out *Strings Magazine*. She folded back the cover to an interview that Dino had given, and began to read.

"'Question,'" Siang squeaked. "'Who or what was your greatest influence?' 'Answer: Well, naturally it was my mother. She was a rose. A wild rose. Beautiful because she was wild. Wild because the world gave her too much beauty. More than could be tamed.' 'Question: Is that a good description of you too? Beauty that cannot be tamed?' 'Answer: I wish it weren't so. Then I could be at peace. Wearing my slippers and smoking a pipe.'"[9]

"What's your point?" I asked.

"That's the name of the painting. It's called *Wild Roses*. It was done by van Gogh."

"I think it should be called *Ugly Flowers on Bland Canvas*," I said.

"I think it is especially beautiful."

"Jeez, Siang. Maybe if you cross your eyes. Maybe if you're color-blind. Or asleep."

"It's beautiful because it was one of his last paintings.

It was done when he was at Daubigny's garden, experiencing his most intensely creative period. Right before his suicide."

---

[9] From Sylvie Partowski, "Master's Chat: Dino Cavalli." *Strings Magazine* (August 2002): 56–60.

The word hung there between us. *Suicide.* This word that is usually so far away from you as to have a sense of unreality. Right then, spoken aloud, it became as real as those ashes, as Dino's eyes searching for villains, as my mother's hushed calls to the doctor.

Siang was trying to tell me something, I knew. Her urgency, these clippings, were both a warning and an attempt to get me to understand something important. I'm sorry, but it wasn't anything I cared to hear.

I gathered the clippings, put them back inside her pack, and zipped it closed. "It's just a stupid painting, Siang," I said.

CHAPTER TEN

You should have seen Ian's eyes. Dark, smeary circles underneath, like someone had set a pair of coffee cups thoughtlessly there without a coaster. I kissed him good-bye one day, and then put my hands in his coat pockets. The underside of his neck was a bright, angry red from the violin.

"Cassie, I've *got* to go." His tone was sharp. He'd never been short-tempered with me before. He was such a gentle person. I took my hands from his pockets, went inside. He called that night to apologize. *I'm just so tired. This schedule is killing me.*

He wasn't the only one looking like hell. Dino's concert was a few weeks away, and rehearsals were scheduled to begin. According to Mom, he had two of the three pieces finished, but was still writing the last one. Worse yet, he'd heard that William Tiero had taken on a new client, the acclaimed female violinist Anna Zartarski. She'd been asked to do the Great Performers Series at Lincoln Center in New York, which would then be shown as a PBS television special. Dino walked around in a perpetual state of anguish. His body was there, his eyes would even look at you, but his replies were random. He went through those horrible cigarettes like Zebe can go through a bag of Cheetos. His paranoia was increasing, though it came in waves. I saw him checking the caller ID repeatedly, and he asked daily about the numbers that appeared there. *That's Zebe's number,* I'd say for the thousandth time. *That's Sophie's.* He pelted my mother with questions about when she went out. If she'd seen anyone hanging around. If she'd heard anything from various people who knew William Tiero. Even if she were meeting with him herself. He looked in the paper twice a day, the same paper, for mention of Anna Zartarski, I guess. We were living with an astrological phenomenon—something like the comets the size of a house that every few seconds break up in the atmosphere as they approach Earth. Daily explosions, not quite disasters.

Irritability was going around like the flu. It seemed like it was just as contagious. My mother had to practice now too, as performances were coming up for the theater she was contracted with. She'd set up in the dining room, but suddenly our house was too small. She couldn't practice when Dino was working, so she waited until the evenings, after he'd holed himself in their bedroom. The low tones of the cello were soothing after the manic, high-strung violins I'd been hearing for weeks. The cello sounds like a kind grandfather, while the violin is the ultimate PMS instrument.

One afternoon, I listened to Mom play for a while as I did my homework in my room. World History had given me the sudden craving for food that boredom can bring, and I had just gotten up to head down to the kitchen when I heard the *thud thud thud* of feet on the stairs, then in the hallway, heading for the dining room. The cello stopped.

"Am I disturbing you?" Mom asked.

"Your playing is grating on my nerves," Dino barked. "I am trying to *rest*."

"You know I have to practice too." I could tell she was on the edge of being really pissed off. Her voice gets this sound of having walls around it.

"That is abundantly obvious," he said.

What came next wasn't exactly silence, because although it was quiet, a thousand things were being said. I hated that part about an unhappy household—that feeling of being perched and listening, the way an animal must feel at night in the dark, assessing danger. Dino must have decided to leave then, because I heard the front door open and close. His car started up in the driveway. My heart felt sick for my mother at the blow he'd dealt. I had Brief Fantasy Number Twelve Thousand and Four, Dino wrapped in the heavy, partly singed dining room curtains. Rolled up like those foil-wrapped candies, twist-tied at the end. After a few moments I went downstairs and into the

188

dining room where my mother stood, holding up Grandfather Cello as if she'd just helped him to the bathroom. She sat back down again in front of her stand, looked at me, and then groaned out a few notes with her bow.

"Damn it," she said.

"That was real nice of him."

"I shouldn't say this, but you know, sometimes he's really an asshole."

"News flash," I said.

"I keep trying to tell myself he's a sick man."

"Yeah, but maybe if he wasn't sick, he'd just be a healthy asshole."

"I'm tired, you know that? I'm going to become a nun."

"Then you'd be married to Christ and he probably wouldn't pick up his socks, either," I said.

"Really," she sighed. "A few more weeks. Four," she said. "He promised he'd go back on the medicine right after the performance."

"If he doesn't crack up before then."

"Please, Cassie. You know? Let's not do this just now. I've got more than I can take as it is."

As I said, irritability was everywhere.

I heard violins in my sleep. I'd actually be dreaming and they'd be playing in the background, or they'd be the focus of the dream, my math class playing them, say, or me performing in front of an audience but forgetting my music. Mostly I dreamed of violins destroyed. People bashing them, violins falling from the sky, or floating on the water. Thrown into the water and sinking. We were a month away from that horrible concert. Just two weeks from Ian's audition.

I began to shut out the sound of those violins whenever they were practicing. Even Ian. What was my only connection to him became a hated sound. The violin was the object of his possession, in the way a bottle of wine possesses an alcoholic before it destroys him. I put on earphones, or got into the car and drove when I would hear the instrument. I would stand out with my telescope under a sky too clouded to see a thing. I would slam the door before I left so that my mother would know how angry I was at where our lives had gone. I felt sorry for her and her obvious unhappiness, but then my pity would just flee the scene and I'd get pissed. I blamed her for bringing us there, for being taken in by genius and fame and some twisted form of love, blinded, so that her own well-being and my well-being had been drowned out by the sound of that music. So, slam—that's how I felt about it all. Let the windows rattle with my fury.

The next time Ian came for his lesson he was wearing his dark coat and his scarf. When he came inside I saw that the scarf had slipped down so that one side was falling down the back of his coat, prevented from hitting the ground only by one small end piece that was doing its desperate best to hang on. It was just luck that kept it from dropping away from him on the way over, lost in a juniper bush somewhere, carted off by some neighborhood dog, dropped on the muddy street and run over by the tires of a telephone company truck. Okay, if I'm sounding a bit dramatic here, it's because I was feeling a bit dramatic. It was symbolic to me, that scarf I gave him slipping and falling, the carelessness he showed in letting it happen. The way it could be lost without him noticing.

He was already in practice mode, so I doubted he even realized that when I pushed past him that day and went outside it was with the same kind of fury and helplessness I slammed doors with. No one was *paying attention*. No one was *seeing*. Our lives were careening downhill, gaining the momentum that only self-destruction has, and no one was even trying to hold on.

My scarf anger turned to surprise when I saw Chuck and Bunny in the Datsun parked at the curb. For some reason I pictured Ian on his bike, the scarf dropping off behind him as he rode on, oblivious to the near miss of it getting caught in the spokes. I hadn't pictured it slipping off in Chuck's backseat, lying there for a nice ride around town amid a couple of old coffee cups, a pair of muddy tennis shoes, a two-disc compilation of Donna Summer hits and some library book titled *Planning the English Garden*.

I poked my head in the open window of the car. "Don't you guys ever work?" I asked.

"Hey, Lassie," Chuck said.

"There's a strike at the Dairigold plant," Bunny said. He was unwrapping the foil from a cheeseburger. "That's where we work. Anyway, I got some money tucked aside."

"We both got our massage therapist licenses, but

there're not many openings here," Chuck said. "Jesus, Bun, eat over your napkin. You see why I don't let him eat and drive? It's a hazard."

"These aren't my clean jeans," Bunny said with his mouth full. He plucked the spilled bit of pickle and lettuce from his lap and popped that in too.

"Massage therapists? You're kidding." That could scare the crap out of you, lying there on some table with only terry cloth for protection and seeing one of them walk in. You'd scream with fear that you were about to be taken hostage and made to wear leather pants and a shirt with some biker chick on it that said BUILT TO RIDE.

"The healing power of touch can work miracles," said Bunny through the cheeseburger. At least I think that's what he said. It could have been "The strength in my hands could break you in half." Or maybe "I should never be allowed to touch anyone because the back of my Harley-Davidson T-shirt says IF YOU CAN READ THIS, THE BITCH FELL OFF.

"Wow," I said, mostly to be on the safe side.

"It is a great release of negative energy," Chuck said. "Flows through your fingers and disperses into the universe, floating away with your cares." He was sounding like a bubble bath commercial.

"Speaking of negative energy," Bunny said. He slurped his drink. He held it between his knees. Hey, Mom had that kind of cup holder in her car, too.

"Have you noticed that Mozart's been a little uptight?" Chuck said.

"Just a little?" I didn't correct him on the fact that Mozart never played the violin—we both knew who he was referring to.

"Frankly I'm getting a little concerned about him," Bunny said.

"His chakras are all blown to shit," Chuck said.

My heart rose a little. I didn't know my chakra from a hole in the ground, as the saying sort of goes. It sounded like something you had in a Greek restaurant with a side of yogurt sauce, but who cared? Someone else was on my side in this, this feeling that things were getting out of control. I felt a surge of energy; the relief of someone helping you pick up the other end of something heavy.

"He looks horrible," I said. "He looks so tired."

"He left the dog out all night."

"He needs a day off, only his mother doesn't see it," Bunny said. "I love her to death, but she can't see the forest for the sea where that violin's concerned."

"Trees," Chuck said. "You moron. Forest for the trees."

"Trees? That don't make any sense. Of course you see trees in a forest."

"That's not what it means," Chuck said.

"I don't care, all right? You know what I'm saying."

"I agree," I said. "He needs a rest."

"Sea," Chuck chuckled. "Heh, heh, heh. Forest for the sea."

"Shut the hell up, Chuck. I heard you sing the 'Twelve Days of Christmas.'"

"So what?"

"Three French men, two turtle doves."

"No one knows all those words. It's a fucking long song."

"Three French men? Wee wee, monsieur. Jacques, Pierre, and Luc," Bunny said.

"It's the stupidest and most boring song in history. I was only trying to jazz it up."

"I don't know if there's anything we can do," I said. "About Ian." I was trying to get them back on track. Something about this reminded me of the time I dropped our old thermometer and mercury bounced crazily all over the bathroom floor.

"Why don't you sit down here in the back for a minute and we'll make a plan," Chuck said. "Crouching over in the window like that's gonna strain your lattisimus dorsi."

"Hey, he's my favorite Star Wars character," I said. "I even had the action figure." I got in the back, shoved over Donna Summer. "Groovy music. Boogie down." I waved the CD around between them.

"Record club. I forgot to send in my coupon."

"Same with this?" I held up the book.

"Literary Guild," Bunny said.

"If you don't mind, I'm leaving the window open," Chuck said. "Nothing worse than the smell of french fry grease when you're not hungry."

"How about we take Ian on a trip?" Bunny said.

"A trip? What kind of trip?" I asked.

"It doesn't even matter. We just stick him in the car and go. Make him relax. The kid's gonna break."

"He's flying out for his audition in two weeks," I said. "We can't really take him on a trip."

"Okay, for the day then," Bunny said. He was folding up the foil wrap from his hamburger into a decisive triangle.

"A day of rest and rejuvenation," Chuck said. "One day off of practice is not gonna kill him. He keeps up like this . . ."

"We'll put him in the car. Pick you up," Bunny said. Something about the three of us plotting there in the parked car made me think of a bad movie with gangsters. "Tomorrow. Do you have school?"

"I'm suddenly feeling a sore throat coming on," I said. "Eck, eck," I coughed.

"We don't want you getting into trouble," Chuck said.

"I haven't missed a day yet this year," I said. I was getting excited. Common sense hadn't quite caught up yet. It was just one of those times where you're so happy to have an idea that you don't quite stop to figure out if it's a good one.

"Mental health day," Chuck said. "I saw it on my calendar."

"Where will we take him?" I asked.

"Just get in the car and go," Bunny said.

"We'll figure something out," Chuck said.

We decided on ten o'clock. I hopped out of the car, feeling like I'd done a good thing. I actually thought I was helping. That night I stayed in my room, afraid that my face would give away my secret. I didn't sleep well, but only because I was excited and hopeful. Let's just make it clear that my lack of sleep had nothing to do with pre-monition of disaster.

Every person above the age of seven knows how to do it—you sag your face down so that your eyes look lifeless, and then slump in a chair like a sweatshirt tossed there by someone with bad aim. You've got to hang over the chair a bit, your head on your arm, too heavy to hold up.

"I feel like crap," I said to Mom. I lowered my eyes, held my hand to my throat. "Hurts."

"I thought we were doing too well this year with no one getting sick," she said. She was hurrying around to catch her carpool, shoving random things in a brown bag for lunch. Someone needed to go to the store. You opened the fridge door, and you could see your own reflection. "Do you need to stay home?"

"I've got a test," I said. "I can't." Utter brilliance. Applause, bow.

"If you're sick, you're sick," she said. "You know how I feel about that."

"I know," I said. Yep, I knew.

She put her hand on my forehead, cold from the fridge. "You *are* warm," she said. And in case this gives the impression that Mom wasn't too smart, I'd better correct that right here. She was hugely smart, read all the time and knew something about everything. But she was some-one who tended to get absentminded when she had a lot on her mind. The week before she'd walked into my math class while it was in session because she was a week early

196

for conferences, and a couple of days before that, she left the water running in the bathroom while hand washing a sweater. I found water spilling over the counter and soaking the rug.

"I'll call the school," she said. "Back to bed." Which would have been the three most fantastic words in the human language if I didn't have better things to do. You may be wondering if I felt the least bit bad about deceiving my mother right then. Or at least maybe I'm wondering it, looking back. And the answer is no, I didn't feel one bit bad. Or at least the parts of me that might have felt bad were silenced by the importance of what I was doing. Sometimes rightness was bigger than lies. And if Mom did get mad over what I did for love, well, hey—what I was doing seemed pretty mild compared to throwing away a home and a man and a family and a shared toaster and vacation photos and a sock drawer with intermingled socks, for the possibility (impossibility) of forever, tortured romance with the Prozac poster boy, *People* magazine's Most Fucked-Up Man Alive.

I went back to bed for a while, and lay there with my eyes wide open and my heart racing, like a kid on Christmas Eve. Mom came up and kissed me on the cheek and reminded me to stay quiet for Dino, as he'd be home working. No problem, I said. I'd be so quiet, it'd be like I wasn't even there.

I watched out my window for the Datsun, and grabbed my coat and went outside when I saw it come up the street. I opened the back door and climbed in beside Ian.

There was a handkerchief lying beside him, as if they had tried to blindfold him or something. It really was like a bad gangster movie. There was even a violin case on the seat.

"So you're in on this, too, huh?" he said.

"Mission accomplished!" Bunny said.

"Partners in crime," I said. "We were worried about you," I said to Ian.

"As long as I'm back before practice," Ian said. "You guys know I've got to get ready." I checked Ian's face for signs that he was pissed off, and saw only the tight, tired face I'd gotten used to.

"Oh, we know you've got to get ready. Yes, sir," Bunny said.

"I mean it, Bun. Two-thirty max."

"Full tank of gas and a road atlas. We'll make it to Malibu by sundown."

"Not funny," Ian said.

"Where we headed?" I said.

"It's a surprise," Chuck said. "You got enough room, or should I move up my seat?"

"Perfect," I said.

And it was. Just being there in the backseat with Ian in his long coat that smelled of coffee and cinnamon, knees touching. Riding down my street with that delicious feeling of everyone else being in their normal routine, poor suckers, while you were having a new day. It was cold but bright out, a nice show of sun that added a couple of notches to the cheer level. I picked up Ian's hand. It was dry and chapped from the cold, as if the last weeks were slowly sucking the moisture from him.

We drove through town, past the Chinese restaurant with its plastic-covered menus, and the real estate office with its pictures of Seabeck homes in the windows. We didn't have many tourists this time of year, so the Gift Gallery, selling wind chimes with ferryboats and tacky sweatshirts with plastic whale decals, was quiet, as was the hemp clothing store (run by the perpetually stoned Mrs. Ramadon), and the bookstore/coffeehouse, which had the best coffee cake of anywhere in the universe. We headed down to the ferry docks, past Ian's house, and Bunny bought a ticket from Evan Malloney's dad in the ticket booth. I wondered if Evan Malloney's dad knew what we all knew about Evan Malloney—that he was already a drunk. The kind that made people so uneasy they steered clear of them. Like anyone whose future you could see (the terminally ill, ninety-year-olds, girls who slept around) it was too much reality to want to look at.

"If we're getting on the ferry, we've got to watch the sailing times," Ian said.

"Would you relax, for Christ's sake?" Bunny said. "That is the whole point of this journey. I'm going to make you do some relaxation exercises."

"Oh, God. Anything but that," Ian said. "I'm relaxed, okay?" He shook his hands and turned his neck in a circle, the way Mom did whenever she was getting a headache. "Mellowness has come." This was the Ian I loved.

We parked in the loading lane behind a camper. Its

license plate read CAPTAIN ED. He had a bumper sticker that said HOME OF THE BIG REDWOODS.

"Just do it. Picture yourself somewhere you want to be," Bunny said. "A beach. A mountain cabin."

"Very original ideas, Bun," Ian said.

"What you want me to say, a Taco Time? A Jiffy Lube?"

"I'm in a boat on a lake," Chuck said.

His head was resting back against the seat. I could see in the window reflection that his eyes were closed.

"Cassie, you too. Close your eyes."

I closed my eyes. Snored loudly. Ian cracked up.

"Find your place of inner peace," Bunny said.

"It's sunny on the boat," Chuck said. "There aren't even any waves. I just had a big roast beef sandwich. I'm thinking I should have remembered sun lotion. Damn, I wish I had a beer."

"Would you shut the hell up, Chuck, I'm trying to relax these people."

"Okay, go ahead. Move along, Bun. I've got my quiet place." Ian poked my leg. He mouthed *bowling alley*.

"School cafeteria," I whispered.

"Airport runway," he whispered back.

"I hear a splash," Chuck said. "I look up. Some asshole in another boat just tossed in an empty can of Mr. Pibb. Man, that pisses me off. I hate litterers."

"Now, start at your toes. You feel them getting heavy. They are totally relaxed. Your foot is relaxed."

I held up one shoe, swirled it around. Ian put a finger through the lace and dangled my foot from it.

"Now your calf is relaxed. Now your shin. Your lower legs have never felt so relaxed." Something about this wasn't right. Maybe I didn't know about these things, but it seemed pretty damn impossible to relax a bone.

"Not the shin," Chuck said, reading my mind. "You don't relax the shin."

"Okay, the leg. The leg. Your leg is relaxed, all right? Go back to the lake, Chuck, Jesus, and let me do my work." He reached for the pack of gum on the dashboard, pulled the little red plastic thread and picked out a stick. He popped it into his mouth, and crinkled up the foil into a little ball and tossed it at Chuck.

"It's like telling you to relax your collarbone," Chuck said. His eyes were still closed. He didn't even notice the foil ball tap his massive arm.

"Meanwhile, back at the legs," I said. I was peeking. Ian was peeking too. It reminded me of the times when my parents were still married and Dad made us go to church. Everyone else would just be praying away while Mom and I were peeking at everyone.

"Legs like Jell-O," Bunny said.

"Lime. Yum, my favorite," Chuck said.

Bunny ignored him. "And then your thighs. Warm and heavy and relaxed. They've never been so relaxed. The warmth spreads to your buttocks. . . ."

This was getting a little embarrassing. In one of my heights of emotional maturity, I started to laugh. It made me think of Aaron Mills, during this science lesson. Mr. Robelard had told the class that the cut of a rock was called a cleavage. After a few snickers, he paused and then sternly told everyone that they had better just get all of their laughs out right then. The class was dead silent, except for Aaron, who just sat in his seat busting up, holding his stomach, he was laughing so hard.

Right then after the warm buttocks, car engines began to spring to life around us, thank God. The ferry was loading, and so I'd never get to find out how Bunny was going to handle what we were going to relax next.

Chuck shook himself as if he had really fallen asleep and was awakening back into the world. "Whew," he said. "Wow. Rejuvenation." He seemed to really mean it. Bunny started the car, followed Captain Ed onto the ferry, squeezing tight behind him. I was hoping we'd be able to see what Captain Ed looked like, but no one got out and the windows were tinted, and Bunny was already zipping up his coat and readying to leave our car.

I could see the couple in the BMW next to us staring at Chuck and Bunny as if they'd better lie low and pretend to be really nice people until Chuck and Bunny got on the ferry, in spite of the fact that Chuck's big butt bumped their side mirror as he tried to squeeze around the Datsun to the ferry door. Already, the noise of the boat filled your ears to the point of bursting, a thunderous roar that appeared to make the brain cells expand to the outer edges of their living quarters. Chuck shouted something that no one could hear, and then pretended to do sign language, moving his fingers in a way that was hugely unpolitically correct and a nice lawsuit for the attorney for the

Deaf People Of America who was probably sitting in the BMW whose mirror Chuck had just knocked askew with his ass.

We walked sideways until we got to the ferry door, which Bunny opened with no problem at all in spite of the fact that those doors usually weighed a thousand pounds. We were suctioned into the quiet of the ferry stairwell.

"You going to be warm enough?" Ian said.

"No problem." I was wearing my wool peacoat from the army-navy surplus store, and you could be in an arctic blizzard in that thing and feel toasty.

The ferry crossing from Seabeck to Seattle is short, thirty minutes tops. Just long enough to have all of the ferry fun without the ferry boredom. Chuck and Bunny sat in the restaurant and ate cheese dogs while Ian and I made a tour of the decks and stood outside in the blasting wind. We stepped out to the farthermost edge of the deck, just watching the water rush at us from below. The land looked as if it was being brought to us, per our instructions. We went inside again to get warm, and bumped into Chuck and Bunny heading our way.

"You got to be outside when the ferry docks," Chuck said. "No matter how cold it is."

"It's like, you've got to take your shoes off at the beach, no matter what. Same kind of law," Bunny said.

"Your guys' hair looks hilarious," Chuck said.

I socked his arm. We walked out with them, though, because they were right about the "laws." I'd add a few to theirs—you had to roll the window down a little bit in the car wash, just to freak out your passenger, and you had to yell wherever your voice would echo. Ian took my hand and put both of ours in his coat pocket. We ducked our heads against the rush of wind that attacked us as we opened the door, walked like Polar explorers to the edge of the deck once more.

Ian put his arms around me from behind, and set his chin by my neck. I let myself forget my drippy nose and the wind that was blasting my face. I just let this good feeling, love, the amazing beauty around us, overtake me. A red carpet of feeling began at my toes and unrolled and filled my heart. I'd been so scared to hand myself over to someone like this, but I'd gone ahead and done it. Love, this letting go, had snuck past the guards and the attack dogs, and now here I was. I was certain that the experience would be akin to putting on nylons (which, if you have any sense, you don't ever do), in the way that when you first stick your foot in, they are going along fine, lying pretty straight, but by the time they're pulled up, they're twisting around hopelessly in some form of leg strangulation. But love hadn't turned out like that. Standing there in the icy wind with Ian wasn't one bit that way. Here was the feeling: delicious and exhilarating. Full to the tiniest pieces.

Bunny was a hypocrite to talk about our hair. You should have seen his. I pointed and laughed, another law. You must always point and laugh when someone you really like's hair looks particularly funny, or when they've spilled food in an embarrassing location on their clothes. "Hey, Bozo the Clown," I said.

"Hey, chick Einstein," he said back at me. Okay, so, my hair was like something you pulled out of a clogged drain.

"Is this amazing or what?" Chuck spread his arm out over the waters of the sound like a game show host displaying the washer-dryer combo.

"Group hug," Bunny said, although I suspect he was just freezing and wanted warmth. He came over to us, wrapped his bear-size paws around Ian and me. Chuck came around the other side and did the same. It *was* nice and warm in there. My nose was smushed up against Ian's chest, and his breath was warm in my hair. I still had a view of the city fast approaching. It was a display of building blocks set up by a genius child, or maybe by his parent after he'd gone to bed. They seemed like they had just been plunked down, rectangles and triangles and squares. It was bright and shiny, the sun hitting glass. We were being delivered to the door, like Dorothy and gang at the gates of the Emerald City.

"Tell me how life gets any better than this," Bunny said. "What could you do to improve this moment?"

And he was right. In spite of the fact that I was squeezed and frozen and had to use the bathroom, he was 100 percent right. I couldn't believe it. I loved my mother and I loved my father, but there in that circle I felt something I hadn't for a long time. It was that something I'd been missing, that I'd been longing for without even realizing it. It was a sense of family. That's what it was. My throat closed up, got so tight I felt like I might cry. You just get to missing that so much, that feeling of everything in its right place. You just feel that loss so deeply that you don't ever give it a name. A hot tear rolled down my cheek. I couldn't believe I was crying, but I just let the tears come. There was so much unexpected emotion that it needed somewhere to go. So much love and pain and absence and cut, living roots. And here, unexpectedly, something to fill that space. You just never knew where you might find your kindred ones. Usually you just walk and walk among people who are not of your tribe, and then suddenly, there you are, in a place that feels familiar and known.

I took my arms out from the middle and reached around this wide group. I hugged back, patted a tattoo.

CHAPTER ELEVEN

Ian stuck a ferry schedule from one of the racks into his pocket on the way back to the car. Everyone squeezed in their vehicles and the guys in the orange vests unhooked the chains so that the cars could *ba-bamp, ba-bamp* off of the ferry. Captain Ed headed off in the direction opposite us. Ian's mind was obviously still on his lessons, and as we drove through the city and headed onto the freeways toward the mountain passes, I could see him looking at the time, watching for the point we'd have to turn back around before he'd be late.

"It's still early," I said.

"If I miss, Dino'll kill me, is all."

"Aren't you ready enough? You've been practicing nonstop for weeks. How much better can your pieces get?"

"Ix-nay on the violin-talk-say," Bunny said. And I thought I was the only one who could never get the hang of pig Latin.

"Dino says I'm uneven. I go from brilliant to shit, in his words. My partita is weak." Bach's *Partita No. 3 in E Major.* One of his hardest audition pieces, far as I could understand. He explained to me that his performance was supposed to demonstrate that he could handle different styles from different time periods, multi-movement pieces, and technically difficult ones. The Bach was in the last category.

"Dino will kill you in the process," I said.

"He's halfway there, if you ask me," Chuck said. "Anyone else hungry? I got Corn Nuts."

"This is a day off from violins," I said. "What have you got, barbeque or ranch?"

"Both," Chuck said.

"Yum," I said. I popped my hand over the seat when the foil bag appeared, and Chuck shook some into my palm.

"There can't be days off until after the audition." Ian watched the speeding scenery. We had driven over one of Lake Washington's floating bridges, long concrete air mattresses that connected Seattle to its suburbs. Then we had passed the wide expanse of Lake Sammamish, which sat to our left, the second lake in five minutes. Mount Rainier was on our right. It looked as if it had been plunked down in the middle of civilization, and not the other way around. That's how we talk about it too. On sunny days when it's visible we say, "The mountain is out," as if a crew of burly guys haul it out only on occasion.

The speed limit had started to increase, and so did the amount of trucks, most of which were piled high with loads of huge, bound tree trunks. We passed the point where humans had sprawled, which meant you started to see only towns with one gas station and a cemetery, bringing to mind the obvious question of where the latter got its customers. Maybe you'd see one or two houses every zillion miles, and you wonder what they do when they run out of milk, and what they do for fun. Watch the rust grow on the broken tractor? Stir up some excitement with another UFO report?

"So when *do* you get a day off?" Bunny asked. "When you're the best in your class? When you win more awards? When you—"

"Quit it," Ian interrupted. "Why are you making me wrong, here?"

"I'm not making you wrong," Bunny said. "I'm making your mother wrong."

"I don't think that's fair," Ian said. "And you know it's not." There was a bite to his voice. Dino's own words flashed in my mind. *Shut this child up about my mother!* Was this the secret to genius violin playing? Unresolved mother issues?

"I don't know it," Bunny said. "Everyone's got their own journey. This is about her pride."

"What? What's going on?" I asked. "Is your mother a frustrated musician?"

"She doesn't even know?" Bunny said.

"Shut up, Bun."

"You don't share these details with your girlfriend?" Bunny said.

"I said, shut up."

"What's going on?"

"I like the ranch better than the barbeque," Chuck said, crunching.

"What, are you ashamed?" Bunny said.

"What?" I said. I took Ian's hand.

"It's just, my family's situation."

"Your mother's situation," Bunny said. "She's broke. Way beyond broke. Seventy thousand dollars in debt."

"God damn it, Bunny. Shit."

"She should at least know what this is all about. Don't you know anything about communication?"

"The biggest stumbling block to a healthy relationship. Next to sex," Chuck said.

"Why didn't you tell me?" I said.

"They lived in their car for a few weeks in California before I heard about it," Bunny said.

"Enough, okay?" Ian said. "Enough." His face was red. He had let go of my hand and was combing his fingers through his hair.

"And child raising," Chuck said. "Communication, number one. Sex, number two. Child raising, number three."

"They were kicked out of their apartment. They used the bathrooms in fast food places."

210

Ian covered his eyes with one hand. "Shit, Bunny," he said. I thought he might cry. I took his hand. The car got quiet. The kind of quiet that hurt.

"I'm so sorry," I whispered. "You could have told me." The words caught in my throat in the way a lie does. I thought about Dino's craziness. All the things I never could say out loud. I thought about saying it right then, but something stopped me. Being poor was one thing. Creeping around in bushes because you think you're being followed and almost setting the house on fire is another.

"It's just . . . I don't know. Not exactly the way to start things out with you. 'Hi, I'm Ian. My stepfather had a long illness and didn't have insurance, and when he died he left us destitute for my mother's lifetime unless I can do something about it. Oh, and by the way, the only reason we've got a roof is my stepbrother's charity. So would you like to go for a walk, because I haven't gone to the movies in three years and couldn't buy the popcorn.'"

"Oh, Ian. Oh, I'm so sorry." I pictured again Ian's mother with her chipped toenail polish. A man in a hospital bed with tubes in his nose and arms. Sleeping in a car. *Living* in a *car*. The Ian that I loved. The hurt of that squeezed my heart. My stomach felt sick. "It's you I care about."

"Okay. Here it is. If I don't get into Curtis, we don't have a chance of getting out of this mess. Number one, it's a full scholarship. Number two, going there would give me what I need to get some good paying performances.

Good paying performances. Recording deals, eventually. The works. We lived on my performance money when my stepdad was sick, but now that I'm older I've got to be much better. I can't be just a cute kid playing the violin."

"Oh, God, Ian." For the first time I clearly saw the choice that sat in front of him. I didn't know what the answer was. I could only sit there in that car, my body filled with the pain of his decision.

"Giving up what you really want—it's not your only option, is all I'm saying," Bunny said. "It's not your job to solve the problem. You don't need to, you know, give up your whole life to do that," Bunny said.

"So what are the other choices? She has her wages garnished for the rest of her life? You feed us, and we live in your house forever?"

"She can stay there till she's eighty, for all I care," Bunny said.

"The average life expectancy is eighty-four," Chuck said.

"Ninety. A hundred. Her job is going well. We deal with the hospital somehow. I don't know. The net will appear. The net always appears if you leap," Bunny said.

"The charity hurts," Ian said. He was looking out the window, his whole body turned away from me.

"Charity, bullshit. She took such good care of my dad. This is family. That's what families do."

"You got it. Exactly. That's why I've got to get into Curtis," Ian said.

"God damn it," Bunny said. "He's obstinate. Hand me

some Corn Nuts, Chuck, the kid is stressing me out."

"I'd try some deep relaxation for you, but you're driving," Chuck said.

I took Ian's hand. Brought it to my mouth and held it there. He couldn't even look at me. That was the worst thing about shame, I guess—its self-destructive power. The way it made you burn the bridges of anyone coming your way to help.

"I'm sorry," he whispered.

"I love you," I whispered back.

"Money, number four," Chuck said. "Communication, sex, child raising, and money."

"Ix-nay on the money-talk-fay," Bunny said.

The car climbed and rose around mountain bends. At first the snow was only scattered in the shady places, but gradually the whiteness grew until the road was buffeted by full-fledged snowbanks, glittery and bright in the sun. The tires crunched over sanded roads, though I could feel the wheels slip a bit on the ice, and Bunny slowed his speed. I was glad to see the summit and the lodge of Snoqualmie Pass, as the driving was getting a little nerve-racking. Bunny must have been glad too—he let out a big sigh of relief as he skidded sideways into a parking spot. The lot was nearly empty, except for a couple of cars with skis still attached to the tops, and an abandoned snow-plow. It was weird. Usually at this time of year the pass would be crawling with people.

"Closed, I guess," Chuck said. "Shit, I've been thinking about hot chocolate and lunch the whole way."

"How can they close it? It's a beautiful day, and we need cheeseburgers," Bunny said. "Let's get out anyway."

"We can just look around," I said. "Eat lunch in the car on the way home." After our talk, I felt anxious to get Ian back to lessons on time. Either that, or have us both run away forever and never return home again.

"No reason we can't play a little," Bunny said. He leaned down, popped the trunk.

We got out of the car, stepped carefully onto the icy ground. The cold air felt great, stinging and fresh. I breathed deeply, as Chuck and Bunny pulled a pair of black inner tubes from the trunk.

"Guys, we got maybe twenty minutes, max," Ian said.

"Enough for a couple trips down the sledding hill," Chuck said. "Yee haw!" He gave the tube a shake over his head, his *yee haw* blowing in a huge puff of white from his mouth.

Bunny slammed the trunk. We walked flat-footed across the parking lot so as not to fall, then cut across the road past the lodge.

Walking was tough. If you trudged in the deeper snow you barely noticed the ice, but my pant legs were already getting soaked. We huffed behind Chuck and Bunny, who could sure haul themselves around for big guys. I was exhausted already, and realized why I'd never been a skier. Just the trip from the parking lot would make me ready to rest for the day by the fireplace in the lodge.

"I'm not sure this is such a great idea," Ian said. "There's no one around."

It *was* a little eerie, the lodge sitting solid and empty, and the lifts deserted and still. It was impossible, though, to really muster up any feeling of warning when the sun was so bright and cheery, and when the snow was glistening like fairy dust in some hokey Disney movie. We pulled ourselves up and up, walking in the deep snow, until I felt like I'd accomplished an amazing Tight Thighs in Ten Minutes. My legs hurt, my butt muscles hurt, my lungs were hot, and I didn't look up until we stopped at what must have been the top of a ski hill. I pictured myself on skis, looking down from this very spot, and realized I'd rather do a two-week punishing stint of math statistics then to throw myself down on a pair of matchsticks from where we stood. The hill was a sheet of ice going straight down, decorated with evergreens that were plunked in death-defying places. I changed my mind about the sledding right then and there.

"No way," I said.

"I agree," Ian said. "Too dangerous."

Bunny sighed through his nose, two straight shots of white locomotive steam. "I guess you guys are right. We'll go back to the baby sledding hill."

"Damn," Chuck said.

And right then, right at that moment before the word was even completely out of his mouth, his foot was yanked underneath him sure as if someone had pulled it. "Whaaa . . ." he cried, and Chuck was suddenly on the ground, a human toboggan, careening down the hill while still clutching his tube in one hand, the black ring skidding and turning as if having the happiest free ride of its little rubber life.

I grabbed Ian's coat sleeve. "Oh, shit!"

"Hang on, Chuck!" Bunny called.

The crazy thing was, there was nothing we could do. We just stood there, watched his limbs fly around until he landed at the bottom.

He was silent for a moment. And still. And then came his voice.

"Fuck," he said.

Bunny stepped forward to call out to him. "Don't worry, Chu—" His voice was lost as he crashed to the ground. Fell on his butt with a thud and whipped and whizzed down that hill like we'd just been shown an instant replay. Bunny held his tube, too, but lost it about halfway when it skidded from his grasp, bounced off one of the trees, then bumped the rest of the way to the bottom until a part of it beaned Chuck on the skull and bounced off.

"Fuck," Chuck said again.

Bunny slid to a stop beside him. His arms and legs were all askew, a toy man tossed by a toddler.

"Bun! Bun! Are you all right?" Ian called.

He lay flat for a moment, unmoving.

"Ow," he said.

"Can you guys move?" Ian said.

Bunny shifted around. "Yeah, everything's working."

"Me too," Chuck said.

"Thank God," I said.

"Do you need us to get you some help?" Ian asked.

He was standing right beside me, right there, and then, *bam!* He was gone. Upright, talking, and then down on his back, his coat flying out behind him, riding down on the seat of his pants, sitting up as if he'd planned it that way. You really would have thought he meant to do it, if it weren't for the yelling he was doing along the way, if it weren't for the crash he had at the bottom, his crying out in pain.

"Oh, God," he cried. He was crying there, in the snow. "My arm. Jesus, my arm."

CHAPTER TWELVE

Of course, I was still at the top of that hill. I was helpless, afraid to move. All we needed was for me to go down with the rest of them and then we'd really be in deep shit. I decided I'd better go for some help, although the chances of finding anyone seemed nil after the looks of that empty lodge. I was holding the real disaster at bay in my mind—Ian's arm, maybe broken, certainly injured, the audition, the way we might have just changed the course of his and his mother's lives—and was trying to concentrate on the more immediate one, namely, how to get three guys, two the size of refrigerators, back into the car and safely home. I stepped back into the deep snow to anchor myself, called down to them.

"I'm going for help!" I yelled, and was glad to see that Chuck was attempting to get on his feet. I struggled back the way we came, a few steps at a time, wondering what the hell I was going to do when I got there. I was beginning to hate the sound of that crunching snow, hated the twinkling, beautiful white, when I heard a roaring sound, a loud zipping roar, like a chain saw almost. It turned out to be a snowmobile in the distance, and when the driver saw me, it quickly headed in my direction. I waved my arms around, which was unnecessary, as he had every intention of heading my way.

The guy was with the ski patrol and was pissed we were out there, wondering how we missed the signs that the place was closed. Apparently, in addition to the extremely icy conditions, there was also an avalanche warning in effect. So, hey, look at the bright side.

I put my arms around the shaking Ian when we were back in the car. I saw his wrist before the patrol guy wrapped it, the bone sticking against his skin as if trying to make a getaway, the color turning quickly to a dark purple. The patrol guy told us to get to a doctor right away and have an X ray, but there was no doubt if you saw what I did that it was broken. The bone wasn't the only thing that had been shattered. I felt the devastation in his trembling; I listened to it in the silence on the car ride home.

If our lives had been losing stitches up until that point, they began a serious unraveling when we got home. I thought of the time when I was a kid and I had pulled one enticing loop from the afghan Nannie was crocheting. I knew I had done something awful and irrevocable, but the more I tried to hold it together, the more it kept coming undone, until the yarn sat in a wrinkled heap. Fragile things become undone at a frightening speed.

I waited in the emergency room with Chuck. Bunny, amazingly in one piece himself, went in with Ian to see the doctor. It was evening before we got out of there. They dropped me off at home, so I wasn't there for the moment that Ian walked into his mother's house with a cast on his arm.

I had my own train wreck to deal with at my house.

"Where in God's name have you been?" my mother said as I walked in. "I've been worried sick."

I walked past her, went up to my room, and shut the door. So what? What was a little more trouble? I couldn't stand to face anyone. After what I'd done to Ian's life, I wanted to drop into a hole and disappear. My own shame made powerful punishment seem certain—it was already withering my insides until I felt I might throw up. I heard Dino in the kitchen. *It's that boy, I know it.* I could hear the smirk in his voice.

I shut the door behind me, lay on my bed in my quilt. I wrapped it so tight around me. I reached out for the bear in the snow globe. I wanted to throw it against the wall, destroy it, but instead I put it under the quilt with me, tucked it right inside that cocooned place.

"Cassie?"

Mom knocked, then came in. She sat down at the edge of my bed. "Cass? What happened? Come on, talk to me."

"I can't."

"Talk to me."

"It's awful. It's terrible." I started to cry. Since I met Ian, I was as bad as the faucet Mom left on when she was washing her sweater. Someone had turned on the emotion and now it wouldn't go off.

"What?" She sounded like she was afraid and trying not to be. "Nothing is that bad."

"Oh yes, it is." I sobbed, just let out these heaves of helplessness. Mom held me.

"I'm here, okay? Whatever it is. Are you pregnant?"

"Holy shit, Mom. No," I said through my crying. I swear, for parents it's always about sex and drugs. "I haven't been arrested for trafficking marijuana, either."

"Okay, Cass, I'm sorry. You know, what am I supposed to think?"

I curled up tight inside that blanket. The glass of the snow globe was cold, and I blew on it to warm it up.

"Should I call Ian's mom?"

"Oh, God, no," I said. "Please don't do that."

Mom sighed. I peeked at her, and saw her just sitting with her chin pointed to the ceiling. She looked so tired. Thin, too. She looked like she was losing too much weight.

"Ian broke his wrist. It was my fault."

"Oh, my God," she said.

"It was my fault."

"Oh, my God," she said again.

"I know."

"What happened?"

I told her the story. She put her arms around me. I could feel her hot breath through the quilt. "Oh, Cassie."

"I'm so sorry."

"You didn't cause it."

"That's not what Dino will think."

"That may be true, but it's not what I think."

I came out of the quilt, just a little. She brushed my hair away from my face. She bent down to kiss my forehead. "I'll always be here for you," she said. But she didn't need to say it. Right then, it was something I knew.

It started like a storm, low rumbling and then louder and louder still until the windows actually rattled and there was a crash of something being broken.

I told you she would ruin this! Did I not tell you she had to stay away from him?

And then my mother's voice, too low to be heard, the rhythms of calm explanation.

My God. It is over for him! I could have helped him. Things could have been different for him than they were for me. How can I help him now? How?

I heard my mother then, clearly. *His situation is different than yours,* my mother said. *He's a boy with options. It's not the same. You are not the same person.*

I could have made things turn out differently. Look what you people have done. You've wrecked him. You want to ruin me.

His voice was gaining emotion; my mother's turned pleading.

This is not about you. This is not about what happened in your life.

I am stuck here in this nothing city because of you.

Calm down, my mother said. She was trying not to get angry. She was saying those words to herself as much as him, I could tell that, too. *You made a choice to be here,* my mother said. *As much as I did.*

You are all the same. You and that bastard Tiero. You want to see that I am a failure. You want to see me fall.

I am not doing this, my mother said more loudly. *I am not talking to you about any of these things. And I will not accept this kind of behavior.*

Where are you going? He was shouting now. I wondered what I should do. If I should do something. It felt bad; I knew this was bad. Should I leave? Call someone?

I'm just going out for a while. So that you can calm down.

Fine! Leave! Run away, you coward.

I heard her coming up the stairs then. She called for me to come with her, and I did. As we went out the door, we heard the shatter from his office. He had slammed the door so hard that the print above his desk had come crashing to the floor, along with a paperweight and a coffee cup that it brought down with it. I made a strange little list in my head as I buckled my seat belt in Mom's car, as she turned the key with a shaking hand. All of the things that Dino had shattered. A wineglass. William Tiero's picture. The painting of *Wild Roses.* Our lives.

CHAPTER THIRTEEN

I spent a few days at my dad's house. That's where my mother drove us, to drop me off there. They had some conversation at the door, after she had told me to stay in the car. It was another one of those moments when I would have killed to hear what was said, but I also would have done anything not to hear it, ever. I was having a lot of those times lately, where what I wanted and what I didn't want were the same thing. I tried without success to keep Mom from going back home. She could stay with Alice, I suggested. Or we could go to a motel somewhere, the two of us, like the time she and I stayed at the Travel Lodge before Dino moved in, when we'd lost power. Yikes—unintentional double meaning, two points for me. The time we lost *electricity*. Losing power to Dino came later.

One of the things that had apparently been discussed

during the porch powwow was my punishment for the Ian caper. Apparently, I could not be disciplined for ruining his life and his mother's life and their chance to save their financial future, but they could make me pay for skipping school. They decided that my absence would go unexcused, which meant that I had to stay after school one day for a detention.

Zebe made fun of me all day after I told her I had to go. I told her I skipped school because I was just sick of being there, but that was all. I couldn't talk about it any more than I already had. It was one of those things that hurt so much that you needed to keep it safely contained in its little box in your gut, because who knew what might happen if it got out. I could see the awfulness spreading like some noxious gas in a sci-fi movie, poisoning a large city. Or at least, eating up my insides more than it had already. Ian's mother, Janet, had answered the phone when I had tried to call Ian to see how he was. *Hi, Janet, it's Cassie,* I had said. For a moment there was silence. And then, *Cassie? Please don't call here. There's been enough damage done already.* Then there was a click. A click and then silence.

I paid my dues in detention, sat amongst the coats that reeked of cigarettes and the notebooks with the Led Zeppelin stickers on them, and tried not to feel like I was a nerdy tourist in a Hawaiian shirt who had mistakenly wandered into the wrong part of town. The whole thing was pointless, because my real punishment was happening every moment, missing Ian, being away from him, feeling as if I'd ruined him. I'd gone ahead and loved him, and it destroyed him. At least, that's how I felt. I under-stood that they didn't want me around anymore, but it made life seem black-and-white, flat and one-dimensional. I craved the oxygen and color Ian brought. He had changed life, and now it just couldn't change back again.

That night Dad was cooking meatballs, rolling them around in the pan over the heat. He was wearing one of Nannie's old aprons that had a parade of smiling fruit on it. She sat on one of the kitchen chairs, arranging her col-lection of salt and pepper shakers that Dad had kept on the windowsill.

"I just can't believe the stoners are still listening to Zeppelin," he said, after I told him my story.

"They were hoodlums in my day," Nannie said. "If I missed a day of school, your grandpa would have beaten me silly," she said to my father. "Kids these days."

"Oh, he would not have," my father said to the meat-balls. "He was the biggest softie. He never lifted a hand to you."

"Maybe not," she said.

"And from what they told me, they couldn't keep you in school if they tied you to the flag pole."

"Top of my class," she said.

"You barely graduated."

"Maybe not," she said. She took a pair of chefs with holes in the tops of their hats and paired them up with two glass Dutch girls.

"Anyway, I've done my time," I said.

"Let that be a lesson to you," my father said. "Though who am I to talk? I missed a college Spanish final and nearly flunked the course because your mother and I were having an argument on the front lawn of the foreign-language building. All that upset, and years later I can't even remember how to ask where the bathroom is."

"*Quisiera el pollo.*" I'd like to have the chicken, is what it really means.

"See? That's why we had you."

"Top of my class in Spanish," Nannie said, and we both ignored her.

"You failed a final. You didn't wreck someone's future and their family's life."

"It wasn't your fault. Did you try to call Ian again? Get the dishes out, these are done."

"I'm afraid to call. After what his mom said? I went by his house, just to *apologize* if nothing else, but no one was there. He must hate me. I keep thinking he'll try to call, but Mom says he hasn't. God, it's just killing me." It was a relief, at least, to finally be able to talk to Dad about Ian. I went to the cupboard, took out three plates and lined them up on the counter for Dad to dish out the steaming food.

"Why your mother is still in that house I do not understand," he said.

"I don't know, Dad. Dino's concert is coming up in only a few weeks. She thinks things will be okay then."

"Things were never okay. Things will never *be* okay. I don't care if he has the most triumphant concert in the history of concerts. She fell in love with an image."

227

"Well, she knows what he's like now."

"He's a lunatic. A bastard lunatic liar."

"Just like my father," Nannie said.

"Your father was a saint," Dad said to her.

"He was a sweetie," she said. "Such a softie."

"Anyway, if there is one more incident like that, I'm filing for sole custody and getting a restraining order."

"Make your feelings known, Dad. Jeez, come on. I'm a little old for a custody arrangement."

"It's my right as a father. I won't have you in that mess. She's not using her brain, and you're the one getting hurt. I won't stand for it."

"I don't want things to get worse, Dad. Can we not make this about your rights? Can it be about my needs? You and attorneys and all that crap again . . . no."

"Maybe there's another way to get that man out of your life," he said.

"Mafioso hit man," I said. "As much as the idea appeals to me . . ."

"Nah, prison food is supposed to be terrible. Something else is . . . happening. Something that may change the way your mother sees things. Grab some forks."

"What do you mean?" Okay, I'm sorry. I had brief Child of Divorce Reunion Fantasy Number Twelve Thousand. A meeting of the minds and hearts that occurred on the front porch step. Flash to Mom packing her bags. Flash to her lighting Dino's compositions on fire, which was maybe getting a little carried away on my part. It's a tad embarrassing to admit. The child of divorced parents is supposed to be over these things when you reach the age of eight. "Is this about you and Mom?"

"God, no. Nothing like that. Just, I'm doing what I can to reveal the bigger picture. I don't know if it's the right time to tell you. Things are upsetting enough for you right now with that wacko."

"Is this my recipe?" Nannie said when Dad placed the plate in front of her. She couldn't cook to save her life. Her favorite used to be creamed corn, which, I can say with some authority, looks like what a chicken might barf up. Nightmare flashback.

"I hate it when you do that, Dad. You drop these little hints of knowing and then, bam, clam up," I said.

"It's not very mature of me," he agreed. He sat down. "I try to do the right thing, but sometimes the wrong thing gets the better of me. The human condition."

"If you know something that has to do with my life, I'd appreciate you sharing it with me," I said.

He cut a piece of meatball, studied it a while. "It doesn't have to do with you. Just, I'm sorry, okay? I wish I could solve this mess, but there's only one person who can do that for you. And she's on a high wire without a net."

"Yeah, and you know she's not exactly the athletic type," I said.

"She's actually an excellent athlete," my father said.

"Thank you very much," Nannie said.

Dad and I stayed up late and watched an old *Die Hard* movie on what must have been a conservative station, because they'd eliminated any hint of swearing. Bombs would be dropping all over and Bruce Willis would face his enemy and say something like, *You rascals!* Of course, the voice that appeared at those times sounded nothing like his, and his lips were forming different words. Our favorite was when he barely escaped being killed by a landing airplane, and he stood up and remarked, *Holy shoot!*

I got ready for bed. I knew I shouldn't do it, but I tried to call Ian. I only let it ring twice before I hung up. I was missing a connection with him so much, that it helped just dialing that number. Maybe he'd hear the ring and know it was me. Maybe at least he'd know how much I cared. I tried to call Mom, too, but there was no answer.

"I'm worried about Mom," I said to Dad when he came into my room to say goodnight.

"She's strong, Cassie. I think she can handle things," he said.

"I know. But sometimes she doesn't . . . I don't know. *See.*"

"She is one of the most logical people I know," he said. "Even if she isn't showing it at the moment."

He was right about that. "She's logical, but then suddenly she gets carried away with a burst of passionate feeling," I said. I was thinking about her own cello playing, her methodical practicing, her sane musicianship. But then I would see her listening to Dino play, the way she closed her eyes and let him bring her to where she couldn't go herself. Like me, I realized. Great, like Ian and me.

"It'd be good if you could have passion without it having you," my father said. He was lost for a moment in his own thoughts. Memories, I'm sure, that he didn't want to share with me. And then one memory he did want to share. "Remember when Mom cut the bushes into the shapes of animals?"

"*Tried* to cut the bushes into the shapes of animals."

"Talk about getting carried away. She just had this sudden idea and whacked away at the poor plants. When I got home, they'd been massacred."

"One really did look like a rabbit."

"You've got to be kidding. A Picasso rabbit."

"And then this one time? She was teaching me to drive," I said. "We were in Seattle. She was doing really well. Not freaking out or anything. She sat there with her hands in her lap and only pushing her foot to the floor mat when she thought I needed to brake. Then we got onto the freeway. I'm trying to merge, right? And this big truck is coming."

"Oh, God," Dad laughed.

"She suddenly screams, 'Oh, shit, FLOOR IT!' Always good advice for the beginning driver."

"I think that's in the traffic-safety manual," he said.

"I practically wet my pants."

"Holy shoot!" Dad laughed. He shook his head, but it was a loving shake, not a critical one. It was strange to be talking like that about her, the two of us, but good, too. Nice. You got so used to keeping both parties separate, Mom here, Dad there, trying to be sensitive to everyone's feelings, that it sometimes got exhausting. No, it always got exhausting. Trying to keep track of the separate piles of emotions and what was to be kept where. Don't talk to Dad about this part of your life; don't mention to Mom about that. Dad will be hurt if he knew we had a good time. Mom will be hurt to know I tried something new when she wasn't there. Dad will be hurt at Mom's new car/vacation/home/baby/clothes/guinea pig. Mom will be hurt at the things Dad's family said about her. Even if they told you a thousand times that there was nothing you needed to hide, that they were both okay about sharing all parts of your life (chapter three in the bestselling *Divorced Parenting for Dummies*), you could still see those brief flashes of feeling pass over their faces. A jealous look, a hurt one. And even if they were sometimes okay at hiding the snide comments, you could still see the feeling there, raw and exposed.

It was good right then, talking with Dad. Just having everything in one pile and it all being okay. Not having to walk the loyalty tightrope. Just for us all being able to love each other in the complicated ways of a family. For one moment we had that thing that I will go out on a limb and say that every divorced kid wants, this sense of family that is still family even if apart.

The possibility of it was sweet, but then it was gone. The human condition again.

"I worry about her too," my father said.

"I know you do."

"The thing I wouldn't tell you?"

"Yeah?"

"She doesn't even know the whole story."

"What?"

"About Dino."

I scooted up in bed. Again, I didn't want to know. A sick warning urge was creeping up my insides, but racing along with it was this adrenaline-fueled desire to hear what he was about to say. Maybe it was the same kind of desire little kids felt with the box of matches in their hands.

"What? Just tell me."

"I know now for sure. He's not who he says he is."

"Who is he then?"

"I don't know the whole story, but I know this. There was no Dino Cavalli born in or around Sabbotino Grappa, then or ever."

"No way. What about all of those people? They've all told their stories. You've read them."

"I don't know. Group hysteria. The desire to be part of the greatness. Reporters coming to this small town and livening things up. Maybe they've come to believe it themselves. Maybe the attention has just become too much fun to give up."

"No. The fig trees, his beautiful mother, the tossing him bread as he played . . ."

"Fiction. All fiction. Good fiction, a great story. But a lie."

"I can't believe it."

"Believe it. Cassie, there was no Cavalli family in Sabbotino Grappa."

CHAPTER FOURTEEN

I made him prove it to me, the things he said about Dino. I wanted to believe in Honoria Maretta, and the Bissola sisters, in lemon trees, and a small boy who made a tiny village happy with his playing.

And apparently the few people of Sabbotino Grappa wanted to believe it too. Whether it happened or not, they were pleased to go along. Same with Edward Reynolds, who must have found out the truth somewhere along the writing of his book. Because there was no Cavalli family in Sabbotino Grappa and there never had been. I didn't know yet what that information meant to me, or what I would do with it, but I did know one thing: my mother wasn't the only one who had fallen in love with an image.

I stayed with Dad long enough to get annoyed when he used up all the hot water when he took a shower and watched way too much of the History Channel at volumes loud enough to make you duck when the allied forces stormed in with guns firing. After the third day when he made my bed for me, I was actually longing for my old routine at Mom's. I missed my routine, even though I did not miss my mother's husband, the psycho liar, the evil stepfather, the Anti-Mr. Brady—Mike Brady with hair grown out and psychological issues and a cigarette. Which brings to mind another inane and mostly irrelevant side note, and that is that *The Brady Bunch* has got to beat out *Lord of the Rings* in terms of the best in sci-fi fantasy. I mean, the kids call their steps Mom and Dad, which we know you'd never do, unless you harbored a death wish or an all-out hatred for your own mother or father. They also never mention their missing parents. What about Carol Brady's first husband? Was he a drunk, a wife beater, or merely dead? And what about Greg, Peter, and Bobby's mother? Adulteress that ran off with Mr. Partridge Family? Decided she was a lesbian and started a new life? Career woman in another state? Also merely dead? And did no one long for their mom or dad? No photos by the bedside, visits to the cemetery, longings to be remembered at Christmas? For God's sake, no one has an attorney. No one even goes to a therapist!

Anyway. Things right then were fairly peaceful but irritating at Dad's. Add to the equation the fifty times a day that Dad said, "I think it's sad what your mother has done to her life," (meaning: what she'd done to his) or "Divorce is such a crime" (meaning: he had nothing to do with it)

235

or "What did she expect?" (meaning: she got what she deserved). I hated the thought of being back with Dino, but I missed Mom and my room and my stuff. I missed the smell of my own pillow.

I talked to Mom on the phone, and she seemed really tired but okay. Okay enough that when she said she thought things were calm enough for me to come back, I went, in spite of Dad's protests. The concert was only a few short weeks away. And Dino had accepted the whole "Ian thing," according to her. It seemed amazing, miraculous and completely doubtful, but I went home anyway. There was a piece of me, too, that felt I could miss Ian better at home. I could miss him more thoroughly, being surrounded by places we had been together. I was beginning to feel that my missing him was all I had of him, and so I wanted it.

I went home the day before Ian had been scheduled to fly out to Philadelphia for his audition at Curtis. I called him again when I got home. His mother answered, and I hung up. I hurt without him. My heart felt like a cave, dug out, dark. I couldn't understand why he wouldn't call me, why we couldn't just *talk*. My fear was that he'd never forgive me, and I pictured him with his cast, hating me with the intensity I felt I deserved. I missed the feeling on the ferry, before it all turned bad that day. I missed the feeling of being where you belonged.

I avoided Dino as much as I could. He avoided me, or else was avoiding everything that wasn't music. He didn't eat, didn't appear to sleep, only built up the cigarette butts in coffee cups and saucers. He only said one thing to me all of that first day. *Turn the handle of the door when you shut it,* he had said. *It makes less noise.* I avoided Mom, too, but for a different reason. I was carrying around this knowledge of Dino that Dad had given me, and it kept bumping between us. I was afraid that if I looked too long at Mom she might see it there in my eyes, or feel it between us in the room. I just lugged this secret around, and how she couldn't see it there, I don't know. It was huge and ugly and powerful. And I kept it close to me, my weapon. This stockpiled bomb that somewhere inside I was sure I would use when the enemy most threatened.

The days were hollow and vast as the sky that I saw through my telescope on those nights, though empty of any of the life that was also out there, stars dying and being born before your eyes, the life cycle taken to its outer edges of time and place. I had all of the vastness, none of the fire. Zebe and Sophie and Brian and Nat were all in rehearsal period for *Anything Goes,* which made things even lonelier. In English class, I sat for an hour as Aaron Urling read his poems aloud. Eleven haiku poems on Darth Vader. *Father and Son. Bonded by Blood. Eternal Destruction.* He had two light sabers in his belt as he read. *My visual aids,* he told the teacher. He snickered to his friends. He thought he was a real crack-up. In science we took a walk in the forest on school grounds to measure distances from trees, and Mr. Robelard called us back in with an elk call. I'm not kidding. It sounded like he was giving birth.

A week and a half until the concert. A week. No Ian. I didn't blame him for hating me.

Your own small universe moves on in surreal ways when you feel a crisis building, building. And when your sanctuary is gone. Walking home, I got stuck having a conversation with Courtney about split ends. Our neighbor, Mr. Frederici, left an angry message that Dog William, in an apparent act of outburst over the withdrawal of the object of his love, had gotten into the Frederici garbage can and spread litter all over his yard. The catsup bottle fell out of the fridge when I was getting some milk and spilled out in a blobby smear of goriness. Life just keeps ticking along.

I invited Siang over. I should have been trying harder than ever to keep her away. Dino's intensity was focused on his music, same as a kid focusing reflected sunrays from a mirror onto paper, hoping it will burst into flames. But it was comforting having Siang around. It reminded me of the simple days when Dino was merely a jerk and Siang would come over and steal his orange peels for her mini-tabletop shrine.

"My father said he's had to give up lattes for, like, six months to afford the concert tickets," Siang said. I had made brownies, hoping to drown my sorrows in three zillion fat calories, and we were taking chunks and eating them out of the pan. I had the feeling that Siang never did these kinds of things. First, she was thin as a sheet of foil, and second, she was going at them like she'd been lost at sea on a rubber dinghy for months.

"Slow down," I said to her. "If you choke, I'm not so hot at Heimlich. I was absent that day in health. I might dislodge something you need, you know, like a larynx. What concert?"

"Cassie! The world premiere of Mr. Cavalli's new work!"

"It was a *joke*. Six months with no lattes? That is so sad. That's like some fairy tale where some woman cuts her hair to buy bread. You should have told me. Maybe I could have helped."

"Those tickets have been sold out for almost a year," Siang said.

"I'm sure we could have done something."

"Wow. Do you know how many people would die to be in your place? Or even mine, sitting in here in his kitchen, eating off his plate?"

"You're bypassing the plate, far as I can tell," I said.

"You probably didn't see the article in *Newsweek*. Or the *New York Times*? FAMED COMPOSER CHOOSES SMALLER VENUE TO UNVEIL NEW WORK?"

"Smaller venue? That's kind of insulting."

"The *New York Times*. Jeez, Cassie."

"As long as you're happy, Siang."

"Is he ready? There are rumors."

"What kind of rumors?" That he's losing it? That he thinks William Tiero is hiding under the table? That his stepdaughter ruined the career of his protégé and now he's cracked? That the only thing he seems to have ingested in a week is a box of truffles sent by his manager and twelve thousand pounds of nicotine?

"Just that the third piece isn't done."

"I'm sure it'll be done." I wasn't sure at all, but, Jesus,

239

Siang seemed so worried, and now so happy with my words. She smiled, brownie in her teeth. "Go like this," I said to her, putting the edge of my fingernail to my tooth. Personally, I hate it when people don't tell you those things.

Siang removed the offending brownie. "I knew he'd be ready. He's a professional. An artist of the highest order."

Maybe we consider a piece of work to be genius in part because it goes places we cannot go. Maybe it is not so much that the geniuses are nuts, but that there is something in the nuts that is genius. That ability to get to not just the seed of emotion, but to the place that exists even before the seed is there. Maybe they live amid the raw materials of feeling before feeling becomes organized; maybe they work with the base elements, like the cosmos in formation. There seems, anyway, an ability to get to truth, the purest emotion, if you can see through the barbed wire of chaos that surrounds it. Maybe that's what we respond to in those works of genius—our own inability to be that emotionally unbound. An envy for the letting go of the tether and seeing what is beyond the frontier, the barrier of self-protection. Maybe the genius is only a letting go, in a way that most of us would be too frightened to. But maybe, too, the genius is just some wacky consolation prize for the pain of living out of this world.

I don't know. But I do know that the most honest, the deepest and purest forms of thought and creation appear to make their owners pay a price. The scientists with the world-changing ideas, the painters that change our vision, the musicians with the soul-altering music—they seem to blow a circuit in the process, or a circuit was blown beforehand that allowed the creation to happen. And sometimes, just before the final break, there is a huge outpouring of creativity. It's hard to know whether the outpouring of creativity causes the break or if the break that is coming causes the outpouring. Before her suicide, Sylvia Plath was writing a poem a day, working at four A.M. while her children slept, and Emily Dickinson cranked out her own poetry during her affair with a married clergyman, then collapsed in a nervous breakdown. And Vincent van Gogh. He had moved to Auvers, France, for peace and tranquility, and painted the flowers of Daubigny's garden, including his *Wild Roses*. He painted seventy canvasses in seventy-five days, and then shot himself in the chest.

I overheard my mother and Dino talking when I got home from school. It wouldn't have been hard to do. Courtney and her media-monster brothers could have overheard them talking, and it would have been better than anything on television.

"For God's sake, Dino, I'm going to call the doctor," my mother said.

"What does the doctor have to do with this? It has nothing to do with the doctor. This is between Tiero and me."

"You're worrying for nothing, okay? He won't be there."

"I know he will. He has never been able to stay away.

He's like a fly on shit. I can feel him nearby. I've always known. He's always come."

"Dino, really. Stop it. If he's come before, it's only because he loves you."

"Love? You call that love? He tried to destroy me."

"Maybe he wanted to help you. Like I want to help you."

Dino had been right. When you turned the door handle, it did make less noise. I had crept up the stairs with my backpack and a box of crackers. I could still hear them. The conversation was giving me the creeps. I almost wanted to look for William Tiero under the bed.

"Maybe you want to destroy me, too."

"Dino, no. Don't do this. I'm phoning the doctor."

"And you run to the doctor whenever I get too close to the truth. Just like he did."

Shit. Weren't these the kind of people who committed horrible crimes? Was my mother in danger? If anything, she was certainly kidding herself in thinking she could manage him. He was not manageable. This had gone way beyond a manageable situation.

"I think you'll feel better if you talk to the doctor a little."

"I'll feel better when Tiero lives his own life and stays the hell out of mine." .

"Look, why don't we just have Andrew call him? We can tell him it's too upsetting for you to have him there."

"Andrew Wilkowski knows where Tiero is? They've talked on the phone?"

"No, they haven't talked on the phone. But it would be

a simple thing to find him. Give you some reassurance that he'll stay away."

"He will never stay away. He can't. He vowed not to."

"It was a long time ago," my mother said. "He's done his job."

"His job will be finished when I die," Dino said.

"Dino, I think he would stay away if you just asked him to. If he understood how much his presence would upset you. He thinks you're just fighting about money."

"And you know what he thinks, don't you? You're two of a kind."

"No, Dino. No, please. I don't know how much more of this I can take." She sounded close to tears.

"You want to destroy me."

"I want you to be well. And that smoking isn't helping anything."

I heard the sound of inhaling, that black smoke curling up inside of him, same as his poisonous thoughts. "If you call him, I will cut you out of my life forever."

Brief Fantasy Number Twenty-Five Thousand Two Hundred and Nine—handing her the phone with William Tiero's number already dialed. I didn't know how much more of this I could take, either. As soon as Dino was gone to rehearsals that night, my mom was on the phone. Dino's doctor. They reached some agreement, something about the doctor coming over. I thought about my mother's marriage to Dino Cavalli. They had run off to San Francisco together and had a judge do the honors at the courthouse. I thought about what my mother's dreams had been that day. Whatever she had imagined their future to be, I was sure it wasn't this.

Mom asked if I wanted to go for tacos. I was glad she was eating—she looked like hell lately, stress-thin. We left and picked up some food, and ate it in the car driving home. I love to eat in the car. There's something so satisfyingly efficient about the whole endeavor, taking care of two needs at the same time, and it's such a challenge of planning, too. Where to put your Mexi-Fries (yeah, right—like we all don't know they're Tater Tots) and your hot sauce; how to balance your drink while keeping the insides of your taco from spilling out of their shell.

Mom negotiated an intersection while taking a sideways bite of her dinner. "I'm sure this goes without saying, but you know I'm expecting you to be at the performance on Friday," she said.

"What performance?" I said.

"Cassie!"

"Just kidding." Boy, that joke got a good reaction.

"You'll have to wear a dress."

"Cruel and unusual punishment," I said.

"The long one from the Thanksgiving party, how about. You won't even have to do pantyhose."

"Okay," I said.

"There'll be reporters and critics," she said.

"They won't even notice me, I'll behave so nicely." I knew why she wanted me there, but I didn't understand why Dino would. I said so.

"Of course he wants you there," she said. "We're family."

I could hear the lie in her voice. "He really has taken the whole Ian thing well, after the initial blowup."

"He's been pretty quiet about that," I said. "But I heard you guys talking today."

"I know, but try not to worry. In two days this performance will be over, and he promised he'd get back on his medication. Dr. Milton is coming over tomorrow, just to help him through."

"You're not a lion tamer, Mom."

"But Dr. Milton is."

"It just seems like there's more than we can handle here. It's just . . . too much. You've been eating Tums and Maalox like candy."

"I'm walking around in someone else's life," she agreed.

Right then I thought about the secret weapon I held, this information that Dino's early life was a concoction, a lie. Everything that she'd already seen hadn't been enough to make Mom leave, so why would this? But maybe it would be enough to tip the scale. I opened my mouth to speak, then changed my mind.

"All this is almost over," my Mom said.

She didn't know, neither of us knew, how right she was.

I'd set up my telescope over the past few nights, hoping and hoping that Ian would come as he had before. But he hadn't come. Still, it was better than being in the house, so after dinner that night I set up again. That night was clear and the sky was still in the hold of the midwinter turbulent atmosphere, the shakiness of the air blurring the images in the telescope, but making the stars twinkle. I gave up and just looked without an instrument, admired Sirius, the most scorching-hot star and the brightest thing in the sky next to a planet. It sparkled blue-white, dominated everything around it. I found Canis Major, the Big Dog, and Canis Minor, the Little Dog, though they looked more like spilled sugar than animals.

I was missing Ian something fierce right then, and I remembered our first touch, right there on that lawn. I packed up, put the telescope into the shed. I was heading up the steps to the front door when I heard his voice.

"Cassie?"

His dark figure came toward me, becoming clearer as he stepped forward, his face nearly white from the light of the sky. It was a dream, I was sure. This figure, approaching me slowly, appearing out of the darkness.

"Cassie?"

"Ian?"

"It's me." One sleeve of his coat hung limp by his side, and the lump of his cast was buttoned inside his coat. I couldn't believe it was him. I just couldn't believe it.

"You came."

"I've been trying and trying to call you."

"You have?"

"I swear, every time I do, Dino answers. I didn't want to make more problems for you, so I keep making up reasons why I'm phoning him," Ian said. "It's getting stupid.

Where have you been, Cassie? What's going on? You haven't called or anything. I figured maybe you were under lock and key or something. Couldn't climb out your window like Rapunzel because your hair is too short. I came over one day and hid behind the neighbor's *car,* because Dino and your Mom were there in the driveway."

"I'm sorry . . ."

"I wanted to come over so bad, but I didn't want to risk getting you into more trouble. I figured it'd be safe now—Dino's got to be at the concert hall every night this week, right?"

"They rehearse in the day."

"Oh, shit—should I go?"

"No! No, Ian. I *have* been trying to call you. Over and over. Your Mom told me not to call anymore. I didn't think you wanted to see me. . . ."

"You're kidding," Ian said. "Man, I had no idea. She . . . she's really upset. God, I worried maybe this wasn't worth it anymore to you. You had enough of all the crap . . ."

"No! I thought *you* . . . after your wrist, and what your mom said. . . . How could you ever even want to talk to me again?"

"I was really worried," he said.

I went to him, put my arms around him, the bulky cast between us. He felt so good. His mouth felt so good. All the pieces came together and made sense again. It wasn't happiness so much I felt, though that, too. There was just this profound relief. His cold mouth, warm breath filling me up again—just such relief.

"Whatever happens," he said. "Whatever, you've got to promise me you won't go away from me anymore."

I put my head against his shoulder. The worry and relief poured out together, lodged somewhere in my throat. My eyes welled up. "I am so sorry, Ian. I am just so, so sorry about your arm." I started to cry. He put his good arm around me.

"Hey," he said.

"I was selfish," I said. "You were working so hard. Please, if you could ever forgive me . . ."

"There's nothing to forgive," he said. "Look, fate decided things for itself. Cassie, look at me." He tilted my chin up from his coat. Kissed each of my eyes. "Look," he said.

I looked. He was right. His face was soft, relaxed.

"Oh, God, Ian. You're happy."

"Happy—I'm *ecstatic*. Worried as hell, but ecstatic."

"I'm so glad. I am so, so glad."

"I didn't have to make the choice. The choice was made for me," he said.

"What's going to happen?" I asked.

"I don't know. Financially . . . God, Cassie, things are such a mess. My mom's a wreck. I feel awful about it. But there's this piece of me in here. It's flying."

"You're free."

"God, I'm free," he said.

CHAPTER FIFTEEN

Three days. Two.

One day and a bad night's sleep. A restless, tense household, my mother making tea at 3:00 A.M. Dino playing in his office at 4:00 A.M. The toilet flushing, doors opened and closed. Me turning my pillow endlessly to the cool side.

And then, the day of the concert.

It's funny about those monumental events that you wait and wait for, the ones that have the big buildup of a rocket launch. There's all the drama and the trauma and then the actual day comes in, soft as any other day, just appearing the way all of the other ones appear. Friday morning, the sun came up the same way it had for a zillion years. I tried to summon some feeling of importance, gather up a sense of the monumental, but instead I just felt cranky and over-tired, got up, and went into the bathroom and checked my face for disaster, as I did every day. When I left for school, Dino was still in bed, and the only sign of an important night was catching Mom downing Maalox in the bathroom, and the newspaper on the kitchen table folded to the article CAVALLI TO PERFORM FIRST NEW MUSIC IN SIX YEARS.

The big thing that happened at school on Friday was that Mr. Robelard, the science teacher, caught on fire during an experiment in his second-period sophomore Life Science class. I was sitting in English class then, listening to Orlando, the gay guy from last trimester's World History class, recite his poetry about love. He flung his arms out dramatically, and everyone rolled their eyes when he described the female object of his desire. Yeah, right. *Her lips were pouting and red,* he panted embarrassingly, just as the door shot open and this sophomore girl ran in yelling, "The teacher's on fire! The teacher's on fire!" Some kid in the back of the class actually laughed until we saw Mr. Robelard run past, the back of his coat in flames. Apparently some alcohol they were using for an experiment got too close to a Bunsen burner, and poof. I wondered how this was going to affect his elk calls.

My own day may have seemed regularly irregular, but the outside music world was greeting it with anticipation. I got my first sense of this at lunch, when I felt a tap on my shoulder and turned to find Mr. King, the orchestra teacher, standing behind me with bright eyes.

"I just wanted to pass on my best wishes for this evening and my sincerest congratulations," he whispered. And then off he scurried, as if the performance had already begun and he was politely leaving the concert hall to use the men's room.

Siang was treating me in that delicate fashion, too, telling me after school that she would not be coming over today, as it seemed best. Some kid with a violin case slipped me a note: *I am a great admirer of yours*, apparently missing the point that the only thing I could do with a violin was make it into a decorative planter.

After school, I started to get a weird bout of nerves. My stomach was rolling and pitching, and I understood Mom's Maalox. I decided I needed something to calm me down. A huge sugar hit, some Twinkies or something. I got a ride from Zebe and she dropped me off at the Front Street Market in town. She took her neon yellow rabbit's foot off of her key chain and insisted I keep it with me for good luck tonight, even though it was creepy.

"People have had them for hundreds of years," Zebe said. "So they've got to be good for something."

"Not for the rabbit," I told her.

I perused the Hostess aisle happily, enjoying all of the beautiful possibilities. Momentarily, all would be joy. I was in the checkout aisle, purchasing more items than I care to tell about, when I heard some familiar voices over by that big ice compartment in the front of the store that you never see anyone near. You get to wondering if a dead body could be stored there, for all anyone ever opens it.

"Hey, Bunny! Chuck!" I said. I was glad to see them. We were bonded by our wonderful and terrible day together. Bonded by our love for Ian Waters.

"Look, I bought happiness," I said, and showed them what was in my bag.

"Whoa," Chuck said. "You won the chocolate lottery."

"Not all chocolate. Fruit pies, too," I said.

"We're just here for ice," Bunny said unnecessarily. The door was open, and big whiffs of white air were escaping the chest. If he stood there any longer, he'd start looking like that abominable snowguy in that geeky Christmas cartoon with the carpenter elf and the Land of the Misfit Toys. "My back is still hurting from that fall I took. You remember that fall I took."

"Vaguely," I said.

"He's sprained his lumbodorsal fascia, but he doesn't believe me," Chuck said.

"Ice, and deep-tissue massage," Bunny said.

"Maybe a chiropractor," Chuck said.

"Hey, get off my back, ha ha," Bunny said.

"After the fiftieth time it's not funny anymore, Bun."

"I'm sorry you're still not feeling well," I said. "Would a couple of Ho Hos help things?"

"Waaay better than a chiropractor," Bunny said.

I shuffled around my loot, found the Ho Hos, and opened the package with my teeth.

"I guess you heard Ian's good news," Chuck said.

"That he's quitting," I said through the plastic. *At ee's kidding.*

"Quitting? No, that he got in," Chuck said.

I'd heard wrong, I guessed. I must have heard wrong.

"What do you mean, got in?"

"Maybe she hadn't heard yet. Shit," Bunny said. "God damn it, Chuck. You and your big mouth."

"What do you mean?" A sick feeling started in my stomach, some horrible dread. My face flushed red.

"He got in," Bunny said. "Curtis."

"How is that possible?" My voice sounded hoarse. I wanted to scream, and my voice sounded like I already had. "No! That's not possible! How is that possible?"

"Mr. Cavalli. He had a tape. He'd taped Ian before he broke his wrist. Cavalli sent it in. Talked to the school and arranged for the tape to be used as an audition."

"No," I whispered. "No."

"I thought maybe he should have asked Janet before he did that, but she's obviously beside herself with happiness," Bunny said.

"What about Ian?"

"I haven't seen Ian," Bunny said.

"No one asked Ian."

"Janet said he was happy. I don't know if this is the best thing for him or not," Bunny said. "All I know is, he's in. He's going to Curtis."

"I've got to go," I said.

"Hey, Cassie. I'm sorry if I said anything before Ian told you himself. I didn't know."

"I've got to go," I said.

I dropped the Hostess loot there on the floor and I got the hell out of there. I ran home. I ran so fast. Fury gave me this speed I didn't know I had. I wasn't myself. I didn't know who I was, but I wasn't me. Dino had taken Ian's life from him. No wonder he'd lost his outrage about Ian's arm. He'd already taken matters into his own hands. Well, now I would take them into mine.

I flung open the front door, slammed it behind me. How was that for turning the knob so it closed more quietly?

"Cassie?" Mom appeared in the kitchen doorway. "I'm glad you're home. We need to eat something before we go. God, what's wrong?"

"Where's Dino?"

"He's getting into his tux. You've got to hurry up and get dressed."

I ignored her, went upstairs.

"Knock, knock," I said to the closed bedroom door. I was trying not to shout. I was doing everything I could to keep those shouts inside. My heart was beating furiously. I was hot all over, from the running, from the anger.

"What is it?" Dino said. He opened the door. He stood there in the doorway in his tux, his tie loose.

"What did you do?" I breathed.

"I cannot handle your dramatics now. I've got to get ready," he said.

My mother arrived at the top of the stairs. "Cassie, come with me to your room," she said. "We'll handle whatever needs handling."

"Why did you do that? Why did you send that tape of Ian to Curtis?"

"So that's what the upset is this time. Always the boy, the boy, the boy. I saved his ass," Dino said. "Daniella, really. Would you kindly remove your daughter from our room?"

254

"He didn't want to go," I said. "He didn't want that."

"It's not always about what we want," Dino said. "If I had what I wanted, we wouldn't be having this conversation. I'd be in New York at this moment, preparing to go to Lincoln Center instead of Benaroya Hall. And do you know why I am not in New York preparing to go to Lincoln Center?"

"Dino, that's not fair," my mother said.

"Because I married your mother, and your mother has you to think about."

"Dino. Stop," Mom said. "Come on, guys. We've got a big night ahead, and . . ."

"You," I breathed. "Are a horrible person. And a liar."

"You're wasting my time," Dino said.

"All of the stories about Italy and Sabbotino Grappa. Who are you, really?" I let the bomb drop from my hands. I let it slip to the floor, where it lay, ticking.

Everyone was silent for a moment. I could hear Dino breathing heavily.

"Because if you're really Dino Cavalli, your history is a lie. No perfect house and mother in a feathered hat. No lemon trees. Maybe not even any bicycles."

"Get her out of here, Daniella. I have a performance to prepare for."

"Cassie. Your room. Now."

"He's not who he says. What, did you pay those people to hide what you really are?"

He turned away from me. I couldn't see his face, which had become so hideous to me. If I could have seen his face, it probably would have been fallen and pale, I know now. Drained of cover and laid bare, just a human.

My mother took hold of my arm, led me out. "Cassie, what are you thinking? Do you know what you're doing? Jesus."

"There are things you don't know."

She closed my door with no small amount of anger. Her face was tight and her eyes flashed.

"I do know."

"No, you don't. Dino wasn't born in Sabbotino Grappa. All of those stories were made up. He never even lived there. What do you think of him now? You never even knew him. It's all a lie."

"I know that."

"What?" I sat down on the edge of my bed. My anger drained from me. Without it, I was suddenly exhausted. "What?" I wanted to cry. I was too tired for that, even.

"I know that. You're right. None of it was true. He made up the story when he was sixteen years old to cover the truth, and he's stuck with it ever since."

"That's crazy. That's absolutely wacko. You knew this? Just one more nutso thing. I cannot believe this."

"He was doing his first interview, and found the town in a book. He chose it because it wasn't a place likely to be visited, and too small to bump into anyone from there. He held a magnifying glass to the picture of the town square, the church, studied the tiny map. The rest . . . he just made up the rest."

"And all those people go along? Like you go along? I just don't understand."

"When Edward Reynolds did the oral history, William

Tiero went to Sabbotino Grappa. He talked to the priest, who then spoke to the handful of villagers. They'd already read about themselves by then in a couple of articles. They thought they were famous. Most didn't need to be talked into anything. They didn't even have to be paid. They loved being part of things. They loved having this bit of excitement. It made them happy. Some of the old people—they started to believe they really did remember Dino Cavalli and his family living in the big house on Via D'Oro."

"I'm sorry, but that's fucking creepy. They all go along like they're in some kind of trance? Come on."

"It's not about a *trance*. It's a small village. It was fun for them, a thrill. They loved it. Some heard the stories so many times, they forgot what the truth was. This is not about *creepy*. This is about filling a boring life with something more interesting."

"You knew this. You knew and it didn't even matter to you. Someone just goes and makes up his whole *history* and this doesn't bother you?" Nothing would matter then, it seemed clear. This was my mother's life, and my life. Nothing was going to change if she didn't have limits of what she would tolerate. I would have to make some decisions. I grabbed my pillow and held it. Put my face down inside. Dad could turn down the heat of his house. Mom couldn't turn down the heat of hers.

"Honey," she sighed. She sat down next to me, just sat there in silence for a while. "Dino needed that history. *Needed* it. And it made those people *happy*. They're part of something bigger than the life they have there. I understood that."

"Why? Why would he need it so bad? Someone just needs to go and make himself up?"

"Dino was born Dino Tiero in the inner city of Milan."

"Tiero? They're *related*?"

"They're brothers. They were desperately poor. God, Cassie, they were so poor that they once had to eat a rat that William caught. Can you imagine that?"

"No," I said. "It's still no reason to lie like that. Being poor . . ."

"His mother was a prostitute. They never knew their father. They saw their mother hanging on the shower rail when he was fifteen. Suicide. He and William found her."

"Oh, my God."

"A teacher, Giovanni Cavalli, had already given him his first violin a few years before. He taught Dino to play. Dino had a natural talent. That part was true. William got him jobs, and the playing kept them alive. Dino changed his name to honor the man who saved his life. William kept pushing, pushing Dino to greatness. They were always running from ghosts."

I was quiet. I felt horrible and cruel. Life could be so beautiful, and it could also be this mess of confusion and cruelty. I didn't know where to begin untangling things.

"I'm sorry," I said finally.

"Cassie, I'm not saying this excuses all his behavior. Just explains some of it."

"Why didn't you tell me before?"

"He didn't even tell me any of this. William did. Dino's doctor did. Dino fired William after he had Dino hospitalized.

He thought he was ruining his ability to create."

"I just don't get it. People would understand. I would have understood. Maybe there would be more compassion for him. He didn't need to worry about the truth."

"I guess sometimes things seem too awful to say out loud." I guess she was right about that. I still hadn't told Ian the truth about what was happening at home. "I'm sorry I didn't tell you. I wanted to protect him, I wanted to protect you. He wanted to protect his mother. He didn't want the world to know her that way."

"I wanted to protect you," I said.

"Oh, Cassie." She looked so, so tired. She put her arms around me. "That's my job," she said. "To protect you. And I'm not doing it well enough."

I hugged her too. "All this has been hard," I said.

"How did you find out about Dino? We don't even know for sure if Edward Reynolds discovered the truth, though I think he had to have. Every magazine and newspaper reporter since has taken their information from that book."

"Dad found out."

"What? Dad?"

"He was worried about you."

"None of this is his business."

"Don't be mad at him. He did it out of love."

Mom sighed. Shook her head. "All the things," she said. "Done out of love."

Karl Lager: Well, then the concerts in the piazza started every Saturday morning. Do you understand what that did to my

259

business? No one went into the store for an hour or more. They came to listen to that horrible child, not to buy peaches.

Father Tony Abrulla: I will confess I am glad he did not choose Sunday! I was just an assistant then, to Father Minelli. I close my eyes and still hear that music. It brought the people of Sabbotino Grappa together as one. For a few hours, this small boy kept Mrs. Salducci and Mrs. Latore from fighting. Even Frank Piccola came outside and stood to listen, and the threat of hell couldn't make him leave his house for Mass on Sundays. Maybe he was depressed. We didn't have depression, then, of course, that we knew of.

Maria Lager Manzoni, grocer's daughter: Father finally gave me Saturdays off. Let me tell you a secret—that's when my Pia was conceived. Eli and I held hands through that child's sweet and tender playing, went home with passion. We barely closed the front door.

Honoria Maretta: No child was ever mine like he was. Like a son to me. I loved that boy.[10]

Here is what I remember about the rest of that night.

Dino puts a coat around my mother's shoulders. His own smells of cigarettes, like the boys in detention. I tell him I am sorry, but it is really more the sadness of his life I am expressing compassion for, rather than my anger at him earlier. There is too much between us for that. And too much that he's done that cannot be excused by the past. Still, I feel bad for the pain he felt. The pain he continues

[10] Dino Cavalli—*The Early Years: An Oral History*. From Edward Reynolds, New York, N.Y. Aldine Press, 1999.

to feel. Maybe he chooses not to see me, as he has chosen to stop seeing other things in his life.

My mother drives. Dino sits in the passenger's seat. I see in the reflection of the glass that his fingers are moving in the air, on the strings of the violin that rides in its case in the trunk.

We take the ferry, stay in the car. I have seen Dino perform only once before, and Mom has seen him several times, but it was never like this. Never a release of new work after so many years, never so much riding on the outcome. Last time he was not nervous, but now his edginess infuses the atmosphere. Mom turns on the radio, but Dino switches it off. She helps him straighten the wings of his bow tie, then he flips the visor down and studies it in the mirror. Unsatisfied, he undoes it, ties it again. His hands tremble. I smooth the velvet of my dress again and again with my hands. I think about Ian, who in a few months will board an airplane for Philadelphia, but will tonight be somewhere in that audience. I think about how everyone is just a small person on a big earth in a bigger universe. I think about how everyone struggles to do the best they can in this imperfect place.

We arrive at the concert hall early, of course. We are backstage, where there is the chaos and noise of people and instruments and bright lights. My mother knows a few performers there, and I can see her watching Dino with sideways glances even as she speaks to them. Dino is using grand gestures and a big voice, but he is sipping water and once again I see his shaking hands. A violist asks me questions about school that I answer as I smile with a politeness that tries hard to hide my impatience. I feel like I am talking to her forever, as she tells me what a shame it is that our schools do not make music programs a priority.

Mom rescues me. She whispers that she feels under-foot, that they want to practice a few measures. The conductor looks relaxed, laughs a lot. She tells me that he will be good for Dino, and that we can go get a coffee. I guess we could use some Optimism in a Cup right then.

We go out into the lobby, where it is mostly quiet still, and where there are huge posters of Dino staring out at us wherever I look. It reminds me of *The Great Gatsby*, which we read in English last year—something about that big sign that signifies death, or something or other that I can't quite remember. We find a coffee stand, share a latte, eat a biscotti, so that Mom must go to the bathroom again to fix her lipstick. By the time the audience begins to arrive, she will have made four trips to the bathroom, not that I can blame her.

It feels like we are waiting forever. My feet hurt in those damn shoes. Whoever decided that high heels were a good idea for women should have had to wear them every day of his life, which would be punishment enough. Everyone smiles at my mother, and my own face hurts from so much smiling. I keep looking around for Ian, but know that with all the people there it will be unlikely that I will see him and have the chance to talk to him about getting into Curtis. The ushers arrive, and Mom decides to go backstage and check on Dino one more time before the show begins. I go back to the bathroom for lack of anything else to do, and to avoid the stares of the Dino posters. His hair is swept back from his face in them, silver and black, and he looks handsome and intense. It occurs to me that he is someone I know, someone I live with. But do I really know him? Anything about him, except the way he wants me to walk down stairs, turn a faucet off, close a door? This strikes me as sad—what a stranger he and his life are to me. In the bathroom, I wish for a vice—smoking, drinking. My best vice, Hostess Indulgence, sounds stomach turning and hugely lacking in vice-ly power at the moment. The bathroom has the paper towels stacked in a basket, and I wonder how long they will last before the dispensers with the twirly narrow handles will have to be used.

The bathroom begins to pack with perfumed women in sequins and big coats. I leave to find that the lobby is filling fast, with rushing people and lingering people, people in heavy jackets and others fanning themselves with their programs. It's amazing how loud it is in there, after the several hours where the only noises were footsteps on carpet. In spite of Dino's complaints about his venue, I know that the hall is one of the best for sound, a building built within a building to keep the life of the street out. Now in the lobby, we are standing in the middle layer, the protective atmosphere.

Mom comes out again, finds me looking out of the glass wall into what is now night. It's dark and has been raining, and the street is glossy. Cars are jammed up all along the road, and a light turns red and someone honks. In every one of those cars there is a story, or a hundred stories. For every light on in all of those huge city buildings, there is a story. No one knows what I am about to face, no one knows my story, and neither do I right then. I think about Ian and I scan the crowd for his face, and kick myself for not making a plan to meet him somewhere here. This place, a night like this, will be his place, too, his night. I wonder if his hands will shake as he takes a sip of water before his performance.

Mom grabs my arm. It's the second time she's done that. She tells me we have to hurry, that we should be seated by now. We walk past the ushers and down the sloped, carpeted ramp. Some of the family of the other performers stay backstage, but Dino has always preferred his support in the audience. I know from Mom's own performances that when you look out from a lit stage, all you can see is a blackness, the sky without stars. You wouldn't even know there were any living beings out there. I guess it's nice to know that there is something familiar and loving in that sea of darkness.

We travel down the rows of seats and I am lucky I don't fall on my ass in those shoes. All of those people in their suits and fancy clothes, holding hands or whispering to each other or reading their programs and scanning the names of all of the contributors to see which of their friends gave money, all of them are here to see Dino, to say that they saw him, to be able to tell the story tomorrow and in the days to come. You can feel the excitement in

264

the air, in that reserved way of people in an elegant place—all good manners and shifting sideways to maneuver past each other and whispered *excuse me*'s.

We sit next to that weasel Andrew Wilkowski, and some other woman who is from the recording company, I think. I can smell her perfume from where I sit, one of those sorts that are not sexy so much as stalking. The strong odor jars me out of the nervousness that I feel, this psychic-hypercommunication that Mom and I have going between us, anxious electricity. The perfume is helpful because now I am just plain annoyed, and the annoyance puts me in full fault-finding gear. The woman has a little run in her stockings right at the point of her ankle. With any luck, we'll see it zip up her leg like a spider crawling up a wall.

I look behind me. Every seat that I can see is full. Every one. No one is even in the bathroom. I know that somewhere behind me, Siang Chibo sits with her parents. I know that Ian is there with his mother, tickets given to them compliments of Dino. I wonder if they can see me, if their eyes are on me. People in the front row turn to us and say things to Mom, shake her hands. They are probably the people whose names you see in the program under CONTRIBUTORS, the ones who have been in our house on Thanksgiving. We are in the second row by choice—my mom hates sitting in the front row. She says that all you get is a view up Dino's pant leg, but I don't understand how this is any better. If I had my choice, since I had to be there, I would rather sit in one of the overhanging pods, those special boxes that remind you of ladies with piled-up hair and opera glasses, or maybe of President Lincoln being shot, but Dino doesn't like us in the balconies. Better yet, I'd sit in the farthest back corner. I'd put my coat around me, close my eyes, and pretend I'm listening to him on a CD. The idea of him on the stage in front of us is too intense. It'd be more comfortable watching the surgery channel on a big-screen TV. This is not some stranger giving us a show—we will bring home his success or failure. We will live with the largeness of this event for days, the monumental fact of this one man with these people in his hands.

The lights dim, and Mom grabs my arm. We look at each other in the dimness, and I'm surprised at how fearful her face looks. We know Dino won't be performing right away, so there is no reason for this stomach lurching just yet. But when the curtain opens and there is such silence, only a few rustles and a throat being cleared, and the symphony is revealed, dressed in black, with instruments held in readiness, you know it has begun and whatever happens is inevitable.

The conductor enters, and we like him already. His hair is loose, and it is as swinging as his walk. He bows to the audience, and his wide smile says he is enjoying every moment of this, that we should relax and come with him where he is about to take us. The crowd breaks into applause—Peter Boglovich is well loved, known for his passion for coffee and pastries and other men. He steps up onto the conductor's stand, and raises his baton to a pinpoint in the air. And then they begin.

There is a frenzy of bowing, the slightly forward tilt of the musicians' bodies, their slight sway. I can feel my mother relax through the piece. I look over at her and see her smiling slightly.

The symphony plays two more pieces. After the third there is silence, and my mother takes my hand and holds it. Hers is sweaty, and I wonder if she has stopped breathing. Peter Boglovich is speaking, although his words are underwater. He turns to face offstage, applauds to Dino, who emerges from the wings. There is thunderous applause, which goes on for a long time, as Dino looks out into the black sea. In spite of all of the people around him, he looks alone, this one man who was once this one young boy. He takes off his tuxedo jacket, hands it to the conductor. Dino takes his place slightly left of center.

The first piece is titled *Giardino Dei Sogno,* Garden of Dreams. It is surprisingly upbeat, almost cheerful. He smiles as if he is remembering something sweet. His white shirt billows softly. The symphony joins him after a while, an easy, lovely mix of a walk in good weather. My mother's eyes never leave him; it's as if she is breathing for him. The piece ends. The crowd's applause is warm and full, but not overwhelming and astonished. Dino bows and his hair falls down over his face. He stands upright, gives the crowd a nod, and then raises up a hand in acknowledgment. This man, whom I share a house with and who uses the same silverware as I do, seems so removed from me that I could forget that I know him at all.

Dino walks offstage, and the curtain closes. The lights

267

come up, and it is intermission. He will play again afterward. I hear my mother sigh a breath of relief, and then
she puts on her smile to receive congratulations of the
people who turn to take her hands again. They are being
polite, I can tell. Underwhelmed. I stand and stretch, look
around. Look up into the crowd and try to meet Ian's eyes,
wherever they are.

My mother is leaning forward and talking to Andrew
Wilkowski, who I notice for the first time is wearing a rose
in his lapel. His wife is talking to the record company
woman, who can't seem to take her eyes off of my mother.
I check out the crowd and have a weird surge of panic at
the sight of one man in our row across the aisle. For a
minute, I think I am looking at William Tiero. I think the
man looks just like him. In fact, I become sure in a
moment that it is indeed William Tiero. This is what living with a paranoid can do; it makes you fear the worst
things. My heart actually thumps around in anticipation
of trouble. When Mom leans back in her seat again, I
point out the man. *Isn't that William Tiero?* I ask.

Don't even think such a thing, she says. And then she
tells me who she thinks he looks like, names someone I've
never heard of, a movie actor probably. She tells me this
man's nose and chin are too round, and that his hair is
wrong. It is not William Tiero.

A woman comes to the front and asks if she can take
my mother's picture. Andrew Wilkowski intervenes and
says no, but my mother says she doesn't mind. The woman
has a hard time figuring out her own damn camera, then

realizes it hasn't been wound forward. Andrew Wilkowski reminds her to keep the camera in her purse during the performance, and the woman snaps something back to him about knowing full well the protocol. She gives us something to talk about until the lights dim again.

The symphony performs one endless piece and then there is Dino again. There is a long silence before he begins, and when he lifts his violin to his chin, he closes his eyes. It is a solo piece, parts of which I have heard again and again, but have never known the title of until I had picked up the program earlier that night. *Amore Dolce Della Gioventù*, Sweet Love of Youth. He begins to play, and for the first time I hear the piece unbroken. I see the entire picture. I know its name. It is strange to me that I have before this moment only known fragments and not the whole. I wonder what made him write it. I wonder if it was memories of his days in Paris as a young man, or if it was something more recent. I hear the notes, this most beautiful, tender arrangement of feeling, and I see him drawing back the curtain of the upstairs bedroom window of our house, see him watching Ian and me on the grass that night. Could he have seen something more than just his anger that night? Or is every person in this room feeling as if he was there the moment they fell in love? When the piece is over there is silence in the hall, and then frenzied applause. Shouts of *Bravo!* The record company woman wipes a tear from her face. He has triumphed.

He barely pauses to accept the applause before he moves to his next piece, the dreaded third composition that has given him so much agony. It is titled simply *Lunetta*. It is a piece that begins with just Dino's single, mournful violin, until the orchestra floats in, it seems, section by section until all the performers are playing so furiously that it is as if their instruments might alight at any moment. He has composed the music for each instrument, written every agonizing note, and it is true—he is a genius. The emotions pour forth, the definitions of love and life and struggle. Dino himself has his eyes closed—he is lost to this frenzied place. He grimaces, as if it is causing him pain; his shirt billows, comes untucked. His sleeves are swaying a rhythm of white, and this close you can see the sweat forming on his forehead. I hold my own breath—it is that kind of music, where you are almost afraid for what might happen next, afraid of where this group cry to the universe might bring us. I look over at my mother, and see her hands clasped in her lap. Her own eyes are closed, and she is smiling. She is gone to wherever music and passion can take her, and I see on her face why she loves this man and what it means to her to simply be part of this moment. I understand that that is what all this has been about—her ability to be here in a way that is more intimate than anyone else in the room. To have a piece of it that no one else has. This is why she has stayed.

I think of my father right then. I think how my mother has needs that he cannot fulfill. In some part of him, held secretly in his palm, maybe, I know he holds out hope that she will return to him. There is a part of me that right then opens up my own palm, unfurls the clutched fingers, and lets the hope out.

The audience is transported, and Dino is the one leading the trip. I am afraid for him—he seems so overcome, so lost and found at the same time that I wonder how he'll manage it. He leans over the violin, and the energy and fire he pours into that instrument is the brightest flash of light, a gamma ray burst, the death of a star and the creation of a black hole. The piece has ended, this piece that has caused Dino so much agony, and the audience explodes with applause, shouts, and rises to its feet. This surpasses triumph, but Dino looks depleted, exhausted to the point of collapse. He just stands there for a while, looking into the blackness of the audience as if wondering where he was and how he got there. *Lunetta*, I learn later means "Little Moon" in Italian. His mother's name.

Someone has the bright idea to turn up the lights a bit so that he can see the people on their feet, their hands in the air. His eyes settle on us, the record company woman, my mother and I, then move across the performance hall.

There are lucky and unlucky things about that night. The unlucky things are obvious. The lucky thing is that someone closed the curtain a bit too early. As the heavy velvet drapes shut, the applause finally quieted, and the rush out began immediately. That was the lucky part, that there were many people who had already made it through the doors before Peter Boglovich and a French horn player lost their grasp on a Dino who was trying to make his way out to the audience through the side curtain. He had thrown his violin down—that's how they knew that he was suddenly outraged and out of control.

Thrown it hard enough to cause a thin crack down the back.

No one hears anything, although Andrew Wilkowski's envelope wife would later claim she heard the splintering of the wood, which was an impossibility and a lie, given the noise in the auditorium and the chatter of the record company woman. We gather our coats. There is supposed to be a brief reception now for a few important people. This is fine for the record company woman, as her perfume is still going strong. I do not know that in less than a minute, Ian will know my secret. That everyone will.

The front rows are still making their way up the ramp when we hear it. This animal cry of rage. *You son of a bitch!* We turn to look, and in spite of everything that has happened up to that point, in spite of all that we have lived with over the past few months, the cry is a surprise, and I have no idea whose voice it is or what is happening. There is that sudden disorientation of trying to make sense of something unexpected.

And then I see him. Billowing white shirt, black tuxedo pants, and he leaps from the stage and stumbles. Andrew Wilkowski is the first one to understand that it is Dino, and that this is a disaster. He rushes down the ramp with a surprising degree of athleticism, but misses Dino coming up the side aisle. Dino is pushing past startled people, reaches the man who bears an unfortunate resemblance to Dino Tiero Cavalli's brother. He grabs a chunk of the back of the jacket the man wears and spins him around. He raises his fist, and with the force of the agony and pain of his lifetime, punches the man in his face, sending him reeling and crashing to the floor.

There are screams—my mother screams beside me. Dino is kneeling beside the man. He is putting his hands to the man's throat. Blood is coming from the man's nose. Andrew Wilkowski reaches them.

Dino looks into the face of the man, and realizes what we already know. He realizes that this is just a man, an aeronautics engineer who played the bass in his high school orchestra and who lucked into good seats through an online auction. This is not William Tiero, who he is certain tried to ruin him financially by getting him the psychiatric help he needed. Who shared the ugly history that Dino tried to escape from but feared he never could. As my mother said, his nose and chin are too round.

This is when Dino rises. The part of him that is sane and rational, if still a perfectionist asshole, looks shocked at what he has done.

Two ushers and a security officer are trying to move down the crowd of people to get to the injured man. Andrew Wilkowski has his arm around Dino's shoulder. But he doesn't know Dino's strength if he thinks he can hold him there. Dino wrenches himself free. He flees out the side door, the fire exit.

He runs out into the night.

CHAPTER SIXTEEN

Later, after the police had gone, the one thing I kept thinking about was Siang Chibo. I wondered if she had seen what had happened, or if she would only read about it in the morning. I thought about her reaction to this night even more than Ian's. I had such a profound feeling of having disappointed her. I kept seeing her finger, straightening that painting of *Wild Roses*.

Andrew Wilkowski was snoring on the couch, and my mother was sitting up in bed with the lights on. She'd told me to go to sleep, and I told her that sleep would be impossible. *Now*, she had said, and I guess she just needed some time alone to think. She had a lot to think about.

I'd been able to sleep, but it was a deep, dark sleep of restless dreams, full of Dino's music, full of the knowledge that he was gone, and that Ian was going away too. Finally I slept hard, woke up late, and emerged from haziness to the awful memory of what the night before had brought. It seemed so unreal that I had to convince myself that it was true. Dino was still gone. I called Ian quickly, and we spoke only long enough to arrange a meeting. There were things he needed to tell me. There were things I needed to tell him, too.

I stayed with Mom all day, on the Dino vigil. Andrew Wilkowski hid the newspaper and made sure the television and radio weren't played. There was no news of Dino from the police or anywhere else. After we tried to eat grilled cheese sandwiches and soup, I left Mom in the capable hands of Andrew Wilkowski, still in his suit, looking wrinkled and exhausted, his music-note tie discarded sometime the night before. Dog William snoozed on the living room rug, looking inappropriately content.

I walked down to the ferry docks. The day had been freezing but bright, too cheerful for what Mom was going through. White wisps of a foggy evening were beginning to form in the dusk, looking as if they could be cleared with a puff of my breath. Ian was there already when I arrived. I saw his dark coat all the way from the ticket window, where Evan Malloney's dad was working late.

Ian faced me, watched me walk toward him. He held out his arms and I got in. I let myself sink there and disappear.

"You saw," I said.

"Yes," Ian said into my hair.

"I heard about you, too, and Curtis."

"Bunny told me he saw you. There's so much to say that I don't know where to start."

"I don't either," I said.

"I knew Dino was . . . difficult. But Cassie, did he just snap?"

"No, not really. I knew something like this was coming. My Mom and I both did. There's been so much happening. . . . I was embarrassed to tell you. There was so much . . ." I still couldn't say the words. *Crazy. Mentally ill.*

"You should have told me. Look at us. We didn't tell each other the most important things."

"I was afraid of what you'd think."

"I was afraid of what *you* would think. God, we can't be so afraid of losing each other. I won't judge you. I love you."

I squeezed him under his coat. "But I *am* going to lose you."

"You're not going to lose me."

"But you're going away."

"Yes."

We stood there, just holding each other.

"It's what you have to do," I said.

"Yes."

"I don't want to talk about this anymore," I said. "I don't even want to talk."

"Okay."

"No sound. No music, no talking."

"Quiet as space," he said. "Is space quiet?" I held my finger up to his lips to tell him to shush. We walked down the dock. We didn't talk about where we were walking; we just kept going forward, in step with each other. We walked back toward town, went to the planetarium. Dave was just leaving, let us in and told me to lock the door behind me when I left. We walked into the dark auditorium, and I kept the lights off, turned on the projector and lit the ceiling with stars. We sat in the plush chairs, side by side and holding hands. Ian leaned over and kissed me, and we stayed there for a while like that. It got uncomfortable, and we lay down on the floor together for a while. What happened after that is nobody's business. It's my sweet, good memory. But I will say that I got my wish for quiet. Quiet except for the sweet, tender notes of *Amore Dolce Della Gioventù* playing in my head, and Ian's breath in my ear.

Alice came over and stayed with Mom when Andrew Wilkowski went home for a little bit. There was still no news of Dino. Alice seemed to know a lot about our life. Mom told more about what went on in our house than I ever did, it seemed. I wonder if my parents' divorce made me get too good at keeping secrets.

Alice brought tea and scones in a white bag. I guess she didn't have time to make them herself. A white bakery bag is one of the reasons life is good, if you ask me, and Alice's calm presence and kind voice did appear to work magic on Mom. Alice had her laughing, telling a story about someone else they knew, and I was glad to see that Mom had good people around her.

So it was Alice, anyway, not Andrew Wilkowski, who was there with Mom when she got the phone call. The call was from William Tiero. Mom was so happy and relieved to hear from him. Dino may have been right in his paranoid feeling that Mom and William kept in contact. They were two people who loved Dino, and they were looking after him. Mom's voice was warm, grateful.

"They found him. Thank God," she said, after she hung up. Dino had boarded a plane, flew to Milan. He had checked into the Principe De Savoia Hotel, was there now. He was alone, in bad shape. She needed to go immediately.

Mom phoned Dino's doctor and Andrew Wilkowski, who insisted on coming with her. The kind Alice called for plane reservations as Mom packed.

I sat on the edge of the bed. "How can I help?" I asked.

"Can you look in the top dresser drawer for my passport?"

I hunted around until I found the small blue book. I opened it up, looked at her picture. It was taken a few years ago, just before they were married. They had gone to Paris for a week for their honeymoon. She looked so young in the picture. I couldn't believe how much she'd changed. "Found it."

"I've never been to Italy," she said. "This wasn't exactly the way I intended going. This is not something I could have ever imagined. I cannot even believe what I am doing right now."

"Is he okay?" I thought about the *Wild Roses* painting. I thought about what Siang Chibo had told me. About what had happened with Vincent van Gogh after he'd painted it.

"You know what Dr. Milton said? Have I ever told you how much I can't stand Dr. Milton? Born with a reptile heart, I swear."

"What did he say?"

"He said I should commit Dino when I get to Milan. If he's alive by the time I get there. That's actually what he said. 'If he's alive by the time you get there.'"

"I still think he's a liar," my father said.

"He had reason. It's not that simple," I said.

"Crazy, then. I don't think anyone will dispute that anymore. That poor man. His nose is broken. I can't believe he isn't going to sue. And that violin. Imagine how much that cost."

I hadn't seen a newspaper in a few days, but Dad had them all. He even had a few from other cities, for God's sake. Nannie was sitting in the chair with the pop-up footstool. She was doing the crossword puzzle in the *Chicago Tribune.* I saw it sitting open on the coffee table later. For "Elvis hit, 1956" she had written *artichoke dip* and had left two squares blank, and for "Hockey legend" she had written *puck,* leaving three squares blank. It just goes to show that if it works for you, great.

"Dino's suicidal in some hotel, Dad. I don't think they're thinking about that aspect of things right now."

"Look at what she chose. And our life together was so bad?"

I kept my mouth shut. Watched Dog William out the window, checking out Dad's backyard with a confused excitement. The gray whales had begun their migration in the sound that stretched out before us. But no one was thinking about whales, and that seemed sad and wrong.

279

"Flower parts, six letters," Nannie shouted. "What's a flower part, six letters?"

"Petals," my dad said.

She ignored him. "Flower!" Nannie said. She counted the letters. "Yep, that's six."

"I guess if your mother puts up with this, she'll never leave him," my father said.

I didn't tell him that I'd had the same thought. Instead, I took his hands across the table where we sat. The Dutch girls were still paired with the chefs—Dad had at last given up on Nannie's rearranging, at least with the salt and pepper shakers.

"I love you, Dad," I said. "I just . . . I wish you would let go, you know? Move on."

"I have moved on," he said.

"Dad." I gestured to the newspapers, spread out all over the living room.

He sighed. "Cassie?" he said. "There's one thing I know. You can't tell a heart what to do."

"All right," I said.

"Oh give me a home, where these roam. Seven letters," Nannie said. She was quiet a moment. Dad and I just sat there, our hands clasped together.

"Monkeys," Nannie said finally.

Mom's voice was there, coming across the ocean by phone. She sounded so close, she might have been phoning from the grocery store.

"I've got to get that doctor's home phone number,"

she said. "You've got to help me. It's an emergency."

"I can ask Dad to help me. He's a master sleuth. What's going on?"

"Just hurry. Call me back as soon as you can. He's gone, Cassie. We got here, and he's gone."

"Are you okay?"

"Something's happened to him. I can feel it. It's like I feel this . . . *separation*. I feel him gone in my gut."

After writing his *Principia*, Sir Isaac Newton collapsed in a nervous breakdown. Abraham Lincoln had several breakdowns, and was obsessed with thoughts of premature death and of going mad. F. Scott Fitzgerald and his wife, Zelda, were the dysfunctional couple of the century. He was wracked by alcoholism, and she died in a fire at a mental hospital. So much painful living, even for the seemingly most chirpy—Dolly Parton (depression), Charles Schultz (anxiety), Dick Clark (depression), Donny and Marie Osmond, for God's sake (anxiety and depression, respectively).

"What if he's dead, Ian?" I said into the phone. "What does dead even mean?" I couldn't get my mind wrapped around the thought. I couldn't picture him really gone. Forever gone, gone where? "I wanted him out of my life, Mom's life. But I never wanted this."

"I know."

"Tell me what dead means," I said.

"I don't know, Cassie. I just don't know."

• • •

Here is what happened, according to my mother. Dino took a cab, all the way down to the center of the country. A cab, if you can believe it, some 130 miles. Through Milan and Bologna. On to Florence, and a short while farther to San Gimignano, Tuscany. From there, just a few miles south to the hilltop town of Sabbotino Grappa.

My mother and Andrew Wilkowski took the train. They paid a man in an old Renault to drive them from the station to Sabbotino Grappa. The man drove with one hand, and held a cigarette in the other, dangling it out the open window. They told him they were in a hurry, and he accommodated, although it seemed that all the cars on the roads drove with the same fury and absentminded recklessness, Mom said. Lots of veering and honking and driving up the curb until they were out of the city and the driver calmed down a bit. It was hot, Mom said, and they had to drive with all of the windows rolled down. You could see Sabbotino Grappa before you arrived there— from the highway it was a tiny town that looked balanced on a pinnacle. The town was built on the lofty hilltop location in the medieval days, so the townspeople could see who might be arriving to destroy them. Dino had done a good job in choosing Sabbotino Grappa, Mom realized. It was too far and too small to be of interest to tourists, and the trip up the winding road to the top too arduous. The village shared one phone, and traveling to that place in an attempt to check facts with the handful of people who lived there and who spoke only Italian would give anyone incentive to believe first Dino's and then Edward

Reynolds's version of events. One look at this place, though, Mom said, and you knew that Edward Reynolds, the author of *An Oral History* made a decision about which story he would give to the world. Because there would be no canals up here. No canals in which to throw a bicycle.

The man in the Renault told them about all of the Americans he knew, asked if they lived in New York City. He'd been there once, and from what he saw of America, he hated it. They wound their way up the hill, arrived at a town so ancient and quiet, my mother was sure it was deserted. The man in the Renault let them out, and Andrew paid him. My mother took a big drink of warm air, looked out over the Tuscan valley, which stretched beneath them. The man in the Renault waved good-bye, the cigarette still smoking in his hand, and beeped his horn. As he headed back down the winding road, my mother worried about letting him go—the town, all yellow stone and small alleyways, seemed completely empty. It looked like an abandoned film-scene set, with its narrow passages and stone walls and buildings so old it was hard to believe anyone that lived there knew what year it was.

In the center of the town was a square, cobbled, with a church and three small stores, just as Dino had described. Just as Edward Reynolds had said. It just seemed so deserted, Mom thought; until she caught the movement of a curtain, saw the bulk of an old woman moving away who'd been watching them. Then she saw the window shade of a store pulled closed, a pair of shutters yanked shut, an old man hurrying off down an alleyway. They walked to the church and went inside. The church was freezing. There were three long rows of lit red candles, and a huge image of Jesus painted right onto the wall, chipped in an unfortunate place. Andrew Wilkowski called out, and an ancient priest shuffled into the church. He stank so strongly of wine, my mother thought she could get drunk just smelling his breath.

The old priest spoke only Italian, and Andrew Wilkowski made his best attempt to speak to him. The old man just shook his head *No, no, no,* until Andrew Wilkowski said Dino's name. When he heard this, he took Andrew's arms in his hands and nodded, gestured to the open doorway. My mother said she felt the most profound relief, until the old priest started shaking his head and mumbling softly, as if it was so sad, so sad.

They followed the priest out of the church and into the warm air of the piazza, followed him across the cobblestones and down a narrow alley. Up a flight of steps to a large wooden door. The old priest knocked with his fist. *Honoria!* He shouted. *Honoria! Apra il portello!*

The old priest kept banging, but no one answered. A cat appeared and curled around his legs, and he swatted it aside with his foot in a very unpriestly fashion. *Honoria!*

Finally he tried the doorknob. My mother and Andrew exchanged a look. Dread filled my mother. She thought she might throw up. The priest pushed the door open, and not knowing what else to do, they followed him into the house, through a dark hall with crooked hanging pictures, and into a kitchen. By that time my mother said she was expecting anything. An empty room, another crazy ride to another strange place, the news of Dino's suicide.

But she did not expect what she saw. He was lying on a couch, an old blanket tucked around him, his mouth hanging open. The nearly deaf Honoria Maretta was setting down a tray of tea and cookies beside him. Dino woke up, propped himself against some pillows, and smiled before he saw the trio come down the hall. He was smiling because he saw what was on the tray. Honoria had made him pizzelles.

CHAPTER SEVENTEEN

As I said, the desire to be near fame and greatness can do odd and amazing things to people. That night, all the good people of Sabbotino Grappa came out to feast the returning son that was never theirs. Mom and Andrew were greeted warmly, now that the villagers knew they were strangers to be welcomed rather than feared. It wasn't too often, after all, that they got visitors. Antonia Gillette, the baker's wife, set up a table in the piazza and everyone brought food. The forever squabbling Mrs. Salducci and Mrs. Latore, both old as time, brought *pinzimonio* and risotto, and broke into an argument about where to place their dishes. Peter, the baker, made focaccia, though his daughter had to carry the plate as she held her father's arm to help him walk. Francesca and Lutitia Bissola arrived, clutching each other for steadiness, chatting and arguing and kissing everyone in sight after they had a few glasses of the wine that Father Abrulla brought from the church. Even Karl Lager came, bringing pomegranates from his store, and bruised apricots and olives. Father Minelli was dead and gone, as was the reclusive Frank Piccola. Almost everyone else, Mom said, was over eighty. She wondered what would happen to the town when everyone was dead, wondered who would live there anymore. The youngest people there were Maria and Eli Manzoni, and they were older than Dino, though Pia and her brothers arrived by car, bringing grandchildren that hid under the table and feasted on Honoria's cookies.

My mother got to see the sunset of Sabbotino Grappa, watched the sun as it dropped down into the Tuscan valley. She breathed in the smell of lemons, of plumbagos. Sat on the stone steps of the church with a plate of *budino di mele* balanced on her knees. Listened to the joyful language she couldn't understand.

And Dino, who had only previously seen this place in a book when he was sixteen and crafting a past for himself for his first interview, lavished in the affection of his "home" and "family." The children put almonds in his pockets, and the old ladies and old men kissed his cheeks. He feasted and laughed. Told stories in Italian. Finally, he picked up the old violin that Mrs. Salducci brought, hopelessly out of tune, and tried to play *Lunetta* for the townspeople. The sound was too awful, and so he gave up *Lunetta*. He played "Ballo di Mattina" (Morning Dance), a Tuscan folk song, instead, and Karl Lager danced with

Mrs. Latore, and the Bissola sisters waltzed in tiny, careful steps with each other, and the children spun themselves in circles, the colors of their clothing bright against that yellow stone.

No wonder, my mother thought then, that Edward Reynolds had decided to respect the version of Dino's life that he had chosen. It was a good story, with wonderful characters, in a beautiful setting. It made everyone so happy. And if you could make a choice, then why not pick happiness?

Late that night, over wine in glass jars and a short, dripping candle in Honoria's kitchen, Dino told my mother that he would be staying in Sabbotino Grappa. We would have to join him if they were to stay together—he had too long been in that second-rate musical city, and he would be near enough to Rome to play there.

My mother told him then what she said she'd wanted to say for a long time. That she loved him and cared about him, but that they could not live together anymore. She would file for divorce when she returned home. He could live with a family that wasn't real, made up of lies and things unsaid, but she had already been doing that for too long. She had a choice, and she wanted to pick happiness, too.

Dino, Honoria's boy, slept on her couch that night, and my mother and Andrew slept on the floor. In the morning, Eli Manzoni drove them to Rome. They stayed in the Grand Palace Hotel, ordered expensive room service. My mother had a bath. They flew out the next day from the Rome airport.

Here was the funny thing. Her baggage never made it home, and she didn't seem to mind.

"You didn't even bring anything back," I said to her. "Not even MY MOTHER WENT TO ITALY AND ALL I GOT WAS THIS LOUSY T-SHIRT."

"Shopping wasn't a priority."

"Did you think for a minute you might want to stay?"

"Not for a second. Not even a split second. Or a split of a split."

"Are you okay?"

"Exhausted, depleted, war weary. Shell-shocked. It's been a long four years."

"It all feels so strange. It's so quiet."

"I know," Mom said. "It's hard to realize that it's done. I've been trying so hard to get everything to fit for so long, but it never did. You keep trying and trying, but you're just killing yourself."

"You've been through a lot."

"We've been through a lot. I've known this was necessary for a long time. But it's not easy to do what you know you should, especially when he's *ill*. God, he was so sick."

I didn't say anything. Just let her talk. I was so glad he was gone. There was air in the house again. Like someone had died, and the body and the illness and the sickroom were now carted away.

"I mean, where should your empathy stop? Your own compassion does you in. Gets in the way of self-protection. You've got an in-love feeling, but the relationship is

289

damaging. When do you stop calling it love?"

"Meanness is still meanness," I said. "It's not a disease."

"It's true. And I've also got you to look after, thank God. I know how this has been affecting you, and I'm sorry."

"Are you going to miss him?"

She thought about this. "I'm sure there will be things I'll miss. I mean, when it was good, it was great. Especially in the early days. I know it's hard for you to understand, but I loved him. I really did. And it was exciting, it really was, being part of his world." She rubbed her forehead as if trying to get the thoughts to order themselves. "Right now, everything just hurts. But I'm also just so *relieved*. Mostly what I can see is that relief."

"Me too."

"You know how just now you asked if I was okay? That's why we're not doing this anymore. A daughter shouldn't have to worry about her mother. That's backward and wrong. And we should both be okay. Yes, it hurts. To get divorced again . . . God. But that's exactly it. A home is where you're okay."

"I'm proud of you," I said.

"I'm proud of us." She held up the coffee pot she was holding. "Here's to lessons learned. Lightness. Peace. Tranquillity. Knowing mostly what the day will hold when you get up in the morning."

I grabbed the nearest thing, a flower vase. We clinked them together. We toasted to a new life.

Siang Chibo still followed me home.

"You know he's not here," I told her. We were at the beginning of my street. I watched Courtney's brothers let themselves in their house, saw the blue glow of the television a moment later. "Even his study is getting packed up."

"You're my friend," she said. "That's why I'm here."

"Okay."

"It doesn't matter to me, you know. What happened that night," she said. "You act as if that changes something."

I stopped before we went in. Slipped my backpack from my shoulder and set it on the walkway. "He let you down."

"Let me down? You've got to be kidding." Her *Indiana Jones Temple of Doom* boy voice grew even higher pitched. "Were you not there? Did you not hear *Lunetta*? Did you not hear *Amore Dolce Della Gioventù*? My father was sobbing."

Dog William was out on the front lawn. We watched him chew someone's tennis shoe. I don't know whose it was. I was hoping he didn't snitch it from Mr. Frederici's front porch.

"I would have thought the rest of the night might've thrown a little cold water on the evening."

"Look what he gave us. Remember his painting? *Wild Roses*. That music. Beauty that could not be tamed. It was magnificent. Unforgettable."

I thought about this. "Yeah. Unforgettable, all right. And roses have thorns."

"Oh, Cassie," Siang said. "I want to be your friend even if you don't seem to get things sometimes."

I watched Dog William. I wondered if we should change his name. I tried a few out.

"Marley," I called. "Hey, Marley!" Dog William didn't look up. "José. Here, José. Archie!"

He ignored me. Kept chewing that shoe.

"William!" I said, and Dog William popped his ugly little chin right in the air, looked at me as if slightly exasperated at being interrupted.

"He is who he is," Siang said.

Ian and I spent the rest of the year together. It was a peaceful time—Janet apologized to me, even made me some cookies, and, of course, Dino was gone. A happy, happy time. Ian left for Philadelphia in August. Janet could not bear to take him to the airport, so Chuck and Bunny drove, and Ian and I rode in the backseat. I couldn't keep the tears from rolling down my cheeks.

"I don't want any blubbering," Bunny said. But he kept blowing his nose and sniffing a lot. Trying to keep the tears back.

It was five o'clock in the morning, already warm and smelling good, the air feeling promising and full of new beginnings. It broke my heart. Ian kept squeezing my hand and looking at me as if trying to get my features deep into his memory.

"Cassie, I . . ." he choked.

"Okay, all of you," Chuck said. "We're never going to get through this." But his voice was wavery, too. "On the count of three, think happy thoughts. One, two, three. Clowns."

"Clowns are creepy," I said.

"Gumballs. Cartoons. The beach. A vacation," Chuck said.

"Real good, Chuck," Bunny said, and honked into his Kleenex again. "Vacation? Travel? Planes?"

"There's so much to say," Ian whispered.

"We're going to be seeing you," Bunny said. Now his voice was hoarse. It was hard to keep back emotion. It always kept pressing, pressing at the edges of you, even if you didn't want it to. "It's not like we're not going to be seeing you."

We took the exit for the airport. The sight of the big planes there, parked and waiting, made my stomach feel sick. The airport was such a wonderful and awful place. For every arrival there was someone on the other side, left behind.

The plan was to pull up to the curb, unload Ian's bags. We'd say good-bye there. We wouldn't prolong it.

Bunny fought the cars and the shuttle buses and taxis, eased into a spot at the airport curb. "Kid," he said. His eyes were full of tears now. He leaned over and hugged Ian hard. "I love you. You be good."

Ian hugged Chuck, too, who was having a hard time holding it together. "Puppies," Chuck squeaked. "Sno-Cones. Heineken."

"Good-bye, Chuck."

I stepped out onto the curb with Ian. He was not wearing his long coat, as it was August and it was packed for a Philadelphia winter, but he was carrying his violin case. He took his suitcase from the trunk and set it down by his feet.

"I love you," he said.

"I love you." I hugged him. We kissed for a while. And then we separated, and I watched his back disappear into the sliding doors. I just watched him go. And like that, he was gone.

"Thank you for showing me how," I whispered.

And then I got back into the car, and let Bunny hold me as I sobbed.

Maybe love, too, is beautiful because it has a wildness that cannot be tamed. I don't know. All I know is that passion can take you up like a house of cards in a tornado, leaving destruction in its wake. Or it can let you alone because you have built a stone wall against it, set out the armed guards to keep it from touching you. The real trick is to let it in, but to hold on. To understand that the heart is as vast and wide as the universe, but that we come to know it best from here, this place of gravity and stability, where our feet can still touch ground.

My mother's divorce from Dino was finalized by the end of the summer. For a while, Andrew Wilkowski phoned her to let her know how Dino was doing. His health was improving, his health was worsening, his health was improving. His music was going well, going badly, going well. So it went. Andrew Wilkowski finally stopped calling with his reports after the record company woman flew to Sabbotino Grappa to discuss Dino's contract and ended up staying.

My mother is calm and happy. She plays her cello with love, not loss. She struggles like hell financially, but she looks more like herself. Her eyes are soft and relaxed. She's been out on a few dates with a poet-slash-advertising executive, a member of the creatively sane. She took in Alice as a roommate, and that worked great until Alice decided to move in with the French horn player in the orchestra. Mom is looking for a new roommate, and in a Bunny brainstorm, is having coffee with Janet to talk over the possibility. I wonder what it would be like to live in the same house as Ian's mom. It would be nice to be close to him in this way, I think, and Dog William would be thrilled to have Rocket on a regular basis.

A few times when Alice was around, Dad came over for a bowl of jambalaya. They all sat around the table and ate and drank wine and played marathon games of Monopoly and made up the rules as they went along. And yes, it felt like family. It was just as you hoped it could be, where everyone decides they can still love and care for each other, married or not. Where everyone just *gets it together*. That's all you really want or need—the ability to love both of your parents, and for them to see that a changed family need not be a destroyed one. I hope that is enough for Dad, to have Mom as family, and I hope he comes over still if Janet moves in. I like the idea of the three of them at that table together.

And Ian. I saw him once, over Christmas, and it was perfect but brief. It is too expensive for him to fly home very much, and long-distance phone calls, too, are few.

We write each other, e-mailing as often as we can. Soon he will be winning awards, performing, traveling. He will make the circuit, following the path to certain success, maybe even fame. When I look at my bear, floating in the globe, I try to see him as free rather than unanchored. I try to think good thoughts about his freedom. More than anything, I try to keep him from spinning out of control.

I don't know what will happen with Ian and me. What I do know is that when I close my eyes, it is him that I see. When I think of love, it is his name etched always in my mind. And it is his music that I hear. When the notes fill my head, I do not imagine anymore the lemon trees and curved streets of Sabbotino Grappa. I do not imagine old ladies smelling of salami and olive oil, or a child running on yellow cobblestones. No, now Ian's music is his own, and what I see is a winter forest of fir and cedar and ever-greens. I see diamond flakes beginning to fall, landing on a joyful, upturned face, drifting to settle in my beloved's hair. I see poplar and spruce, solid and sure, covered in the softest, quietest white. The snow glitters like a sky filled with stars, like a galaxy on a planetarium ceiling.

Turn the page for a peek at
another novel by Deb Caletti:

the nature of jade

Humans may watch animals, but animals also watch humans. The Australian Lyrebird not only observes humans, but from its forest perch, imitates them, as well. It's been known to make the sound of trains, horns, motors, alarms, and even chainsaws . . .
—Dr. Jerome R. Clade, *The Fundamentals of Animal Behavior*

When you live one and a half blocks away from a zoo like I do, you can hear the baboons screeching after it gets dark. It can scare the crap out of you when you're not used to it, as I found out one night right after we moved in. I thought a woman was being strangled. I actually screamed, and my mom came running in my room and so did my dad, wearing these hideous boxers with Santas on them, which meant he'd gotten to the bottom of his underwear drawer. Even Oliver stumbled in, half asleep in his football pajamas, with his eyes squinched from the light my parents flicked on.

The conversation went something like this:

Dad: God, Jade. Zoo animals! *Baboons*, for Christ's sake.

Mom: I knew we should never have moved to the city.

Oliver (peering at Dad with a dazed expression): Isn't it August?

I was told once, though, that we really would have something to fear if there ever were a big earthquake, like they're always saying is going to happen at any moment here in

Seattle. Then we'd be living in the most dangerous part of the city. See, all the electrical fences are, well, *electrical*, and so if the power went out for any length of time there'd be lions and tigers (and bears, oh my) running loose, panicked and hungry. You hear a lot of false facts around the zoo—you've got the husbands incorrectly correcting wives ("No, ha ha. Only the *males* have tusks, honey"), and you've got those annoying eight-year-olds you can find at nearly any exhibit, who know entirely too much about mole rats, for example, and who can't wait for the chance to insert their superior knowledge into any overheard conversation ("Actually, those teeth are his incisors, and they're used for protection against his greatest enemy, the rufous-beaked snake"). But this bit of frightening trivia came from one of the Woodland Park zookeepers, so I knew it was true.

That's one of the reasons I have the live zoo webcam on in my room to begin with, and why I see the boy that day. I don't mean I keep it on to be on alert for disaster or anything like that, but because I find it calming to watch the elephants. I also take this medicine that sometimes revs me up a little at night, and they're good company when no one else is awake. Besides, elephants are just cool. They've got all the range of human emotion, from jealousy and love to rage and depression and play-fulness. They have one-night stands and then kick the guy out. They get pissed off at their friends and relatives or the people who care for them, and hold a grudge until they get a sincere apol-ogy. They are there for each other during all the phases of their lives. A baby is born, and they help it into the world, trumpet-ing and stamping their feet in celebration. A family member dies, and they bury the body with sticks and then mourn with terrible cries, sometimes returning years later to revisit the bones and touch them lovingly with their trunks. They're just this group of normally abnormal creatures going through the ups and downs of life with big hearts, mood swings, and huge, swingy-assed togetherness.

When we moved into our brick townhouse in Hawthorne Square by the zoo during my first year of high school, I had this plan that I'd go there every day to watch the gorillas and take notes about their behavior. I'd notice things no one else had, make some amazing discovery. I had this romantic idea of being Diane Fossey/Jane Goodall/Joy Adamson. I liked the idea of bouncy, open-air Jeeps and I liked the outfits with all the pockets, only I didn't really want to live in Africa and be shot by poachers/get malaria/get stabbed to death. Bars between gorillas and me sounded reasonable.

I went over to the zoo and brought this little foldout chair Dad used for all of Oliver's soccer and baseball and basketball games, and I sat and watched the gorillas a few times. The only problem was, it felt more like they were watching me. They gave me the creeps. The male was the worst. His name is Vip, which sounds like some breezy nickname a bunch of Ivy Leaguers might give their jock buddy, but Vip was more like those freaky men you see at the downtown bus stops. The ones who silently watch you walk past and whose eyes you can still feel on you a block later. Vip would hold this stalk of bark in his Naugahyde hand, chewing slowly, keeping his gaze firmly on me. I'd move, and just his eyes would follow me, same as those paintings in haunted-house movies. If that wasn't bad enough, Vip was also involved in a tempestuous love triangle. A while back, Vip got gorilla Amanda pregnant, and when she lost the baby, he ditched her for Jumoke. He got her pregnant too, and after Jumoke had the baby, Amanda went nuts and stole it and the authorities had to intervene. It was like a bad episode of *All My Primates*.

So I moved on to the elephants, and as soon as I saw Chai and baby Hansa and Bamboo and Tombi and Flora, I couldn't get enough of them. Baby Hansa's goofy fluff of hair is enough to hook you all by itself. They are all just so peaceful and funny that they get into your heart. When you look in their eyes, you see sweet thoughts. And then there's Onyx, too, of course. One notched ear, somber face. Always off by herself in a way that makes you feel sad for her.

I didn't even need the little soccer chair, because there's a nice bench right by the elephants. I went once a week for a few months, but after a while I got busy with school and it was winter, and so I decided to just watch them from home most of the time. There are two live webcams for the elephants, one inside the elephant house and one in their outdoor environment, so even when the elephants were brought in at night, I could see them. Twenty-four hours a day, the cam is on, for the pachyderm obsessed. I got in the habit of just leaving the screen up when I wasn't using my computer to write a paper or to IM my friends. Now I switch back and forth between the cams so I can always see what's going on, even if the gang is just standing around sleeping.

I never did really write anything in my "research notebook" (how embarrassing—I even wrote that on the front); making some great discovery about elephant behavior kind of went in the big-ideas-that-fizzled-out department of my brain. But the elephants got to be a regular part of my life. Watching them isn't always thrilling and action packed, but I don't care. See, what I really like is that no matter what high-stress thing is going on in my world or in the world as a whole (Christmas, SATs, natural disasters, plane crashes, having to give a speech and being worried to death I might puke), there are the elephants, doing their thing. Just being themselves. Eating, walking around. They aren't having Christmas, or giving a speech, or stressing over horrible things in the news. They're just having another regular elephant day. Not worrying, only *being*.

That's why the elephant site is up on my computer right then, when I see the boy. I am stretched out on my bed and the elephants are cruising around on the screen, but I'm not even really watching them. My room's on the second floor of our townhouse, and if you lie there and look out the window, all you see is sky—this square of glass filled with moving sky, like a cloud lava lamp. Sometimes it's pink and orange and purples, unreal colors, and other times it's backlit white cotton candy, and other times it's just a sea of slow-moving monochrome. I'm just lying there thinking lazy, hazy cloudlike thoughts when I sit up and the computer catches my eye. The outdoor cam is on, which includes a view of the elephants' sprawling natural habitat. Chai is there with baby Hansa, and they are both rooting around in a pile of hay. But what I see is a flash of color, red, and I stop, same as a fish stops at the flash of a lure underwater.

The red—it's a jacket. A boy's jacket. When the outdoor cam is on, you can see part of the viewing area, too, and the people walking through it. At first it's this great big voyeuristic thrill to realize you can see people who are right there, right then, people who are unaware that you're watching them from your bedroom. There's probably even some law that the zoo is breaking that they don't know about. But trust me, the people get boring soon enough. It's like when you read blogs and you get this snooping-in-diaries kind of rush, until you realize that all they talk about is how they should write more often. People's patterns of behavior are so predictable. At the zoo, they stay in front of the elephants for about twelve seconds, point to different things, take a photo, move on. The most excitement you get is some kid trying to climb over the fence or couples who are obviously arguing.

But this time, the red jacket compels me to watch. And I see this guy, and he has a baby in a backpack. The thing is, he's young. He can't be more than a year or two older than I am, although I'm pathetic at guessing age, height, and distance, and still can't grasp the how-many-quarts-in-a-liter type question, in spite of the fact that I'm usually a neurotic over-achiever. So maybe he's not so young, but I'm sure he is. And that brings up a bunch of questions: Is he babysitting this kid? Is it his huge-age-difference brother? It can't be *his*, can it?

The boy turns sideways so that the baby can see the elephants better. Baby? Or would you call him a toddler? I can't tell— somewhere in between, maybe. The boy is talking to the baby, I can see. The baby looks happy. Here is what I notice. There is an ease between them, a calm, same as with zebras grazing in a herd, or swallows flying in a neat triangle. Nature has given them a rightness with each other.

My friend Hannah, who I've known since I first moved to Seattle, would say I am interested in the boy on the screen only because he's cute. Hannah, though, seemed to wake up one day late in junior year with a guy obsession so intense that it transformed her from this reasonable, sane person into a male-seeking missile. God, sorry if this is crude, but she had begun to remind me of those baboons that flaunt their red butts around when they're in heat. Talking to her lately, it goes like this:

Me: How did you do on the test? I couldn't think of anything to write on that second essay question.

Hannah: God, Jason Espanero is hot.

Me: I don't think it's fair to give an essay question based on a *footnote* no one even read.

Hannah: He must work out.

Me: I heard on the news that a fiery comet is about to crash into the earth and kill us all sometime this afternoon.

Hannah: He's just got the sweetest ass.

It *is* true that the guy on the screen's cute—tousled, curly brown hair, tall and thin, shy-looking—but that's not what keeps me watching. What keeps me there are the questions, his *story*. It's The Airport Game: Who are those people in those seats over there? Why are they going to San Francisco? Are they married? She's reading a poetry book, he's writing in a journal. Married literature professors? Writers? Weekend fling?

The boy doesn't take a photo and move on. Already, he is not following a predictable path. He stands there for a long time. The baby wears this blue cloth hat with a brim over his little blond head. The boy leans down over the rail, crosses his arms in front of himself. The baby likes this, pats the boy's head, though the boy is probably leaning only to relieve the weight of the backpack. The boy watches Hansa and Chai, and then Hansa wanders off. Still, he stands with his arms crossed, staring and thinking. What is on his mind?

His too-youthful marriage? His nephew/brother on his back? The college courses he is taking in between the nanny job?

Finally, the boy stands straight again. Arches his back to stretch. I realize I have just done the same, as if I can feel the weight of that backpack. You pass a bunch of people in a day—people in their cars, in the grocery store, waiting for their coffee at an espresso stand. You look at apartment buildings and streets, the comings and goings, elevators crawling up and down, and each person has their own story going on right then, with its cast of characters; they've got their own frustrations and their happiness and the things they're looking forward to and dreading. And sometimes you wonder if you've crossed paths with any of them before without knowing it, or will one day cross their path again. But sometimes, too, you have this little feeling of knowing, this fuzzy, gnawing sense that someone will become a major something in your life. You just know that theirs will be a life you will enter and become part of. I feel that sense, that knowing, when I look at this boy and this baby. It is a sense of the significant.

He stands and the baby does something that makes me laugh. He grabs a chunk of the boy's hair in each of his hands, yanks the boy's head back. Man, that has to hurt. Oh, ouch. But the baby thinks it is a real crack-up, and starts to laugh. He puts his open mouth down to the boy's head in some baby version of a kiss.

The boy's head is tilted to the sky. He reaches his arms back and unclenches the baby's fingers from his hair. But once he is free, he keeps his chin pointed up, just keeps staring up above. He watches the backlit cotton candy clouds in a lava-lamp sky, and it is then I am sure this is a story I'll be part of.

Feisty. Flirty. Fun. Fantastic.

LAUREN BARNHOLDT
author of two-way street

sometimes it happens

LAUREN BARNHOLDT

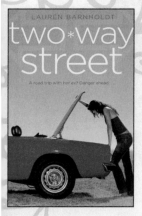

Intense . . . Romantic . . . Real.

THERE'S A FINE LINE
BETWEEN *bitter* AND *sweet*.

bittersweet

SARAH OCKLER

AUTHOR OF *TWENTY BOY SUMMER*

STORIES OF LOVE, LIFE, AND LETTING GO

ELIZABETH SCOTT

TWO HEARTBREAKING AND GUT-WRENCHING STORIES ABOUT FRIENDSHIP, LOVE, AND LOSS

HER AND ME AND YOU
Lauren Strasnick

Lauren Strasnick
NOTHING LIKE YOU

"Candid and quick-paced, with characters you can't help but want the best for."
—DEB CALETTI, National Book Award Finalist

Lauren Strasnick

EBOOK EDITIONS ALSO AVAILABLE

FROM SIMON PULSE
PUBLISHED BY SIMON & SCHUSTER
TEEN.SIMONANDSCHUSTER.COM